WIT

THE CHRONICLES OF FAERIE

THE
LIGHT-BEARER'S
DAUGHTER

Dublin City

COUNTY
DUBLIN

Duff Hill

Sally Gap

River Dargle

POWERSCOURT   Enniskerry

Powerscourt
Waterfall   Bray

Luggala   Djouce

Knocknacloghoge   Bray
              Lough Tay   Great   Head
Cloghoge River   Sugar Loaf   Little
                                        Sugar Loaf
Lough Dan

                              Glen of the Downs

            LEGEND   The Murrough
        — — — County Line
                            N11   Irish Sea
        - - - - Wicklow Way
            (designated hiker's trail)

MOUNTAINS

THE CHRONICLES OF FAERIE

THE LIGHT-BEARER'S DAUGHTER

O. R. MELLING

Amulet Books • New York

Library of Congress Cataloging-in-Publication Data:

Melling, O. R.
The Light-Bearer's daughter / by O.R. Melling.
p. cm. — (The chronicles of Faerie ; bk. 3)
Summary: In exchange for the granting of her heart's desire, twelve-year-old Dana agrees to make an arduous journey to Lugnaquillia through the land of Faerie in order to warn King Lugh, second in command to the High King, that an evil destroyer has entered the Mountain Kingdom.
ISBN-13: 978-0-8109-0781-2 (hardcover w/jkt.)
ISBN-10: 0-8109-0781-X (hardcover w/jkt.)
[1. Messengers—Fiction. 2. Voyages and travels—Fiction. 3. Fairies—Fiction. 4. Magic—Fiction. 5. Ireland—Fiction.]
I. Title.
PZ7.M51625Lig 2007
[Fic]—dc22
2006033517

Permissions

The author wishes to thank Pádraigín Ní Uallacháin for permission to use verses from her songs "Cara Caoin" ("Beloved Friend"), on page 62; "An Leannán" ("The Beloved"), on page 213; "Gleann na nDeor" ("Valley of Tears"), on page 238; and "An Phog" ("The Kiss"), on page 264. All songs are from her CD Ailleacht (Beauty), Gael Linn CEFCD 187, used with the kind permission of the singer/songwriter.

Chapters Twenty-seven and Twenty-eight were inspired by Glendalough: A Celtic Pilgrimage, by Michael Rodgers and Marcus Losack (Columbia Press, Ireland, and Morehouse Publishing, USA)

There are various quotes throughout the book from the King James version of the Bible

Printed and bound in U.S.A.
10 9 8 7 6 5 4 3 2 1

HNA
harry n. abrams, inc.
a subsidiary of La Martinière Groupe
115 West 18th Street
New York, NY 10011
www.hnabooks.com

For Michael Scott, mo chara, *dear friend*

ACKNOWLEDGMENTS

As always thanks to many: my daughter, Findabhair, first reader and advisor; Georgie-mum for her constant support; sister Pat Burnes for fabulous photos; my editor, Susan Van Metre; agents Lynn and David Bennett of the Transatlantic Literary Agency Inc.; the Second Sunday hiking group for research adventures in the Wicklow Mountains; the staff at the Tyrone Guthrie Centre at Annaghmakerrig; Dr. Nena Hardie, dear host in Toronto; John Duff and Brian Levy, dear hosts in New York; Piers Dillon-Scott, my Webmaster; Joe Murray, my computer angel; Brenda Sutton and all the gang at the Mythic Imagination Institute; and last but not least, *Na Daoine Maithe*, for their assistance and permission. *Go raibh míle maith agaibh!*

One

A year and a day after the fiery blast, it shuddered into consciousness. Hidden in the undergrowth, barely alive, it could not grasp its name nor even its nature. There was only the memory of blinding light and the searing pain that came in its wake. Then a fall into darkness.

But now as it woke, it began to move.

─── ⌀ ⌀ ───

She stepped through the spinney of tangled trees that crept over the back of the small mountain by the sea. The green hem of her gown brushed the damp grass; the earth felt cool underfoot. Stopping to press her ear to the bole of an old hawthorn, she closed her eyes to listen. With a smile, she sang the refrain that coursed through the tree's veins.

Tá grian gheal an tsamhraidh ag damhsa ar mo theach.

The summer sun is dancing on the roof of my house.

She left the spinney and came to a cliff that plunged down to cold waters. Her smile faded. A confusion of memories clouded her thoughts; shadows of another self, another life. She gazed down at the waves that struck the rocks in a fury of white spume. Why had she come here? What had drawn her to this place? Her skin shimmered faintly with a tint of gold. Her hair was wreathed with white blossoms. She stared around her, lost.

Then she froze.

It was like a wound in the earth: a gash of red mist like vaporized blood. Writhing through the grass, it trailed over the stony summit and into the mountains beyond.

She let out a cry.

The wind caught her cry and cast it through the air like a net, a summons. Out on the sea, a gray seal broke the surface. From overhead came the skirr of bird wing and the screech of gulls. A robin landed on her shoulder. Small animals scurried from their hideaways to form a circle around her—foxes, hares, field mice, badgers. On the slope above, a horned goat and a wild deer emerged from the dark of the mountain.

"A demon has entered the kingdom. A shadow of the Destroyer."

Her words were met with noises of dismay and terror. She herself was undone. Trembling, she struggled to keep her voice firm.

"Be of good courage. I will bear this news to the King. You will not be forsaken."

Deep in the mountains, the giant stirred. Something had entered the kingdom that did not belong. He tried to rise but couldn't. All around him was darkness. Were his eyes sealed shut? The smell of earth and stone was suffocating. A great weight lay upon his chest. What enemy had laid him low? What battle was lost on the plain that saw him defeated and entombed? He could hear a song spinning around him, words twisting like cords to bind and restrain. Whose spell enthralled him? He struggled like a wild man, striving to break free, but it was no use. He was blind and powerless. How did this happen? Even as he sought answers in the shadows of his mind, the words pulled him deeper into the darkness, where he drowned in layers of storied memory.

Two

Standing at the front window of his living room, Gabriel watched his daughter play soccer on the road. Their street was lined with small terraced houses built in the 1930s that faced each other across scrappy bits of lawn. Like the dwellers within, each house was different, painted in various shades of yellow, blue, pink, and brown. Some had low stone walls and others, iron fencing. They were either owned by the town council, as was Gabriel's, or purchased after years of rental. It wasn't a prosperous or even a peaceful neighborhood, but Gabriel had been happy enough to rear his daughter in it. Behind the line of red-tiled roofs and brick chimney pots rose the Wicklow Mountains, their green hills patched with hedge and speckled stone.

In scruffy jeans and a none-too-clean T-shirt, Dana was the only girl in the soccer game and the loudest to boot. Taller than most twelve-year-olds, she had shot up suddenly that summer and looked underfed and scrawny.

Gabriel winced at the thought that she needed new clothes as it meant an expedition to the charity shops on the main street. He was vaguely aware of the contrast between his daughter and the gaggle of girls who watched on the sidelines. The other girls were dressed in the latest styles, their hair sparkling with clips and bands. His income didn't allow for fashion and Dana herself had no interest in girlie things. Still, there were days when she came home hurt and angry, and eventually she would tell him the unkind remarks. Girls could be cruel. Far worse than boys who just punched each other.

Dana had taken control of the ball. Chest heaving, dark hair flying, she headed for the goalpost.

A big lad with a face like a clenched fist ran to cut her off.

"Get outta my way!" she yelled.

If he meant to intimidate her, he hadn't a hope. With the ball spinning between her feet, Dana wove deftly around him and laughed out loud.

Gabriel winced. The boy's fury was unmistakable. There would be payback.

The goalpost was a crack in the road. If Dana kicked the ball over it, the game was won. Face screwed with resolve, she sped toward it. Scrums and fights broke out on all sides as her teammates blocked the opposition. Gabriel was reminded of June bugs scrambling over each other.

The girls on the sidelines screeched encouragement.

Two dogs in the crowd began to bark, a shaggy-haired mongrel and a fractious Jack Russell. "Mutt and Jeff," as Gabriel liked to call them. They had watched Dana keenly throughout the game and would growl if she appeared in danger. She was champion and provider to all the neighborhood animals, collecting bones from the butchers to distribute among the faithful and feeding any strays. Even the King of Cats, the fiercest warrior tom on the street, acted like a gentleman in her presence. And whenever the inevitable fights broke out, Dana thought nothing of running into the fray, often at considerable risk to herself.

Now the boy she had outsmarted charged again. It was obvious he meant to crash into her. Technically it wasn't against street rules and it happened regularly—a fall, a sprawl, a head split open. All the players had been stitched up at one point or another. There was no use forbidding the game. They would only play elsewhere.

Gabriel tensed as the boy bore down on Dana's right side. She was concentrating on the ball and didn't notice. But the Jack Russell did and suddenly shot from the crowd. Someone grabbed him and hauled him back though he yelped and snapped. The boy was gaining on Dana. Gabriel sucked in his breath, but kept his eyes open. A father had to see what a father had to see. He was used to being afraid for her. She was so competitive it made her reckless, even dangerously so. He suspected she was the one who invented that terrible craze the previous summer—kids dashing in front of cars on a dare. Though she denied ever doing it, his heart still jumped every time a tire screeched. The only control he had in such matters was the threat of grounding. Dana hated being trapped indoors and was too restless to read or watch television. The only time she sat still was when he read to her himself or told her stories.

The moment of truth had arrived. Dana closed in on the goalpost. The big boy closed in on Dana. Without lifting her head, she made a feint in his direction that threw him off guard. And then, before he knew it, her foot shot out to trip him.

With a scream of rage and pain, he hit the ground.

With a yell of triumph, she kicked the ball over the crack.

Dana's teammates roared their approval and so did the spectators. The two dogs howled. When the Jack Russell was released, he leaped into the throng that surrounded the victor. Gabriel relaxed. His daughter had managed to win without getting hurt. Then he tensed again, for he himself was about to hurt her and he could put it off no longer.

Leaning out the window, he shouted at Dana to come in for lunch.

Flushed with victory, Dana bounded into the back-yard that was almost a garden. Wildflowers and tufts of grass sprouted through the broken concrete. The stone walls glared white in the sunshine. Clothes flapped on the washing line. The rickety picnic table in front of the shed was Gabriel's handiwork, as was the hutch that stood nearby, the former home of Millie the rabbit who was still mourned. Seashells and candles marked her grave under the hawthorn bush. There were no pets in the house at present as the last three hamsters had lived out their pampered lives in "Hamsterdam," as Gabriel called Dana's bedroom. A trip to the animal shelter was long overdue, but he had managed to forestall it so far.

Dana's eyes widened at the sight of the feast laid out on the picnic table. A white sheet stood in for a tablecloth and all her favorite foods were there: slices of pale-green melon, a jar of dill pickles, halves of avocado with lemon and olive oil, egg salad sandwiches cut in quarters, a tub of coleslaw, and a big bowl of raspberries.

"What's up, Gabe?" she said, delighted. "New job? Big gig? Festival in Europe?"

"A new job, yeah," he said uneasily. "Did you wash your hands?"

"'Course," she lied, wiping them on her jeans.

She was too busy wolfing down her food and reaching for more to be aware that he was only picking at his. Nor did she see him fidget nervously. In between mouthfuls, she chattered about the game, slipping in a hint that they needed a new soccer ball. Her face glowed with the health of summer sun and fresh air. Whenever the tangle of raven-black hair fell into her eyes, she pushed it back impatiently. She was a child but not a child, for maturity was slowly dawning in her features: the curve of her cheekbones, the fullness of her mouth, the arch of her eyebrows. She would be a beauty, like her mother.

Gabriel felt a twinge of the old wound and let it pass. He had to focus on the moment. He had to tell her they were leaving.

She had almost finished her lunch. Dividing the raspberries evenly between them, she stuck hers on her fingertips and began eating them one by one.

"Dana, you're not going to like this, but I need you to hear me out."

Her reaction was instant. She straightened up, eyes hard, ready for a fight. Another attempt to ban her from soccer? A lecture about the state of her room? New rules to increase her share of the housework? Whenever these moments arrived, she faced him as an equal. Living together as a little family of two, they had forged their relationship over the years. He encouraged her to speak up for herself, often to his own chagrin. She would hear him out all right, but that didn't mean she would agree or comply.

"Professor Blackburn rang this morning. He put my name in for a job at the University of Toronto. Teaching music and Irish language in the Celtic Studies program."

"Toronto? As in *Canada?*"

She saw it coming. How could she not? Though they lived in Ireland, the country of her birth, Gabriel was Canadian. From time to time, he would broach the subject of going home, but it was always a vague and unlikely notion. They were well settled in Bray, and the low rent on their house provided security against the vagaries of a musician's earnings. There was no reason for them to move.

"It's not just the job," he pointed out. "It's for you as well. Look, you're growing up fast and I'm clueless here. Remember the whole fiasco about getting you a bra and—"

"*Da!!!*"

"See? We can't even talk about that stuff together. Your aunts Dee and Yvonne will be like big sisters. They'll help you out. And your grandmother."

"I don't want to go to Canada! This is my home!"

"Canada is your home too. My family's there."

"They're here too! Great-aunt Patsy and Uncle Sean. All the cousins. You're always saying we've got too much family! This is our home! We're Irish!"

"I was born in Canada," he insisted quietly. "And I grew up there. I'm Irish *and* Canadian. And so are you."

Gabriel started to fiddle with the silver ring in his ear. Then he rubbed his hand over his head which he had recently shaved. These were the things he did whenever he was upset. Though he was nearly thirty, he looked a lot younger and rarely acted his age. Dana sometimes treated him like an older brother. She liked his music, a fusion of Irish trad with jazz and folk, and her friends thought he was cool. They both knew that his status as an artist, as well as a foreigner, helped to counter the stigma of being poor and a single-parent family. But Dana had once admitted to him that she wished he were more normal, like her best friend's dad who worked in a bank. Gabriel didn't even own a suit.

"I want to go back," he said quietly. "I haven't been there since . . . before you were born. I know it'll be hard for you at first, but you'll love it in the end. Canada is a great country."

It was the quiet tone that convinced her his decision was final. She stared at him speechless. Had she been the sort of girl who cried, she would have burst into tears. Instead, she gritted her teeth and spat out her words.

"You didn't even ask me! We didn't even talk about it! Like it's got nothing to do with me! You're just a . . . a dictator! *I hate you!*"

Jumping up from the table, she stormed into the house.

Minutes later, he heard the bedroom door slam.

Gabriel stared at the last of the raspberries pooling in red juice at the bottom of the bowl. The days ahead would be a nightmare. He knew what to expect—quarrels, tantrums, and sullen silences. But wasn't that at the heart of his decision? Not her moods or defiance, but his inability to handle them. His own fears and lacks. There were times when he simply didn't know what to do. While he had managed to muddle through her childhood with reasonable success, the past year had unnerved him. There was no manual for rearing an adolescent girl on one's own. He needed help. His mother was eager to see more of her grandchild, and his two younger sisters were like teenagers themselves. When things got rough, he could call in the cavalry.

Gabriel started to clear the table. Yes, it was the right decision. For both of them. Now all he had to do was convince his daughter.

THREE

Deep in the woods, the spoor of red mist trailed through the trees. Squirrels sat up in their dreys, alert. The chirr of insects ceased. A fox stopped in its tracks, nose to the air, hair bristling. A wild rabbit thumped the ground. Warning. Danger. All held themselves rigid, awaiting catastrophe.

At first the demon clung to the fetid shade of the undergrowth, avoiding the light that worsened its pain. In misshapen and inchoate form, it instinctively sought life to feed upon, consuming the insects that crossed its path. Killing brought relief. It grew ravenous for more. The mother bird screeched helplessly as her young were devoured. The hare tried to outrun its fate but to no avail. And the great antlered deer fought with ferocious courage before it, too, fell.

As the shadow's strength grew, shreds of image and memory coalesced into thought.

It had a mission.

A target to destroy.

What? Or who?

It knew that it did not belong to this place, yet it had been here before. Before the fiery blast that had ravaged its mind.

So much was lost. So much it needed to remember! And even as it grasped for knowledge, it sensed the two worlds that existed around it, peopled with many different beings. One world was solid and visible; the other of a different fabric, lapping against the first like waves against the shore. In which of these worlds would it find its prey?

And how could it carry out its mission in its crippled state?

It needed to grow, to learn, to know.

Creeping through the half-light of dusk, under cover of the forest canopy, it came to a clearing where a bonfire burned. The warmth and brightness of the flames repelled it, but it did not flee. Already it sensed some kinship here. Cloaked in gloom, it watched and waited, brooding upon the scene.

A band of brave companions sat together, laughing and talking. Drinking cups were passed among them and plates of cheese and oaten bread. The chieftain was a robust man with a weathered face and a hearty laugh. There was a flame within him as bright as the campfire itself.

With the firelight flickering in his features, the chieftain put a question to his comrades.

"What is the most beautiful sound in the world?"

They cheered at each other's replies.

"The calling of a cuckoo from a high tree."

"The song of a lark breaking suddenly over a field."

"The belling of a stag across the water of a lake."

"The laughter of a lovely girl."

"The whisper on a beloved's lips."

"What do you think is the most beautiful sound in the world?" they asked him in turn.

He let out a great roar.

"The music of what happens. That is the finest sound you will ever hear."

Their merriment was painful to endure, but the demon felt drawn to the circle. For there was one in the company who was not unlike itself. Yet it had to be careful. Already the leader suspected its presence and was peering around the campsite with a frown. One of the women shivered. The chieftain stood up, signaling to his lieutenant to scout the area.

Too late.

It was already moving among them, hiding in the shadows they cast themselves.

Four

A sea breeze blew through the open windows to cool the stuffy interior of the old Triumph Herald. Air conditioning could not be expected in a car built in the 1960s. The leather upholstery was sweaty and Dana's legs kept sticking to the seat. She didn't complain. She had grown up in that old car: naps in the backseat during long drives through the country, picnics on the side of the road in the rain, journeys by ferry to Brittany and the Outer Hebrides when Gabriel played in Celtic music festivals.

She threw a furious glance at her father. All that would go too! As the first shock of his announcement wore off, she faced the magnitude of what lay ahead. How much she would lose. Her best friend. Her soccer gang. Her street. Her life.

"Once you start school, you'll make new friends," Gabriel had said that morning, in an effort to cheer her up.

"It won't fix what's gone! Nothing can. You know that!"

As soon as the words were uttered, she was sorry. He looked as if she had hit him.

"Oh Gabe . . . Da . . . I didn't mean . . ."

He stood up to put the kettle on for tea. She flinched when she saw the slump of his shoulders. He was more sensitive than she, more easily hurt.

They continued their breakfast in silence. The toast felt dry in her throat and she started to choke. He handed her a glass of orange juice and rubbed her back. She smiled apologetically through the tears caused by her coughs. He smiled back.

"Let's go to the glen today," he suggested. "I need to talk to the lads. Maybe you could see a tree house?"

It was a peace offering, almost a bribe. He had refused to let her near the tree houses built by the eco-warriors in the Glen of the Downs. She had been begging to climb up to one since the environmental protest began earlier that summer.

It was an old story befalling an old country that had suddenly found itself new and rich. Economic progress was rampaging across the land. Green fields were being smothered in concrete and tarmac, small villages swallowed by urban sprawl. Winding roads lined with hedgerows were disappearing into webs of roundabouts and motorways. Though the Glen of the Downs was a Nature Reserve protected by law, the government had approved the widening of the road that ran through its heart. Great tracts of trees were marked for felling in order to accommodate a four-lane highway. Eco-warriors had arrived from around the world to join the protests of Irish environmentalists. Setting up camp in the endangered woods, they halted all work at the site by living in tents on the ground and tree houses in the branches.

Gabriel slowed the car as the speckled peak of the Sugar Loaf Mountain loomed ahead. Past the mountain, the road wound like a snake through the Glen of the Downs, a deep gorge torqued by the tidal forces of an ancient glacier. On either side of the road, the slopes rose skyward for over three hundred feet, cloaked with forest. To the right, above the tree line, an old famine wall crested the ridge like a broken crown. Painted crudely on the stone in great white letters was the cry: WHO WILL FIGHT FOR THE GLEN?

Turning left into the parking lot, Gabriel drew up the Triumph under a banner strung between two trees. NO MOTORWAY HERE. Dana was out in an instant. They were already inside the forest, surrounded by tall beech, birch, and oak. Only a few yards behind them, the road was hidden by greenery. The susurrus of the speeding cars blended with the soughing of the wind in the trees. The understory was lush with nettles and purple foxglove. It had rained earlier and the air was rich with the smell of loam.

Dana loved the glen. She and Gabriel often hiked its trails. When the protest began they had joined up immediately, helping with petitions, supplies, and fund-raising. Though many locals viewed the eco-warriors as hippies

and troublemakers, there was widespread support in the
community for "the tree people."

GIVE TREES A CHANCE.

THE EARTH DOES NOT BELONG TO US.
WE BELONG TO THE EARTH.

IN WILDNESS IS THE PRESERVATION OF THE WORLD.

THE DEATH OF THE FOREST IS THE
BEGINNING OF THE END OF OUR WORLD.

The banners and signs were everywhere, hanging
from the trees like gigantic catkins. Dana raced past them
and into the clearing where the eco-warriors had set up
their central command. The area was surrounded by
Scots pine, with a carpet of brown needles and cones that
crunched underfoot. Here the protestors gathered around
the campfire for meetings and meals, and companionship
when they weren't on duty. Though legal action was being
taken to evict them, they were using the time to build support for their cause.

After weeks of living and sleeping outdoors, the eco-
warriors looked a little rough, as if gone to seed. In muddy
boots and soiled clothing, with straggly hair and unshaven
faces, they sat around the fire on old chairs and a burst

sofa. Dana thought of them as a gang of outlaws, like Robin Hood and his Merry Men. Big Bob was the leader, a broad-shouldered bear of a man with laughing eyes and a booming voice. His hair was sandy-colored and so was his beard, and he wore faded dungarees tucked into his boots. An organic farmer from County Monaghan, he had left his farm in the hands of his wife and grown children in order to lead the protest.

"Seems right to go when you're called," he would say.

The moment he saw Dana he hurried over to give her a great hug.

"How's the youngest eco-warrior in Ireland?" he roared.

"Ready to fight the good fight!" she shouted back, as always.

"That's my girl! Got a barman joke for me?"

"I do!" she said, delighted. She had been saving it. "A priest, a rabbi, a minister, a blonde, and a dog went into a bar. 'What's this?' said the barman. 'A joke?'"

Big Bob laughed loudly and clapped her on the back.

"Goodgeon!"

The others made room for her at the fire. A blackened kettle sat in the flames, boiling water for tea. Cracked cups and mugs were passed around. Everyone smelled of burnt wood. Though occasional breezes caused clouds of smoke to billow around them, no one moved. Instead, they sat like ghosts in a fog.

Dana smiled over at Billie, an English backpacker with piercings in her ears, nose, lips, and eyebrows. The tattoo of a blue serpent ran up her arm. Next to her was Murta, Big Bob's lieutenant, a wiry man who rolled his own cigarettes and was always talking on a cell phone. Several new arrivals introduced themselves to her, but it was a while before she noticed the other stranger, the one who hovered in the shadows of the trees, leaning against an old oak. He wore a black wide-brimmed hat with green leaves tucked into the band. His jacket, jeans, and T-shirt were also black. He didn't join the circle but seemed to be watching them from under the rim of his hat. The others ignored him, but Dana kept glancing in his direction. Something about him made her uneasy.

The talk around the campfire concerned the illegal dumps found in the Wicklow Mountains.

"Tons of toxic waste," Billie said, shaking her head, "polluting the soil and the groundwater."

"It's no longer a matter of politics or economics," Big Bob declared passionately. "The ecological crisis is a moral issue. It's a battle between what's right or wrong for the Earth!"

Dana listened for a while, but once they turned to injunctions and legalities she lost interest. With nothing to distract her, she was left with her own gloomy thoughts about the move ahead.

Big Bob noticed her unhappiness.

"As the barman said to the horse, 'Why the long face?' Da giving you a hard time? Do you want me to box his ears?"

Gabriel signaled to him to let matters lie, but it was too late. Dana sensed an ally.

"He's taking us away! Off to Canada!"

Big Bob looked dismayed. "You're not leaving us, Gabe! When? Why?"

Gabriel shrugged. "I've been offered a job. The money's too good to pass up. And I think it's time. Time to go. Time to let go . . ."

His voice trailed away as he stared into the flames.

Looks were exchanged among his friends. Billie got up to pass around a packet of chocolate biscuits. Murta made more tea.

The conversation moved on to ways of raising money for the cause.

Dana's heart sank as her hope of support vanished. Would no one take her side? Was she all alone? She heaved a sigh, scuffed the ground with her feet. And to make matters worse, by the time the cookies reached her, the packet was empty.

Billie caught her eyeing it ruefully.

"There's more in the cave. Help yourself."

She didn't need much encouragement. Dana loved nosing around in the clapboard shack where they kept their supplies. Set back in the trees, the cavernous shelter had wooden shelves from floor to ceiling cluttered with groceries, books, tarpaulins, and sleeping bags. Rain gear hung from hooks on the walls. Cupboards were crammed with cooking utensils, tinned goods, and sacks of rice and potatoes. Dana was rummaging through the foodstuffs when a blast of wind buffeted the shack. Everything rattled and shook, but nothing was disturbed except for a packet of chocolate biscuits that landed at her feet.

"Hey! Great!"

As she stooped to get it, she was suddenly aware that she was no longer alone. She straightened up. There stood the man with the wide-brimmed hat. She hadn't heard him enter the cave. A strange nervousness came over her. There was something about him that she didn't understand. Was he young or old? She couldn't tell. His features were striking, pale and handsome. His red-gold hair was tied in a ponytail that draped over his shoulder. But it was the eyes that really struck her: bluer than any blue she had ever seen.

Shyly she offered him the packet of biscuits, but he declined with a smile.

"Follow the greenway."

Though he spoke quietly, his voice resonated in the air. She was reminded of Gabriel's blackwood flute.

"What?" she said.

He lifted his hand to his hat. She thought he was saluting her, but he plucked a green leaf from the brim and handed it to her. A ticket? An invitation?

"My lady awaits you."

Again he spoke softly, yet the words were unmistakably a command. She would have asked questions but he didn't give her the chance. Tipping his hat in farewell, he stepped out of the cave and back into the forest.

"Wait a minute!" she said.

Another blast of wind shook the trees. He was gone.

"That was weird," she muttered.

But then none of the eco-warriors were what you would call normal. They were all "odd sods and bods" as Gabe would say. In fact, that description applied to most of his friends.

Dana stuffed the leaf into her back pocket and returned to the campfire. More tea was being brewed. More plans were being made. She groaned. They would be there all day. Slow death by boredom.

"Da, when can I see the tree houses?"

Before her father could answer, Big Bob responded.

"Let her go, Gabe. She's safe here. We're all over the place, like guardian angels."

"All right then," Gabriel agreed. "But no going near the road. And don't climb any trees. You can look at them from the ground and I'll bring you up later. After lunch. And shout if you need me. And—"

"Aye, aye, captain," Dana said quickly.

Then off she ran, before he could think up more rules.

• • •

Big Bob grinned as Dana disappeared into the trees.
"She's getting big. Heading for womanhood."

"Don't I know it." Gabriel sighed. "It's one of the reasons I want to go home. She can be a handful."

"Twelve is a tough age," Big Bob said, nodding with sympathy. "Half kid, half teen. Betwixt and between. I'm glad my lot are well out of it."

"She needs a mother," Gabriel murmured.

"Aye," his friend said gently, gripping his shoulder.

FIVE

Swimming through layers of storied memory, the giant clutched at fragments of words and images. Were they pieces of a true tale that belonged to him? Or were they slivers of the spell that pinned him down?

Imdha toir torudh abla,
Imdha airne cen cesa,
Imdha dairbre ardmhesa.

Plentiful in the east the apple fruits,
Plentiful the luxuriant sloes,
Plentiful the noble acorn-bearing oaks.

Fado, fado.

Once upon a time, long, long ago . . .

. . . there was a Mountain Kingdom that curved like a chain on the blue throat of the sea. It was a place of dark forests and windy peaks, of sunny glens and rushing rivers.

The lakes and streams brimmed with trout and silver salmon. The trees rang with the song of bright birds.

The King of the Mountain, the King of the Woods, was tall and broad-shouldered, of courteous speech and gentle manner. He did not care for war or battle. His chief delight was to roam the hills in the company of wild creatures, great and small. In the light of day, his peals of laughter rolled over the highlands like summer thunder. In the shadows of the evening, he swam in cool waters under the moon. Oh, how tranquil was his world! How green its valleys! How sweet the air and clear the waters!

And when springtime thawed the white frost of winter and everything living bridled with new joy, the Mountain King's people would call out to him.

"Will you not marry?" chirmed the birds.

"Will you not take a wife?" hummed the bees.

It was a question they always asked and one to which his answer never wavered.

"I am waiting."

Then falling silent, he would gaze upward into the glimmering night, and hope would dim his eyes till he was almost blind.

Six

Dana hurried along the trail through the woods, ducking under the overhanging branches and jumping over roots and rocks. To her right, a burbling stream bordered the road, half hidden by thickets of hazel and ash. To her left, the ground sheered upward, covered with trees and a dense undergrowth of fern. The call of a wood pigeon echoed over the treetops. The air was pungent with the scent of wild garlic. She stopped for a moment to glare at writing gouged into the silver-gray trunk of a birch. How would people like it if trees carved names on *their* skin? *Oak loves holly. Rowan was here.* When she rested her hand against the scars, she startled a treecreeper. The tiny bird scrabbled up the trunk like a little brown mouse, but not before issuing a *tssst* to express its annoyance.

"Sorry," she called softly. "Didn't see you!"

Leaving the trail behind, Dana climbed the slope, pushing her way through bracken and fern, avoiding the prickly patches of holly and bramble. She didn't see the green tent until she was almost on top of it. Low snores rumbled from inside; someone catching up on lost sleep after a stint of night duty. She checked the branches over-head. Like the tent, the tree houses could be camouflaged; she might be missing them.

Setting out again, she was surprised to hear a twig snap behind her.

"Hello?" she said, looking around.

Was someone following her? The strange man from the camp? Or maybe it was an animal. Though they were rarely seen in daylight, foxes and badgers lived in the glen. The woods seemed suddenly ominous, pressing against her. She shivered. For a moment she considered going back. *Don't be silly. There's nothing to be afraid of.*

As Dana continued upward, she spotted a rope ladder hanging down the trunk of a tall beech. Craning her neck, she spied the tree house above her, resting in the branches like a great disheveled bird. It was built of wooden pallets and covered with blue sheets of waterproof plastic that crackled in the breeze.

"Anyone home?" she called.

No answer.

She didn't think twice about going up. A safety rope dangled alongside the ladder. Tying it around her waist, she started to climb. Looking down made her dizzy, but she also felt exhilarated. She had never gone this high before.

When she finally reached the tree house, she found it crude and rather shabby. There were two musty sleep-ing bags on dank pieces of carpet, some books and papers,

and candles in glass jars. Nonetheless, it was exciting to
be there. When the wind blew, the house swayed with the
branches. Dana remembered a book her father had read
to her, *The Tree That Sat Down*. She had always wanted
to sleep in a hammock— like the girl in the story—strung
high in the treetops, under the stars.

She gazed out over the forest canopy. Below her curved
the road and the ribbon of stream. The sound of the cars
and the water was muted, like the fall of soft rain. Smoke
from the campfire wisped through the trees. Wouldn't
Gabe have a fit if he could see her!

A flash of light caught her eye. On the slope above her.
One of the eco-warriors signaling with a mirror? There
it was again! A burst of gold. Not a mirror. Too big, too
bright. As if the sun were caught in a net of branches.
But the sun was overhead. She had just decided to go
and investigate when she spotted something else nearer
to her. Something or someone moving through the trees.
She couldn't make out the shape as it was hunched and
half crawling, as if trying to hide. It was coming toward
her. One of the tree-house dwellers? But why so sneaky?
Dana was suddenly overwhelmed by the sense that she
wasn't safe.

The fear of being cornered sent her into a panic. Without thinking, she threw herself onto the ladder and forgot to grab hold of the safety rope. In her haste, she lost

her balance and her foot slipped. The ladder swung. The world spun around her. With a cry, she clutched the rungs till the ladder steadied. Then she hurried down.

She had just reached the bottom when someone broke from the trees. Murta, Big Bob's right-hand man. Dana was immediately wary. He had always given her the creeps; the way he stared at her chest when no one was looking. A chill ran through her. The campsite seemed suddenly far away. Gabe's constant warnings raced through her mind. *Stand strong. Stare them straight in the eye. Make it obvious you'll fight. They don't like that. If attacked, go for the groin. Or the eyes, if he gets that near. Punch, kick, bite, whatever you need to do. Yell as loud as you can. Shout "fire." People respond to that.*

"Is my Da looking for me?" she demanded. "I'm on my way back."

"No, no," said Murta, licking his lips nervously. He managed a weak smile. "I thought you might like to see a tree house. Maybe this one?"

"I've already seen it," she said coldly. *As if I'd go anywhere with you.*

"There are other ones you could see," he said, stepping closer.

She backed away instinctively and bumped into the tree behind her. He appeared to be huge, blocking her path. She kept staring at his fingers, stained yellow with nicotine.

Then she heard it, high up in the air. A stream of music so sweet it brought tears to her eyes.

"Gabe?"

It sounded like his flute, the silver one. A surge of relief flooded through her. He liked to practice in the woods.

Murta looked around quickly. The swift change in his features gave her a shock: the hatred that burned there.

She didn't stop to wonder. The instant he was distracted, Dana made a run for it.

She headed for the camp, but in her panic lost her bearings. Behind her she could hear Murta crashing through the underbrush. He was breathing heavily. Smoker's lungs. She scrabbled higher up the slope to make it harder for him.

And all the time the silvery notes danced through the air, leading her onward.

The way itself grew more treacherous. She had to fight against the tall bracken; the smell of bruised greenery was suffocating. There was no time to maneuver around briars or brambles, and she was scraped and stung. Her sense of direction was skewed. She had no idea where she was. Then a gust of wind rolled down the mountainside, making the leaves on the ground swirl around her. Startled, she saw little faces in the eddy: narrow eyes and wide mouths and brown crinkled skin. She blinked. They were gone.

The sight had brought her to a halt. And the music had also stopped.

She was almost at the top of the ridge, in the farthest

reaches of the glen. A great oak tree stood before her, far taller than any she had ever seen. A ladder of twined ivy hung down its trunk, and above was a tree house impossibly high in the branches. Even from that distance, she could see it was different from the other one. This had a natural grace and form, as if it grew from the tree itself.

Dana's skin tingled. She could hardly breathe. More than anything else, she wanted to get up there. Fear and daring battled inside her. Could she climb that high? What if Murta caught her there? There were no sounds of pursuit behind her, only a soft whisper in the leaves above.

Follow the greenway.

Grasping the ladder, Dana hurried upward before she could change her mind. Clusters of oak leaves brushed against her as she climbed higher and higher. Though she tried not to look down, she couldn't help but see the valley unfurl below her. The forest canopy was like a carpet of curly kale. In the distance, to the east, rolled the smooth lawns of a golf course, and beyond them, the blue glimmer of the Irish Sea. She felt light-headed. Her hands trembled as she gripped the next rung. There was no safety rope. Shouldn't she go back?

She continued on.

At last she reached the crown of the oak to find the loveliest tree house imaginable. Slender branches wove together to form a green dome stippled with primroses, bluebells, and pink and white foxgloves. The windows were openings like big round eyes. A natural arch made the door. Dana lowered her head to enter. The interior was dappled with a gentle green light. The scent of wild-flowers tinted the air. The whole structure rocked gently, like a boat on the waves.

Magical.

But no more magical than the person who waited inside.

A young woman of startling beauty sat cross-legged by a low wooden table. Her gown was of green silk threaded with silver. White blossoms wreathed her long fair hair. Her skin seemed to shimmer with a trace of gold.

Was she a hippie girl, Dana wondered, an English traveler like Billie? But the label didn't fit. There was something too . . . queenly . . . about her. An eccentric aristocrat perhaps? There were plenty of those involved in the cause. Some of them lived in the big house above the glen. Dana was suddenly conscious of her own appearance. Her clothes were soiled from climbing the ridge and she was covered with scratches. Mumbling apologies, she started to back out the door.

The Lady smiled.

"*Fáilte romhat,*" she said, beckoning Dana to join her. "I welcome thee to my forest fane."

Her voice was musical, silvery.

Not a hippie, Dana decided, but definitely eccentric. Both the Irish and the English sounded odd.

With the same breathless excitement she had felt before climbing the tree, Dana sat down on a mat of soft moss.

"Eat and drink with me," said the Lady.

A little feast was laid out on crystal dishes. There were bowls of luscious wild berries and roasted hazelnuts, tall glasses of a dark purple wine, and elegant seedcakes dripping with honey.

The moment she sampled the fare, Dana wanted more. Never had nuts tasted so rich and nutty, while the berries burst on her tongue with tart zest. As for the little honey-eyed cakes, they tasted like sunlight dusted with sugar. She was about to cram another one into her mouth when she stopped. A tiny alarm had sounded in the back of her mind. Some warning about not eating? Her hand dropped into her lap. Her eyelids felt heavy. The alarm in her mind was louder now, urging her to leave, but she was reluctant to do so.

"We are in need of thy help," the Lady said.

Dana's thoughts were muzzy. It took some effort before she could speak.

"Da and me . . . we're doing . . . he's . . ."

The Lady shook her head.

"You alone, dear heart. The *Ard Rí* needs you to be his messenger."

"*Ard Rí?* . . . High King? What—?"

The Lady's gaze was steady. Where had Dana seen eyes that blue before?

"Do you not know who we are?" the Lady asked her.

Dana was bewildered. She felt as if something was pressing against her so that she could hardly breathe.

"Aren't you . . . one of . . . the tree people?"

The Lady nodded gravely.

"That is one of our names: the Tree People."

A shiver ran up Dana's spine. She sensed the capital letters and the huge significance that lurked behind them. Now the Lady was saying even more baffling things.

"I am of the Tree People behind the tree people. We inspire their work. The destruction of the forest is the beginning of the end of our world."

Dana was growing more nervous by the minute. This was more than eccentric; it was weird and kind of scary. Were drugs involved? She wanted to leave but couldn't move. Something in the food? She opened her mouth to scream for help, but found herself yawning instead. Her eyelids felt heavy and began to close.

Watching her keenly, the Lady grew upset.

"Thou art *fairy-struck*, Dana! Do not be spellbound! Come, we have need of thee!"

Some part of Dana wanted to please the Lady, especially after she had given her such nice things to eat. But it was too difficult. Her eyes had closed to shut out the impossible, and she was drifting away into the safe harbors of sleep.

The Lady buried her face in her hands.

"Lost to me are human ways and speech! I cannot gain her trust nor secure her assurances. I have failed the Summer Land!"

The tears and laments didn't wake Dana, but the sudden transformation that followed did.

"Omigod! You're only a kid! How could I possibly send you on a dangerous mission? It's worse than abduction!"

Dana's eyes sprang open. The North American accent was like a cold splash of water. What was going on? She rubbed her eyes. Everything was different. Though the young woman was still pretty, she had lost her *glamour*. The golden sheen was gone from her skin, and the startling blue eyes were now hazel-green. Her blond hair was in knots, strewn with daisies and leaves. Instead of a shining gown, she wore faded jeans and a grimy T-shirt. She looked very like a hippie, and a scruffy one at that.

Dana was stunned.

"Who are you?"

"I . . . I'm not sure."

The voice was the biggest shock. The silvery tone had disappeared to be replaced with an accent that was clearly recognizable, as it was so like her father's.

"You're not even Irish!"

The older girl, little more than a teenager, looked as surprised as Dana.

"I . . . I was . . . I don't . . . I'm kinda new to . . . This has never happened before!" She regarded her clothes with dismay. "Maybe I was so freaked out about not getting through to you that I returned to my former self. You see we . . . They . . . You're really needed, Dana. Bigtime. Something evil has entered the Mountain Kingdom. We've got to get a message to the Tánaiste. You're the only way we can reach him."

"*Tánaiste?*" Dana was growing more confused by the minute. "You mean in the government?"

"No, not your Tánaiste. *Our* Tánaiste. The second-in-command to the High King of Faerie. He's the King of Wicklow. Lugh of the Mountain, Lugh of the Wood. We haven't been able to contact him. His borders are closed and—"

"I don't know what you're talking about!" Dana jumped to her feet. It was time to get out of there. "Look, I can't help you. And even if I could, why should I? I don't know you. This has nothing to do with me."

"Please don't go!" the other begged. "Hear me out!"

Dana hesitated. Though it was all too bizarre, she found herself feeling sorry for the girl. Between her bedraggled look and desperate pleas, she was like a homeless waif.

"Go on," said Dana reluctantly.

"I'll be as honest as I can," the young woman said, both relieved and anxious. "I seem to have forgotten a lot of things. I guess because I've reverted. All I know is this:

you're the best person to do the job. You're the only one who can reach King Lugh. As for your question about why you should do it?"

Her eyes flashed with mischief, and the grin was so infectious Dana couldn't help but smile back.

"Well, get this," the girl said in a conspiratorial tone. "If you do something for Them . . . I mean us . . . in return, we owe something to *you*."

Dana was caught.

"What kind of something?"

The other shrugged and then giggled.

"Your heart's desire. Whatever you wish."

SEVEΠ

W here was she? A green valley lush with life. She smiled
to see its beauty.

The vision lasted but the length of a heartbeat.

Then they came.

At first they appeared to be a storm on the horizon, a
dark squall rolling over the sky. Then, as they drew nearer,
she saw they were ragged crows with their eyes sewn shut.
As they swarmed into the glen, they attacked everything
that lived, ripping out plants and stripping trees, tearing
apart animals, devouring birds and the tiniest of insects. The
silence of the slaughter was more terrifying than screams. A
red fog of blood obscured the scene.

And when the demon birds departed, there was nothing
left.

Dim shadows descended over the desolation. The earth
lay barren without a single blade of grass. No bird sang. No
creature stirred. A venomous wind wailed over the landscape,
hot and dry and choked with dust.

She sensed the suffering of the land. It seeped into her
body and withered her soul. Was this Dún Eadóchais? The

Fort of Despair? Or was it Dún Scáith? *The Fort of the Shades?*

A deep dread crept over her. She grew aware of the ground beneath her bare feet. Deathly cold and slimed with oil, it yielded too readily. Each step she took sank further than the last. Generations have trod, have trod, have trod. *With dawning horror, she realized she was not walking on solid earth, but over a cesspit of noxious substances. Foul draughts of air rose to assault her nostrils: the sweet, sickly scent of putrefaction.*

And even as the nightmarish thought struck her, it began to happen. She felt herself sinking into a pit. The noisome mud gurgled around her, opening like a maw to gorge on her. She fought like a wild thing, twisting violently, clawing against the trap.

She screamed for help.

But her screams fell like stones into a bottomless well.

She screamed again.

And again.

Eight

"*MAMA! MAMA!*"

Dana woke screaming. As always, she changed her cries when Gabriel came rushing into the room.

"*DA! DA!*"

"I'm here, princess. It's all right. I'm here."

He gathered her up in his arms and held her tightly.

She was shocked and trembling. It had been a while since that particular nightmare attacked her. By the guilty look on Gabe's face, she knew he believed it had come from the news about their move. She herself believed differently.

"I shouldn't have touched the feast," she muttered.

"What feast?" Gabriel asked, humoring her.

"At the glen."

It was a valid suspicion. She had grown up on tales that warned against taking food or drink from "the Other Crowd."

"The cups were pretty manky," Gabriel agreed. "But as your grandmother likes to say, 'you have to eat a peck of dirt before you die.'"

"Yuck," said Dana.

But she let him think she was referring to the eco-warriors. She hadn't told him about the Lady in the woods, nor of the pact they had made. In return for a wish, Dana had agreed to go into the mountains to carry a message to the King of Wicklow. Not something to tell a parent!

"How about a midnight snack?" she suggested.

They padded down the stairs in their pajamas. It was three o'clock in the morning, the usual time for Dana's night terrors. Some were worse than others. The really bad ones were always treated with hot cocoa and a bite to eat.

Their terraced house was small and narrow, with two bedrooms upstairs and a living room, kitchen, and bathroom below. The living room was Gabriel's work space, cluttered with his instruments, amplifiers, and computer. The sofa and television were crowded into the kitchen along with bookshelves, appliances, table and chairs. When weather allowed, they always ate in the backyard.

Dana poured milk into a small pot, while her father popped brown bread into the toaster and set out their assortment of jams—homemade marmalade, blueberry, black currant, and plum.

"It's been a while since you rode a night mare, eh?" he ventured.

"Yeah," she said with a shrug.

She leaned over the stove to watch the pot. Her hair

got in the way and she pushed it back. It was tangled from all her tossing and turning, and her eyes felt puffy. The gas flame flickered blue and orange. The milk began to bubble. She tested the temperature with her finger. The last trails of the dream wormed through her mind, but she thought about the Lady instead and the wish she had promised.

"Look, Dana," her father began carefully. She could hear the remorse in his voice. "How about we agree just to try it? Maybe a year or two? If it doesn't work out . . . if you're really miserable . . . we'll come back. I swear."

Without stopping to think, she asked the question that burned in her mind.

"If we move to Canada, Gabe, how will she find us?"

It was like a great soft blow. He almost staggered back. When he spoke at last, he fell over his words.

"Dana . . . sweetheart . . . I thought . . . We've been through all this. You know very well . . . *Your mother's not coming back.*"

Her features hardened.

"You don't know that! Things change. Anything can happen!"

His dismay was obvious. She was upset herself that they were talking about it. She felt the memory of a stone in the pit of her stomach. Neither of them had spoken of her mother in years. Dana remembered exactly when she stopped asking about her. It was Mother's Day. She was six years old. For some reason she had got the idea into her head: *this is the day missing mothers come home.* Without explaining to her father, she had taken a bath, put on her Sunday dress, and brushed her hair. Was Gabe uneasy that day? Did he suspect? All she could remember was sitting on the front step, hour after hour, looking hopefully up and down the street. There were no tears when the day ended, but a stone had dropped inside her, cold and heavy. Whenever Gabriel mentioned her mother, Dana would turn her head away. Eventually he stopped raising the subject altogether. As far as Dana was concerned, her mother didn't exist.

The meeting with the Lady in the woods had changed all that. No sooner was the wish proffered than hope surged through Dana and shattered the stone. *I'll find her at last!*

Gabriel was floundering. Even as he measured out his words, she recognized the tone: the one he used in the days when she still begged him to search for her mother. *She must be lost, Da! Like the time on the beach when I couldn't find you! We've got to go look for her!*

It was not his way to avoid the issue. He always told her the truth. What else could he do?

"You know the story, kiddo. But I'll keep telling it to you as long as you need to hear it. It all happened a long time ago, before you were born. Your mother and I were madly in love, but we were very young. Kids really, both in our teens. Way too young to marry. We rented an old cottage in the Glen of the Downs. You were born a year later. We were poor but happy. Your mother grew vegetables, made her own bread and just about everything else we ate. Okay, we were hippies. I played in pubs, took on a few students, even busked in the streets. We got by, and it was a good life, believe me. And you were a great baby, always laughing."

His face shone as he remembered.

Then his features tightened.

"It was like a bolt out of the blue. That's the only way I can describe it. I left a happy home that morning and when I came back for lunch, everything had changed. Changed utterly."

Dana put her hand on her father's shoulder. He didn't cry. Like her, all his tears had been shed years ago, but his body was clenched as if in pain.

"I found you in the house alone, crying your heart out. She was gone. Without warning or explanation. Not even a note. The police thought maybe an accident, maybe something worse. They searched the glen, the mountains, the bogs, the lakes and rivers, but no sign of her. In the end, they called her a runaway and closed the case."

Gabriel gazed out the kitchen window. Dawn was creeping through the sky to light up the backyard. The wild roses trailing over the shed blushed red in the dimness.

"And that's when we moved here," Dana murmured,

ending the story the way she used to when she was little, "to Wolfe Tone Square in the town of Bray where we lived happily ever after, just you and me."

Yet something in her voice implied that the ending was no longer satisfactory.

"Why can't I remember her, Gabe? I try to picture her in my head and I can't."

"You were only three. But you've seen the photos."

Dana's mouth twisted wryly. How intently she had once studied those few fuzzy pictures taken with a disposable camera! Always searching for clues and memories. There was one of the wedding at the Registrar's Office. Her mother wore a dress of green lace with a string of pearls, and a sprig of honeysuckle in her hair. There were several of the celebration back at the cottage, all their friends laughing and drinking, mostly young musicians and artists. Dana's favorite had always been the one of herself as a baby in her mother's arms. Yet no matter how hard and how long she had stared at those images, the pretty young woman with the strawberry-blond hair remained a stranger to her.

"I mean a picture in my head. Of *her* looking at *me*. I can do it with you, even from way back. I shut my eyes and there you are, smiling at me."

Dana closed her eyes. Her face lit up, reflecting her father's love for her. But when she opened her eyes again, they glinted darkly.

"When I try to do that for Mum, nothing comes. Nothing's there. Gabe, did she hate me? Is that why she left?"

For the second time that night, he was speechless. A deep shudder passed through him. He reached out to grip her arms, his voice shaking and urgent.

"Jesus, Dana, how can you think that? We went over this again and again when you were little. *All* kids blame themselves if their parents leave or split up or even die! You've got to believe me. *It wasn't your fault!* It had nothing to do with you! How could it? You were an innocent baby! A three-year-old! Maybe I was fooling myself and I was doing it all wrong, but the way I remember it, the three of us were happy. Really happy. I can tell you this for certain—she loved me and she loved you."

"Then why did she go?"

Dana's demand was almost a wail. They had arrived at the point inevitably reached whenever they went this way: a dark place of defeat and unknowing. A dead end.

Gabriel sighed and shook his head.

"Like I said, we were very young. Just kids. Maybe it was too much for her. The truth is, honey, I can't answer that question and I've given up trying. I don't know why she left. I guess we'll never know."

ПiпE

The giant roared like a wounded beast in the night, maddened beyond all sense. The mountain closed around him like a tomb. The weight of stone bore him down. Tripling in force, the spell worked its magic with more songs and more words to tighten his bonds.

Seothó, a thoil, ná goil go fóill,
Seothó, a thoil, ná goil aon deoir,
Seothó, a linbh, a chumainn's a stóir.

Hush, dear heart, no need to cry,
Hush, dear heart, no need for tears,
Hush, my child, my love and treasure.

Now an image flickered in the darkness of his mind. A great bonfire burning on a distant hill. He strove to draw nearer, to see more clearly. The night sky was dusky with the warm breath of midsummer. Was it he who stood in the flickering shadows, surrounded by creatures of every kind? Not only animals but elemental beings of the woods and the *waters, shimmering like the stars above. He was laughing with the others, yet he did not join the circle that danced around the flames. His eyes were constantly watching the sky.*

Then he raised his arms, for he knew the time had come, and he let out a cry that flew like thought.

Let her come to me now, she for whom I have waited so long!

Tᴇɴ

Dana was beginning to panic. More than a week had passed since the meeting in the woods. The Lady had told her to wait for a sign, but time was running out. The airplane tickets were booked. In less than a month, she would be leaving for Canada.

There were moments when Dana wondered if it had really happened, if such a thing were possible. The leaf she was given in the cave had already dried and crumbled to dust. Was it just make-believe? Her own wishful daydream? And what if it wasn't? A trace of fear always mingled with her hope. She knew these matters were beyond the ordinary. She recognized their nature from the stories she had grown up with; all those tales of a half-glimpsed world beyond the veil of the visible. A world that was both beautiful and perilous. Didn't the Lady herself speak of danger?

Dana knew she would go regardless. Having caught hold of a long-lost dream, she wasn't about to give it up. She had begun to think of her mother again. Early memories were trickling in. That time she found the box of clothes in her father's wardrobe. Was she four or five? The dresses and skirts were mostly light cottons with flowered patterns. Crushing the fabric against her face, she had inhaled the lingering scent of apples, as she sobbed her heart out. Then there were the times she had lain in bed at night, listening to the sound of a sweet voice in her head. *Hush, dear heart, no need to cry. Hush, dear heart, no need for tears.* Her pillow was always damp when she woke in the morning.

And there was something else. Behind the snippets of memory, Dana sensed the shadow of some terrible moment; an event both monstrous and hidden. Too amorphous to recall, it only left her baffled.

She wished she had someone to talk to, but her best friend was in Spain on holiday and her soccer gang were useless. They would only make fun of her. No one believed in magic at their age. Gabriel did, of course, or so he always said, but he was the last person she could turn to. *Hey, Da, I've got to go off into the mountains on a dangerous quest!*

Things were already tense at home. Since her father held a Canadian passport, he had to prove his right to take Dana from her birthplace. Officially the mother's consent was required. Notices had to be posted in newspapers and public places to allow her the chance to come forward to claim her child. It was harrowing for him. Though he didn't involve Dana, she knew what was happening and she could see the haunted look in his eyes. Under normal circumstances, she would have been tormenting him about the move, but she wasn't able to. He looked too miserable.

It was Sunday when she found him sitting alone in the kitchen staring at the wall. His eyes were red and she knew he had been crying.

"Let's go out for dinner," she suggested. "Take my pocket money for the month. We should celebrate your new job!"

She had to turn away quickly. It was obvious he was about to cry again.

The Hanuman House was their favorite place in Bray, not only because it served delicious food, but because they knew its owners, Aradhana and Suresh, who had arrived from India only a year before. Two flights of stairs led upward to an airy dining room overlooking the stone bridge that crossed the River Dargle. The walls and even the ceiling of the restaurant were painted with scenes from the Hindu epic the *Ramayana*. Dana loved looking at the pictures that told the story of the hero, Rama, who saved his beautiful wife, Sita, from the evil demon, Ravanna. In the evening, when candles were lit at the tables, the murals seemed to come alive. The flickering light made the figures breathe and move, while the music of tambours and sitars swept softly through the room.

Aradhana was on duty that night, not her plump and jocular older brother. Slender and graceful, with great dark eyes, she mirrored the mythical beauty of Sita. The silk of her red sari, threaded with gold, rustled as she walked. Her long dark braid was plaited with jasmine. This was how she dressed for work. When they met her on the streets or in the shops, she was usually in jeans and a T-shirt, with her hair in a ponytail.

Dana and her father were also dressed up. Gabriel wore beige linen trousers and a faded blue shirt. Both his head and his silver earring gleamed in the candlelight. Dana sported her best clothes, bought for her Confirmation: a denim skirt that fell to her ankles, a yellow blouse with embroidered sleeves, and high-heeled sandals. She caught the critical look of a girl her own age who sat at another table, and shrugged it off. Fashion was not something she understood or cared about.

"How is my Irish Barbie this evening?" Aradhana asked as she brought them to their seats.

Dana would have hated to be called this by anyone else, especially since she had never owned a doll, but it somehow seemed less objectionable coming from Aradhana. And Dana wasn't the only one the young woman charmed. Gabriel always acted oddly around her. When Dana once teased him about being too cowardly to ask for a date, he had answered seriously, "My girlfriends don't last. You know that. Radhi's special. I wouldn't want to wreck our friendship."

Now Dana watched wryly as her father puzzled over the menu to keep Aradhana beside him. Enquiring after various dishes, he requested her opinion on this one and that, knowing full well what he meant to order. He and Dana always ate the same meal: white basmati rice with vegetables cooked in a balti sauce, peshwari bread stuffed with nuts and raisins, and two frothing glasses of mango lassi.

While Gabriel dragged out the process as long as he could, Dana left the table and wandered over to gaze at the murals. There was Rama with his great bow, shooting arrows that never missed their target. His skin was sky-blue, a sign of his otherworldly nature as he was the son of a god. At his side stood Sita, the daughter of a king, who fell in love with Rama the moment she saw him. It was when the couple were exiled in the forest that the ten-headed Ravanna, half demon, half human, abducted Sita. In his fiery chariot, he carried her away to the island kingdom of Lanka. Only after many adventures and the help of the monkey-god Hanuman did Rama defeat the demon and rescue his wife.

As Dana gazed at her favorite scene, the reunion of Rama and Sita, an old woman hobbled up beside her. Leaning on a blackthorn stick, she wore a long crimson skirt and a black shawl with a green fringe. Wisps of smoky gray hair framed a narrow face that was wrinkled and whiskery. Her eyes were like two black beads.

"*Is breá an tráthnóna é,*" she said to Dana. "A fine evening indeed."

"'*Sea,*" agreed Dana politely. Educated in a Gaelscoil, she was fluent in Irish. "*Conas atá tú, a mháthair?*"

The old lady didn't answer the question but clutched Dana's hands.

"You must come, my child! You must come to the mountains! I will meet you there."

Then she scurried away with surprising speed out of the restaurant.

Flushed with excitement, Dana returned to her table. The sign she had been waiting for!

"Gabe, I need you to take me hiking in the mountains."

"Since I've nothing else to do."

She knew that face. It wasn't open to negotiation. But by the time Aradhana brought their dinner, Dana had a plan.

"When's your next day off?" she asked the young woman.

"Dana—" Gabriel started, but she was too quick for him.

"Didn't you say you've never been to Powerscourt?"

Aradhana nodded. "There are many places I would

like to visit, but first must come the business. No time for holidays just yet."

"But you get a day off," Dana pointed out, and she turned to her father. "Let's take her on a picnic, Gabe! To the waterfall. Give you a break from the packing. A little farewell party."

"Packing? Farewell?" Aradhana's voice quavered. She avoided looking at Gabriel. "Are you going away, my Irish Barbie?"

"Not that I want to," Dana said, appreciating the unexpected support. "He's dragging me off to Canada!"

Aradhana's face brightened.

"Ah, Canada. It is a wonderful place. Many Indian people live there. I have cousins in Toronto."

"That's where we're going!" Gabriel said, surprised and delighted.

Dana frowned. The two were staring at each other as if they had been rescued.

"Are you emigrating so?" Aradhana asked softly.

Gabriel shook his head. "I'm going home. My parents are Irish, but I was born in Canada and grew up there."

"You are like me, then. In two places also."

Dana heard the wistfulness in her voice. It was the same tone Aradhana had used when she spoke of the Indian community in Canada. There wasn't much of one in Ireland. Was she lonely? Was she homesick? Who else did she have besides her brother and the few men on staff, all older and married? Dana felt a pang of guilt for using the young woman as bait to get into the mountains. But the plan had succeeded. Gabriel was already enthusing about the picnic. As soon as Aradhana named her day off, the date was confirmed.

It was later, when they were eating their dessert of deep-fried bananas drizzled with cream, that Dana spotted the young couple waiting near the takeaway counter. At first glance they looked like any teenaged pair, entangled in each other's arms. The girl was dressed in the briefest of skirts with a skimpy pink top. Her blond hair was piled on top of her head. She kept laughing as her boyfriend nuzzled her ear. He was tall and lanky, in tight jeans and a black T-shirt. The leaf-brimmed hat was nowhere to be seen, and his red-gold hair fell over his shoulders.

They began to kiss each other languidly, oblivious to everyone around.

"Hey, look at the fairies!" Gabriel exclaimed.

"What?" gasped Dana.

He pointed to the mural behind her. She spun around. It was one of the early scenes in the *Ramayana*, before Sita was kidnapped. Rama walked with his wife in the forest. And there to the left of them, in the leafy undergrowth, were figures Dana had never noticed before. Dark-eyed and blue-skinned, with the faint hint of wings, they watched the two lovers from the shadows.

Gabriel called Aradhana over to ask her about them.

"Oh yes," she said. "We have fairies in India, with many different names. Some call them *devas*. The artist must have known this. I cannot remember her name, but I think she lives somewhere up in the mountains."

"I bet she does," Dana muttered.

She looked over at the counter. The couple were gone.

ELEVEΠ

She tumbled from the sky like a falling star, trailing fiery dust behind her. Old as the world, young and beautiful as the day, she was one of that tribe who herd the shining spheres across the heavens. Spéirbhean. Sky-Woman. As she fell to the earth, she clutched her light in her hands.

When she landed by the bonfire on the mountain she stared around her, dazed. She had journeyed far to reach him, through paths of light and shadow, suffering much upon the way.

"Are you the King of Evening?" she say'd.
"If you are the Queen of Night," he replied.
"Are you the Morning Lord?" she bade.
"If you be the Lady of the Day," he sighed.
"Will we dance all summer long?"
"We would pass the time in pleasure."
"Will your love hold true and strong?"
"You would be my treasure."

Oh how different they were! He was as brown as the amber rivers that flowed through the mountains; as steadfast as the ancient rock. She was as pale and glimmering as the moonlight that played upon the foam of the sea. His eyes were green like the hills in springtime; his hair black as the peat in the deepest bogs. Her eyes were a starry cerulean blue, and her hair flowed around her like living flame.

She was a daughter of Slua na h'Aeir. *The Fairy Host of the Air. One of the* Sídhe na Spéire. *The People of the Sky. He was a son of* Na Daoine Uaisle Na Gnoic. *The Gentry of the Hills. One of the* Sídhe Slua na Sliabh. *The Fairy Host of the Mountain.*

There were those of his Court who proclaimed their union doomed to fail, yet he would not hear it. He knew she was more than a dream of love, and the one for whom he had yearned since time began.

Three gifts did the Mountain King offer to woo his Sky Bride.

A crystal crown carved in the shape of doves' wings.

A pendant of blue light gathered from a mountain lake in the morning.

A golden ring fashioned in the image of two swans entwined.

As he knelt before her, he sang the song of his heart.

Siúil liomsa, a chara dhil, suas fá na hardaín,
Ar thuras na háilleacht' is an ghileacht amuigh,
Le go ndeánfaimid bogán de chreagán a' tsléibhe,
Is le páideoga lasfaimid dorchadas oích'.

Rise up, my love, and come along with me,
On a journey of beauty in nature's sunlight,
To smooth every stone as we walk on the hillside
And with rush candles light up the dark of the night.

Ní laoithe an bhróin a cheolfainnse duitse,
Ná ní caoineadh donóige nó doghrainn daoi,
Ach le silleadh a mhillfinnse méala an chumha
Sa phluais sin go maidin ar shliabh na caillí.

No sighing of sorrow I'd ever sing for you
Nor wild lamentation, or sad foolish song;
With a glance I'd disperse the dark clouds of longing
In the cairn on the mountain, from dusk to dawn.

And when the Mountain King asked would she consent
to marry him and be his wife forevermore, this is the answer
the Sky-Woman gave him.
I do.

TWELVE

Powerscourt was an old country estate refurbished by a viscount in the late nineteenth century. The palatial mansion was built around the stone shell of a castle, and the surrounding lands sculpted into gardens and parks. Two miles from the manor house, the demesne ran wild into a lush green valley that was once a deer park. Here fell the highest waterfall in Ireland, like the silver hair of a giantess cascading down a dark-blue rock face. The ridge was steep and unscalable, cloaked in oak, bracken, and heather. Beyond its height was the Wicklow Way, a hiker's trail that led into the mountains.

At the foot of the waterfall was a deep pool surrounded by great stones like broken plates. From the pool, a stream meandered across the valley floor through a scattering of oak and monkey puzzle trees. Children played in the clearing with Frisbees and footballs, and there were picnic tables, a shop, and a public lavatory as well as a parking lot camouflaged by greenery.

While Gabriel and Aradhana were unloading the car, Dana ran to find a place for their picnic. She had almost reached the waterfall when she spotted a familiar figure. There by the pool stood Murta, staring upward toward the top of the ridge. With a shudder Dana recognized the look on his face, the same rage he had shown when the music sounded in the glen. She was backing away so he wouldn't see her, but then Gabriel called out to him. Murta's face shifted into a friendly mask.

Gabriel joined him, introducing Aradhana and waving Dana over.

Murta clutched his cell phone in his hand like a weapon. His eyes swept over the two females. Dana flinched, noting that Aradhana did the same.

"Off duty today?" Gabriel asked him.

"I'm supposed to meet a contact here." Murta lowered his voice, implying a secret. Gabriel moved closer to hear, but the other two didn't. "One of *An Taisce*'s people. She can't be seen to support us." He shrugged. "Cloak-and-dagger stuff. She must've got waylaid. I'd better head back."

It was obvious he didn't want to linger.

"I won't keep you," Gabriel said quickly. "Tell Big Bob I've booked the Enniskerry community center for the concert. The North Wicklow Set-dancers will be part of the lineup."

Though Gabriel was evidently pleased with his own news, Murta nodded indifferently.

"I'll give him the message."

Dana was more than relieved to see him go, and led her father and Aradhana to the spot she had chosen.

"This is a most perfect place," Aradhana said as they rolled out the blanket and unpacked the picnic. "Listen to the birds singing! It is very beautiful."

"You can hear the nightjar at dusk on a summer evening," Gabriel told her.

"Really? What sound does it make?"

"Haven't a clue," he admitted. "I read it in the brochure at the gate."

They laughed.

Dana frowned. They were doing a lot of laughing.

"Let's paddle!" she suggested, catching Aradhana's hand.

It was a warm sunny day. They kicked off their sandals and climbed over the huge stones that cradled the pool. The water was the color of amber and icy cold. The spray from the falls cooled their faces. The dark wet cliff was rimed with green moss and filmy fern. Kestrels preened their feathers on the highest ledges.

Aradhana had rolled up her trousers to the knee. Her clothes were of a soft loose-flowing cotton, beige and cream. A burnt-orange scarf draped her shoulders. Her jet-black hair gleamed in the sunshine, strands curling around her face. Eyeing her surreptitiously, Dana felt scruffy in her cutoff shorts and faded T-shirt.

"What do you think of that creepy guy?" she said suddenly.

Aradhana looked uncomfortable.

"It would not be right of me to speak badly of your father's friends."

"He's not a friend," Dana stated. "Just someone we know." But she was satisfied. It was clear that Aradhana didn't like him either.

"Is there something you wish to tell me?" Aradhana spoke carefully, but her eyes were filled with concern.

"Nah. I just don't like him."

They circled each other in the sunlit water. Dana picked some wood sorrel from a cleft in the rock and offered it to the young woman.

"Gabe calls it 'chip chop cherry.' Tastes like cherry-flavored gum."

Aradhana chewed it thoughtfully.

"Tart but tasty. I will try it in a salad, perhaps also a sauce." She smiled at Dana. "I shall miss my Irish Barbie."

"I don't want to go to Canada. It's not fair that Dad gets to make all the decisions."

"It is unfair," the other agreed. "But once you grow up, you will be in charge of your own life and it will all be up to you."

"Roll on that day," Dana said with a sigh.

She sat down on the rocks and kicked her feet in the water.

"We are alike, you know," Aradhana said, sitting down beside her. "I was reared by my father also. There was only Suresh and me. Our mother died when we were very young and our father never remarried. His heart was broken and could not mend to love another."

"That's sad," Dana murmured, but she felt uneasy.

She had known instinctively that this was the reason Gabriel's girlfriends never lasted. But though she wanted him to be happy, she didn't want his heart to mend just yet. Aradhana was different from the others and if there had been no hope at all—no hope of finding her mother—then . . . but there *was* hope now and Dana would do anything to see it fulfilled. If she earned her wish, she would find her mother and reunite her parents. Then they could stay in Ireland and live happily ever after.

"Do you believe in fairies?" she asked suddenly.

Aradhana smiled.

"This question of belief is a difficult one for people in the West, yes? It is not so if you are born a Hindu. You grow up knowing many gods and goddesses, many kinds of spirits and beings."

"Irish people believe in a lot too," Dana pointed out. "God and the Mother of God and angels and saints. Da says he believes in fairies and that he's not the only one."

"And you?"

Dana shrugged. "Well, weird things can happen." She tried to sound casual. "But they're just for little kids, aren't they? Like Santa Claus?"

Aradhana gazed up at the great falls that tumbled

toward them. Where the sunlight shot through the spray, silver spicules needled the air like miniature spears.

"I would not want to live in a world without gods or fairies," she said softly. "I am happy to think that life is filled with mystery."

Before Dana could respond to this, Gabriel called to them.

"Hey, you two mermaids! Come and join a poor mortal who's starving to death!"

He had emptied the wicker picnic basket that he was so proud of, the one he had bought at an antiques market for a lot more money than he could afford. It came with a linen tablecloth and napkins, blue china dishes, and tarnished cutlery he had spent days polishing. There was plenty of food: a stick of crusty French bread, goat's cheese from the deli and cream cheese from the supermarket, a jar of dill pickles and another of olives, a green salad with herbs, a bag of apples, a punnet of mandarins, and a box of chocolates for dessert. A bottle of cold white wine lay in the cooler for the adults, and one of cola for Dana. To the delight of the other two, Aradhana had brought vegetable samosas and spicy pakoras, along with crispy poppadoms and a raita dip of yogurt with cucumber and fresh mint.

"Yum!" cried Dana as she dived on the feast.

While they were eating, Gabriel told Aradhana about the movie *Excalibur*, and how some of the scenes were filmed by that very waterfall. Then with all the verve of a natural storyteller he recounted the tragic tale of King Arthur and Queen Guinevere, and the French knight Lancelot who stole the Queen's heart.

Aradhana listened, enrapt, and so did Dana. Her father's voice was like his flute, resonant and musical. She closed her eyes, overcome with happiness. It was as if her world was suddenly complete, as perfect as a pearl. Startled, she opened her eyes. The feeling had been strangely familiar, as if she were remembering another picnic, another moment like this. Guilt and panic swept through her. It was all wrong. This was not the family she wanted. This was not her life made whole.

Angrily, she scanned the park. *Where were they?* She had done what she was told to do. She had come to the mountains.

Lunch was almost over when it began to happen, and Dana was the only one who noticed. A silvery breath of mist rose from the earth itself, whispering through the grasses and around the trees. Like the sea come to shore, it flooded the valley. Dana stared at the lustrous haze, mesmerized. It even hung from the branches of the trees like icicles. The world around her had utterly changed. She was looking at the same scene, yet it was not the same. Everything was infused with an intensity of light that made her eyes ache. *What was it?* Some secret message pressed against her heart till she could barely breathe. Then she suddenly understood, without knowing how or why, that the other world hadn't come to her, rather she herself had entered it; and instead of falling under a spell, she had woken to the truth that Faerie was all around her.

Then came the second shock.

Both Gabriel and Aradhana were frozen in their places, stopped in mid-motion as if turned to stone. And so, too, was every man, woman, and child in the park and everything else besides. The waterfall hung like sculpted ice. Not a trickle of water plashed. Nor did a single leaf on any tree stir. And no birds sang.

It was time to go.

For a moment Dana balked. Here was the price to be paid for her hopes and dreams. The sacrifice to be made. She would have to leave her father. Without warning or explanation, she would have to abandon him even as her mother had. The thought of the pain this would cause him was almost unbearable.

Now a sighing sound surrounded her, though she couldn't see anything.

Follow the greenway.

Invisible hands began to tug at her clothes. When she didn't move, they grew more insistent, pushing and pulling her.

"Stop it!" she hissed.

She stood up to beat them off, but she couldn't see what she was fighting. As she spun around, she caught sight of a slight figure above the waterfall. It was the Lady, waving at her! There was something urgent in her movements, as if she were entreating Dana to hurry.

"All right, I'm coming," she muttered to the air around her.

She grabbed her knapsack. It was already packed for a journey, with jeans, sweater, running shoes and socks, a waterproof jacket, matches, and a flashlight. She shoveled in some leftovers from the picnic, plus the bottle of cola and the box of chocolates. Now she turned to her father. Frozen in mid-act, he was passing a glass of wine to Aradhana. Dana's heart tightened as she saw the look in his eyes. In real time he could hide it, blinking shyly. Caught in that moment, his love shone like a beacon.

Dana didn't want to look at Aradhana. She was afraid for Gabriel, who might be rejected; afraid for herself, not wanting the complication; and afraid for her mother who might be replaced forever. Yet look she did. And there, like the sun on the surface of a lake, the same love was reflected in the young woman's eyes.

Any last doubts in Dana's mind disappeared in that instant. She had to find her mother before it was too late. Before things progressed. Before people got hurt.

She hugged her father's still body and kissed him good-bye. "Love you, Da. Be back as soon I can. I promise." Then she whispered in Aradhana's ear. "Look after him for me."

Dana had only begun to climb the ridge when she heard footsteps echo from the parking lot. Someone else was moving in the park! She couldn't turn around to see, as the invisible hands were dragging her upward. She didn't fight them off this time. The cold prickles at the back of her neck told her all she needed to know. Whatever was coming behind her wasn't good.

THIRTEEN

The demon was beginning to remember. Though the fire in its head still caused it agony, torturing it into fits of madness, it grew stronger and more knowledgeable each time it fed. The host body it possessed was aiding it too, nourishing it with the essence of human wickedness.

An image had already taken shape in its mind, a faint imprint of the memory of what it was sent to murder. A dormant power. A sleeping giant. One who must be destroyed while still weak and defenseless.

It knew it had to act furtively, to use its ability to creep and hide. In its own maimed and vulnerable state, it could not risk being captured or killed.

Everything rested on the mission. The final step of the Great Plan. All else had been put into place. This shedding of blood, the red rite of slaughter, would seal the beginning of the end.

For it had come in the name of the Destroyer of Worlds.

Fourteen

Dana scrambled up the steep ridge, past warning signs staked in the earth. DANGER. DO NOT CLIMB. ABSEILING PROHIBITED. Didn't Gabe say these cliffs claimed at least one life a year? She found a trail too narrow for human traffic, most likely forged by the sika deer that ran wild on the upper slopes. The way was rough going. She had to push through bracken taller than herself, and the ground was wet and slippery. Higher up, she stumbled over knotted roots and patches of gorse that pricked her. Whenever she slowed down, the invisible hands hauled her upward. She was now glad of their help. She would never have made it without them.

The silvery mist had begun to recede from the valley, but the deathly silence remained, unnerving her. On her right, the waterfall hung eerily still, as if made of glass. Alert for any sound, she instantly heard the small stone that fell behind her as it clattered over the rock. She looked back quickly. Some distance below, the green sea of bracken wavered, though no wind blew. Her heart skipped a beat. Was something following her? For a moment she thought of running back to her father, but she knew he couldn't help.

A voice called from above.

"Hurry, Dana! Hurry!"

The Lady sounded distressed.

The invisible hands were more insistent now, dragging her over rock and through nettles and briar. As she crashed through a clump of fraughan bushes the bilberries burst, staining her clothes and skin red. Dana didn't object. Panic coursed through her. She had to get to the top. She had to reach safety.

She was almost at the summit when life returned to the park. Like the roar of a wave, the sounds broke over her—the rush of the waterfall, the chatter of birds, the cries of children playing. The invisible hands were gone. The Lady stood above her, extending a slender arm to help her onto the ledge.

"Something's after me!" Dana said, gasping for breath.

The Lady peered down the slope with a frown. "I feel I know this thing and yet I do not. What can this import?"

Despite her manner of speech, she looked like a normal young woman in khaki shorts and a halter top, with leather sandals on her feet. A blond ponytail jutted from the back of her white baseball cap, and she wore stylish sunglasses.

"I have sent the others to investigate," she continued, "but it has already taken flight."

Though her voice was calm, she looked worried.

"What——?" Dana began, but stopped when a cry rang out below.

"*Dana! Where are you?*"

It was Gabe. He sounded surprised.

"That's me Da," she said with a pang.

The Lady drew her quickly away from the ridge and into the woods beyond the waterfall. Her grip was firm, reminding Dana of the invisible hands.

Gabriel's shouts were coming faster now, echoing that mix of concern and annoyance peculiar to parents.

Dana stopped to look back.

The Lady's grasp loosened as she, too, stopped to listen. A wistfulness came over her features. "I had a father once . . ." Then she bit her lip. "This is all wrong." She shook her head. "What am I doing? How can I send you into the mountains alone? How can I put you in peril?"

Now Dana was the one who was doing the pulling. She clutched the young woman's arm and hurried her through the trees. Behind them, Aradhana had begun to call too and Gabriel's cries were growing more frantic. She had to escape them. It wouldn't be long before they tried to climb the ridge. Any misgivings Dana had were dissolved by the Lady's wavering. The fear of losing her wish made her all the more adamant.

"You can't back out now! This was your idea! You got me into this!"

Deeper in the woods, beyond earshot of Gabe's cries, Dana slowed down.

"Yes, it is my fault." The Lady's sigh was like a breeze in the branches overhead. "I have lured you to this. And when I'm like . . . Them . . . I don't have a problem with it. That's just the way things are done. They use mortals for their own ends without thinking about it. Yet I have human feelings sometimes."

They had come to the heart of the wood. The Lady linked arms with Dana in a more casual manner. Dana noticed how the briars and brambles gave way before them. Deer peeked shyly from behind the trees. An otter slid from the riverbank and into the water. The air was filled with trills as songbirds swooped around them in arabesques of flight. When they passed a clump of wild rose, a flurry of pink petals showered their path.

At first her companion seemed oblivious to their surroundings. Then Dana glimpsed something different at the corner of her eye: a vision of the Lady in a flowing green gown and a crown of white flowers, waving graciously to all around her.

But it was an ordinary young woman who argued with her.

"Look, you're just a kid. I should find someone else to do the job. Someone older. It's usually teenagers who go on these missions."

Dana almost choked. She recognized the tone in the older girl's voice, the same one her father had used when he told her they were going to Canada. The finality of the adult who held all the power; the certainty that they knew best. A rebellious fury surged through her.

"You made a pact! You promised! I want my wish and I'll do anything to get it. I'm nearly thirteen. I'm as good as any teenager. You can't take this away from me!"

The Lady hesitated. It was obvious she wanted to be convinced. "The High King says you are the one . . . He says mortals always underestimate their young."

"He's right!" Dana insisted. "We can always do more, just no one lets us. I can do this! I know I can!"

The Lady looked no happier. They had reached the edge of the forest. As they stepped from the trees, they looked out over a landscape of heathered hills that swelled into the distance like a green grassy ocean. They had arrived at the threshold of the Wicklow Mountains.

And the way was barred.

A great gray standing stone blocked their path. The monolith was scored with a hieroglyphic script that curved like the hills themselves.

The Lady rested her hand upon the stone.

"It declares the borders of the Mountain Kingdom closed. There are more around the perimeter. How long they have stood here we do not know. The mountain folk are a solitary people and rarely mingle with the High Court or the rest of fairy-kind. There are spells on the stones to keep intruders out, but even if there weren't, we would defer to their wishes. Every kingdom in Faerie sets its own laws."

She gazed into the distance.

"Do you know of the mountain called Lugnaquillia?"

"The highest in the chain," Dana said, nodding. "Da and I climbed it last summer."

The Lady looked pleased, and a little relieved.

"Lugnaquillia is the site of the palace of our Tánaiste, Lugh of the Mountain, Lugh of the Wood."

Dana blenched. From where they stood, Lugnaquillia was at the farthest point of the range, beyond many peaks and valleys. It would take days to get there. And that meant she would have to spend nights in the mountains alone. A hard task for anyone, never mind a twelve-year-old who didn't have a tent or enough provisions.

"Right, I'm off to Lugnaquillia," she said, with forced heartiness. She couldn't let the Lady see her fear. The mission was already hanging on a knife-edge. "To find Lugh of the Mountain, Lugh of the Wood. What's the message?"

Looking anxious again, the Lady frowned at Dana.

Dana held her breath, doing her best to appear relaxed and unconcerned.

The Lady spoke carefully.

"_A shadow of the Destroyer has entered the land. Where is the light to bridge the darkness?_"

Dana was baffled.

"What does it mean?" she asked, a quaver in her voice.

"The Tánaiste will know. The message is for him. Your mission is simply to carry it to him."

But the Lady's unease was peaking. Her eyes were dark with concern.

Dana shivered, feeling suddenly cold. Slipping off her knapsack, she took out her anorak and pulled it on.

The older girl began to fuss over her, tightening the hood on Dana's head and tucking in stray strands of hair.

"Keep your ears covered. The winds will be colder out in the open. Have you brought food and drink? Travel always westward. Into the setting sun."

"I know what to do," Dana said, backing away from her. "I'm all right."

She wanted to leave immediately, before the other could change her mind.

The Lady brightened suddenly.

"Wait, I almost forgot! I can give you something! It's tradition. A special gift. To help you on your way."

Dana half expected her to produce a Swiss Army knife from the pockets of her khaki shorts; but instead it was a little golden box with a jeweled clasp. Inside was a red pomade that smelled of apples.

"Close your eyes," the Lady said. As she dabbed the sweet-smelling balm onto Dana's eyelids, she explained its use. "This will let you see what mortals cannot. Your eyes will pierce the veil that cloaks our world. You will know that Faerie is all around you. And those who think they are hidden will be made visible, yet they will assume you are blind. This will give you time to judge friend from foe."

A chill ran through Dana. There would be other enemies besides the shadow she had spoken of? It wasn't a question Dana could raise, for fear that the older girl would get upset again. She was clutching Dana's hands, reluctant to let her go.

"Okay, I'm off!" said Dana, breaking away. "Goodbye!"

And hurrying down the trail that led into the mountains, she didn't stop to look back till she was some distance away.

There stood the Lady in the shade of the forest with boughs of oak leaves overhead like a green canopy. Her gown shimmered with dappled light. Her long fair hair was wreathed in white hawthorn.

"My blessings go with you," she called out in a silvery voice. "May you be of good courage as you follow the greenway."

FIFTEEN

H iding deep inside its human host, the demon returned to track the Bright One unbeknownst to her. It suspected she was its prey, for it could sense the power beneath her mortal guise. Crawling through the greenery like a serpent, it dared to draw near. Thus it heard of the mission and the message.

Where is the light to bridge the darkness?

The words caused a storm of confusion. The Bright One herself sought something more powerful! Doubt needled its tortured mind. Was she not the one it was sent to destroy? She spoke of a King. Was he the light? Or the key to the light? And what of the child?

It lay in the understory, gnawing on its thoughts like a starving beast who had unearthed a pile of bones. The child must die before she warned the King. And then the King. But not before it had torn from him what it needed to know. One way or another, the light would be extinguished.

Devising the plan helped to cool its feverish brain. Caution was essential. It was not yet strong enough for open battle. There was also the struggle with the one it possessed. Despite their dark kinship, their wills did not meld.

Hours passed before it crept from the shadows of the trees. As it approached the marker that declared the borders closed, it hesitated for only the briefest of moments. Then it passed the great stone and set out on the road into the Mountain Kingdom.

Sixteen

Dana stepped gingerly along the hiker's trail that wound through the Wicklow Mountains. The great hills rolled all around her, like great mottled beasts lolling in the sunshine. To her right rose the pointed peak of Djouce Mountain, its purple flanks of heather brindled with gray stone. Ahead lay the wooded vale of Lough Tay in the shadow of Luggala and beyond it, the glen of Lough Dan below Knocknacloghoge. It would take her the rest of the day to reach Lough Dan and that was only a third of her journey. She stopped to study the map she carried in her knapsack. So many mountains to climb, valleys to cross, lakes and forests to pass! And she had to avoid populated areas and the paths more commonly used by hill-walkers. Once the alarm went up that she was missing, there would be search parties and rescue teams. She would have to skulk and hide.

It wasn't going to be easy.

Though she had set out bravely, she was already despondent. Hiking alone was no fun. She and Gabe had always gone with their local hill-walking group. Many

were amateur naturalists who used magnifying glasses
to peer at miniature wildflowers and the lichen on rocks.
They would ask her the Irish names of trees and plants as
she was the only one fluent in the language. *An cuileann.*
The holly tree. *An dair ghaelach.* The Irish oak. *Méiríní
sídhe.* Foxglove or fairy-fingers. *Méaracán gorm.* The
same name for both bluebells and harebells. And when
they sat down on the hillsides to eat their lunch, everyone
shared whatever they had brought—hot tea or cocoa from
steaming thermoses, every kind of sandwich, crisps and
fruit, sweets and chocolate.

She began to yearn for company. The vast solitude of
the landscape was overwhelming and she soon suffered
from lonesomeness and a slow, creeping unease. Now the
mountains seemed like sullen giants, brooding over her.
She tried not to think of the thing at the waterfall; tried
not to wonder if it was out there somewhere. Watching
her. Hunting her. She kept looking over her shoulder.
Nature was beautiful when you felt safe within it. When
you didn't, it was terrifying.

She had deliberately taken one of the trails less traveled, crossing the uplands. Even if she was able to convince any adults that she was fine on her own, it would
only be a matter of time before they contacted Gabe. She
flinched whenever she thought of her father. The state
he must be in. She hated to think of him making countless phone calls, rounding up their friends, searching the

mountains . . . going crazy. She had tried to write him a note, but couldn't think of what to say that would make any sense to him or ease his mind. *I'm away with the fairies. They've promised me a wish. If I get it, I'll come back with Mum.*

If I get it . . .

And there was no point telling him where she had gone. He would only come after her and ruin any chance of her getting that wish.

She quickened her pace. Wasn't she doing this for him as well as for herself? Once she brought back his wife to him, it would make everything worthwhile, even the pain.

Dana had been walking for several hours when she spotted a vague shape on the path ahead: a humped figure on a stone in the midst of thorny briars. For a moment her heart jumped, and she thought of running away, then she recognized who it was. The old lady from the Hanuman House in Bray. She ran to meet her.

"Here I am! Like you said!"

The beady eyes were the same, dark and merry, but the face seemed to have grown more whiskers.

The old woman smiled and cocked her head.

"Do you hear it, *mo leanbh? Éist nóiméad.*"

Dana did as she was told and listened a moment. She had grown used to the wind hawing through the mountains, but now she also heard a low booming note.

"How I have longed to hear that sound," the old lady said. "The song of the bittern. She was driven from the bogs by hunters and drainage, but she has come back. Not all that is gone is gone forever."

Her words were reassuring.

"*Go raibh míle maith agat,*" Dana thanked her.

The whiskery face crinkled with laughter.

"You have good manners, for a motherless child. Let me guide you on your way. Hurry up this hill as fast as your feet can carry you, with a heart as wild as the hearts of birds, and you will find a splendid surprise. *Hind's feet in high places.*"

Though Dana didn't really understand, she loved surprises and she loved to run.

"Thanks again!" she called behind her, as off she raced.

Dana took the steep track that wound through the bracken. Patches of pink foxglove waved her on. At one point a lone hawthorn tree, stooped and twisted by the winds, offered her a friendly branch to pull herself up. She hurried without thinking, filled with an inexplicable excitement. Her heart beat rapidly, as wild as a bird's, and when she reached the top, breathless, she gasped with delight.

They stiffened at her arrival. Heads up, ears pricked, soft eyes staring, antlers branching: a great herd of wild deer.

She could see they were shy and a little nervous, yet they didn't bolt. She stood still herself, not wanting to startle them. One of the does ventured forward and nuzzled her hand. The others followed after and Dana was surrounded by a wild sweet smell as they jostled her gently. She sensed they were about to run and that they wanted her to run with them.

"Not sure I can," she murmured anxiously.

Then they breathed on her, their warm green grassy breath, and a whisper echoed through her mind. *Follow the greenway.* She felt a tingling in her legs. Her muscles began to twitch. Her feet pushed her upward till she was standing on her tiptoes. Now the knowledge surged through her like the green sap of spring: she could be one of them.

Oh the joy of running with the deer! *Hind's feet in high places.* Supple pelts rippled alongside her, rising and falling like tawny waves. Hooves drummed and thrummed upon the earth. All ran with one mind as if of one body. At the heart of the herd, she too ran wildly, her humanity shed like clothes in the wind. She was still two-legged, but her feet were cloven and antlers jutted from her brow, and her heart beat with the wild heart of the herd.

Up the airy mountain and down the rushy glen.

The landscape blurred around them with the speed of their passing. Hurtling downhill in a blind descent, they kicked up stones and soil behind them. Now they plunged into a dark forest of oak and birch, weaving around the trees like a brown mountain stream. Then out again and into a green valley, splashing up the Cloghoge River. The blue water of Lough Tay gleamed ahead. Over it loomed the high cliffs of Luggala. Dana could never have scaled that talus of scree alone, yet up it she sped, along with the others, *hind's feet in high places,* scattering the loose stones in a cloud of gray dust.

Over the open summit of Luggala they charged and down its western slope, then upward again in another ascent. It wasn't till they reached the top of Knocknacloghoge that the herd finally halted. Pressing against Dana, they butted her gently to say good-bye.

"Thank you, thank you," she kept repeating, already saddened at their parting.

Then the deer sped off down the hillside, the way they had come.

As Dana looked around her, she saw how far the herd had brought her and almost cried with gratitude. They had done in an hour what would have taken her the day. But now as she gazed into the west, toward her destination, she felt a cold grip on the back of her neck. What was that on the horizon?

Shielding her eyes against the sunlight, she squinted into the distance. For a moment she could hardly believe what she saw. Then she remembered the Lady's pomade and knew that it was working. For there amidst the granite spine of the highlands was the silhouette of a sleeping giant. The gigantic body was made of rock and earth, covered with blanket bog. Its face was craggy, yet it did not seem unkind. Was this King Lugh? His head rested against Lugnaquillia as if it were a pillow. But if it was he, what could have made him close his borders and lie down among the mountains?

Even as she studied the sleeping giant, he underwent a change. Storm clouds gathered in the sky above him, making his features look dark and strained. As rain poured down, streams of water ran over his face as if he were weeping. Then the clouds moved on and sunshine broke out and he smiled in his sleep. Dana was bewildered. Was she imagining it all?

There was no time to wonder. The rain clouds were scudding over the hills and heading her way. The open summit offered no shelter. The air was already chill. Quickly she changed into jeans and sweater, replacing her sandals with socks and running shoes. She was glad she had brought her waterproof jacket with the hood, but soon wished she had packed the wet-pants as well. As always in the hills, the rain lashed sideways. Minutes after it arrived, her jeans were soaked and clinging to her legs. Things could only get worse.

Missing the deer, Dana started down the western scarp of Knocknacloghoge in sight of Lough Dan. The descent through heather and moor grass grew trickier still as the ground got drenched. She kept sliding and slipping. A climbing stick would have helped. She promised herself to look for a strong branch the next time she passed a tree. Her stomach was rumbling, but she ignored it. She had to keep moving. Though it wouldn't be dark for a good while yet, the afternoon was fading. The dread question of where she would spend the night loomed in her mind. The burden of the task began to oppress her—the drizzle and the mud and the dreariness of the hike. It wasn't fair. How did they expect her to do it without any help? She started to sniffle, then got angry with herself. *Suck it back! You're the one who said you could do it!*

When she reached the bottom of the hill, she had to fight her way through another sea of bracken till she came to a small river. As she struggled across it, she skidded on the stones and fell to her knees. Now she was bruised and even wetter. Would it never stop raining? Before her lay a sodden field bristling with sedge. Beyond it was the rocky slope of Scarr Mountain. To her right lay the dark-blue waters of Lough Dan. She spotted a group on the trail nearest the lake, their colored jackets like bright birds in the rushes. All had lowered their heads against the rain and didn't appear to see her. Nevertheless, she hunched down as she hurried away.

By the time she had begun her climb up Scarr, Dana had to force herself to keep going. Placing one foot in front of the other, she counted her steps and stopped for breath after every ten. Though it had finally stopped raining, her feet were soaked, her legs aching, and her knapsack felt like a bag of bricks. The mountainside was moving shakily beneath her, and she thought she might faint. Plunking herself down in a patch of heather, she grabbed a handful of chocolates from her knapsack and crammed them into her mouth.

Life's shite, eat dessert first.

She was chugging on the bottle of cola when something caught her eye. It was moving down the ridge on the far side of Lough Dan. For a moment she thought it was a deer, and her heart lifted. Then she went cold. *What was it?* She couldn't see clearly at that distance, and the thing itself kept scuttling behind the rocks. Then she got a clear sighting. Human. With limbs and a head. She almost laughed. Things were bad enough, why was she scaring herself? Still, she kept watching it. Then came the moment when it emerged from a rock once again and she saw something else: a reddish body, oddly segmented, with too many legs.

As the waves of terror washed over her, Dana scrabbled up the hill. Was it the thing from the waterfall? Or some other enemy? Had it seen her? Was it coming after her? Fear gave her new energy. Drove her onward. She could hardly breathe. Her lungs were heaving. Her panic made her careless. At one point she almost fell backward. Steadying herself, she stopped to look behind. There was nothing in sight.

A moment of relief.

Then she spied a flash of red near the spot where she had crossed the river. She almost cried out. It was following her scent, like a dog. *It was hunting her.*

The last few feet to the peak were a blind dash of dread and hope. No longer caring about anything else, Dana prayed that someone would be at the top. A group of hill-walkers. A lone hiker. Anyone. *Please.*

When she reached the summit, her heart plummeted. Nothing but rock and coarse heather. She was alone and defenseless against an unknown predator.

SEVENTEEN

There were a few moments when Dana lost all control. She ran in frenzied circles, like a terrified toddler. *A monster's coming after me! A monster's coming after me!* She didn't scream, but only because her fist was jammed into her mouth. Then she drew up abruptly. Forced herself to think. *What can I do? Where can I hide?* The grassy summit was pocked with outcrops of rock and several small cairns. Searching quickly through them, Dana found a narrow opening overgrown with heather. There was enough room inside. Crawling backward to allow herself to see out, she did her best not to disturb the heather that provided some cover. In each fist she clenched a sharp stone. If cornered, she was prepared to fight like a wildcat.

The wait was harrowing. She was cramped and wet, shivering with cold and fear. Breath held, stomach knotted, she peered through the greenery, dreading what might come. Footsteps approached. Slow and heavy. Loose stones were kicked out of the way. Instinctively she cringed, as if to make herself smaller. Then a figure came into view. She nearly gasped out loud.

Murta!

In the first moment of relief, so glad to see a familiar face, she almost scrambled from her hiding place. Something stopped her. She remembered the creepy feeling she got whenever he was near. What was he doing there? And wasn't it too much of a coincidence that he had been at the waterfall too? A sick feeling came over her. What could this mean?

Murta sniffed the air as he looked around. Was he searching for her? Her mind insisted on a reasonable explanation. She had been missing for almost half a day. Search parties would be combing the mountains. But if he was part of one, why was he alone? And he didn't look like he was on a rescue mission. He didn't even have a rucksack.

Murta's cell phone rang out, piercing the quiet. He pulled it from his pocket and stared at it a while. Slowly he raised it to his ear.

"Yeah?. . . No . . . I'm . . . I've . . . got business."

Dana shuddered to hear his voice. It sounded strange and sluggish. Now he put away the phone and with a last glance around him, stalked away, disappearing down the western slope.

She didn't come out till she was sure he was gone. Her mind was in turmoil. What was going on? Nothing made sense. And what should she do now? She needed to go west, but didn't want to be seen by him. She would have to take another route. Detour around Scarr. She had just decided to have something to eat and consult her map, when she froze in new horror. There, near the cleft where she had been hiding, something protruded from under a big rock.

Two legs and feet!

She screamed.

A male voice croaked in response from beneath the stone.

Someone trapped!

"Are you all right?" she cried. "Are you hurt? Can you move?"

She started to push frantically against the rock, shouting encouragement. The person underneath had begun to move, twitching his feet and yelling also. She worked all the harder, thinking he was in pain; but when the stone finally rolled over, she discovered he was shouting at *her*.

"What in the name of all that's holly and ivy are ye kickin' up such a racket for?" he roared.

Speechless, Dana gaped at the little man. He was yellowy-brown and as wrinkled as an autumn leaf. Both his hair and beard fell in thick knotted strands that curled around his feet like a bird's nest. His shirt and trousers appeared to be made of brown paper tied with twine, making him look like an abandoned parcel.

Now footsteps sounded on the western ridge and Murta came into sight. He was breathing heavily, eyes darting around. He seemed bigger, darker, red-faced, and terrifying. His glance passed over the little man, but he jerked back in surprise when he saw Dana. Then a ghastly grimace distorted his features. She knew in an instant that she was in danger.

Dana stood transfixed, unsure what to do. At the corner of her eye, she searched for the stones she had dropped. She needed weapons.

Murta licked his lips as he bore down on her.

The little man had stopped yelling to stare at Murta, and now turned to Dana.

"Are ye with the likes of that, *girsearch?*" he asked her.

"No."

She had meant the word to be emphatic, but it was more like a whimper.

Murta was almost upon them. His eyes were burning. Dana tried to force her feet to run but she was paralyzed with fear.

"I thought not," said the little man.

Rooting in his clothing, he pulled out a dandelion with its thistledown still intact.

"Hold on to yer britches," he said, catching hold of Dana's hand. "We'll be away in a hack."

He puffed on the weed.

And blew the two of them away. Right off the mountain!

It was the oddest sensation, like being sucked into

a vacuum cleaner. With a *whoosh* the landscape blurred around Dana in streaks of green and brown with a blue blotch of sky.

Then she found herself on another mountain peak entirely, dizzy but relieved.

"Thanks!" she said fervently. "That man scares me to death!"

"Man?" said her companion, blinking through the tangle of hair that fell over his eyes.

Dana regarded him curiously. Was he some kind of leprechaun? And had he helped her because she set him free?

"Are you okay?" she asked. "Were you imprisoned in that rock or did it fall on top of you?"

"Are ye a complete eejit or what?" he said. "I was having a lovely kip when ye rousted me out of it."

"But I thought . . ."

Dana stopped. He was having a nap? She felt a little light-headed. Between the huge relief at escaping Murta and the antics of this funny little man, she couldn't help but giggle.

"Are you a fairy?" she asked him.

"Do I look like one?" he said testily.

Her giggles died.

"Sorry," she said quickly. "The Lady told me—"

He raised a grubby hand and his voice softened.

"Stop the lights! I have ye now. Yer the Lady's messen-

ger. She sent word to watch out for ye. Is that why yer able
to see me when none of yer kind do? They're always pas-
sin' me by with their big banjaxed feet and bags o' grub.
They all sit down on Yallery Brown's bed—the Traveler's
Rock, they call it—and divil a one of them offers me a bite
to eat. You'd think I didn't have a mouth on me."

He eyed her knapsack hopefully.

"I was just about to have my tea," she told him.

Yallery surveyed the peak around them and pointed to
a large flat stone nearby.

"There's a handsome piece of furniture," he said. " 'Twill
do for our table."

They settled down on the stone and Dana laid out her
fare—a chunk of cheddar cheese, a leftover salad roll, four
samosas, some pickles, several apples, and a little heap of
chocolates.

Yallery eyed the samosas.

"I never seen the like o' dat before."

He picked one up and held it to his nose. His whiskers
trembled. Holding the pastry with both hands, he began
to nibble it daintily, starting at the corners.

Dana had to fight back another bout of giggles. He
ate like her hamsters. She herself wolfed down the sandwich of lettuce, tomato, red onion, and chopped peppers.
She was starving. It was hours since the picnic at the
Powerscourt Waterfall. After all that had happened, it
seemed like days. She stared up at the sky. The sun was

lower. Evening was coming. Rummaging in her knapsack, she pulled out her map and spread it on her lap.

"Can you tell me where we are?" she asked him, her
mouth full.

Yallery Brown peered down at the map. It was a three-
dimensional image of the Wicklow Mountains, showing
peaks and valleys, lakes and rivers.

"There," he said, placing a grubby finger on Duff Hill.

"Oh," she said, dismayed.

He had blown her north, way off course, adding at least
another day to her journey. Doing her best to hide her disappointment, she offered him another samosa. Perhaps if
she kept him in good humor, he might be persuaded to
use another dandelion.

Gnawing away on the second pastry, Yallery stretched
out his legs.

Dana noted the two left feet but didn't comment.
It was time for dessert. She doled out three chocolates
each, mindful that reserves must be kept for the road
ahead.

Yallery licked the edges of a coffee cream with his pale
pink tongue.

"Give us an oul *scéal*," he said. "I haven't heard a
human tale in ages."

She looked confused.

"You mean like a fairy tale?"

"Nah, sure they're old hat and a load of blatherumskite.

Too much use of the imagination. Ye always have to guess what's really goin' on. Give me a human tale any day. All facts and feelings. Will I tell ye a story about Johnny Magorey?"

She nodded, chewing on a toffee.

"Shall I begin it?"

She nodded again.

"That's all that's in it!"

His cackles ended in a fit of coughing.

Dana laughed too.

"Good one. I'll tell it to me Da when I get home."

The sudden thought of Gabe brought a sharp pang and her mood changed.

Yallery gave her a thoughtful look. He began to chant in a singsong voice.

> *Skinnymalink melodeon legs,*
> *Big banana feet,*
> *Went to the pictures*
> *And couldn't get a seat.*

She was laughing again.

"Your turn," he said. "A poem or a song or a tale."

"I can't," she pleaded. "Da's the storyteller in the family. How about a joke?"

Before he could object, she launched into one.

"A grasshopper goes into a bar and the barman says,

'Do ye know there's a drink named after ye?' 'Really?' says the grasshopper. 'There's a drink named Bob?'"

Yallery Brown blinked, perplexed.

"There's a drink called a grasshopper," she explained.

"What? Are ye tellin' me yer kind drink grasshoppers' blood? The poor wee craters!"

"No, no," she said, and tried to explain again, but it was no longer funny.

"Asha, that won't do at'all at'all," he said, relentless. "What about yer own tale? Isn't everyone the grand hero in his own life story?"

"There's not much to mine," Dana said. She thought a moment. "Well, to start off. My name's Dana Faolan. I belong to the Faolans of Wicklow, that's me Da's people. His mum, my gran, is a Gowan from Wexford. She lives in Canada. I don't know anything about my own mum's family. She left before I could ask her about them." Dana was quiet a minute. "She left before I could ask her about anything." She heaved a deep sigh. "I've only got half a story I guess."

Yallery Brown patted her hand.

"No matter, *a leanbh*. Sure, yer still inside your tale. And what is it that yer kind do be sayin'? *It ain't over till the fat lady sings.*"

The latter was said with such an awful attempt at an American accent that Dana couldn't help but laugh.

Satisfied, Yallery brushed the samosa crumbs out of

his beard and produced another dandelion from inside his clothing.

Dana scrambled to gather up her things.

As the little man blew on the downy clock, his last words sailed through the air.

"Fare ye well on the journey, girl. *Follow the greenway.*"

And then with a *whoosh*, like water sucked down a drain, he disappeared.

Dana looked around her. Yallery Brown was gone and she was still on top of Duff Hill.

"Damn!"

Eighteen

If Dana hadn't been so cheered by Yallery Brown's company, she would have been devastated. All around her ranged a wilderness of rock and damp grass under endless sky. She was on the northern flank of the Wicklow Mountains, on a long ridge that wound through windswept bog. She was nowhere near the trail that would take her to Lugnaquillia.

Glumly she stared at the map. She would have to stay on the ridge, of which Duff Hill was a part, and continue westward to Mullaghcleevaun. From there she could head south for the Wicklow Gap and west again to her destination. Just looking at the route, she knew it would take days. Her only choice was to hike as far as she could before it got dark, then camp out for the night. Perhaps in the forest below Stoney Top.

With that decision, Dana heaved her knapsack over her shoulders and set out. Westerly winds blew down the exposed corridor. She wished she had brought her wooly hat and gloves; neither hood nor pockets could fend off the cold that gnawed at her ears and hands. The landscape

itself was bleak and miserable. Though a few sheep strag-
gled over the lower fields, there was no sign of a house
or farm. No evidence of humanity. Yallery's retreat had
taken her far off the beaten track. Faerie appeared to favor
the more forsaken regions. Were its people hiding out in
the last scraps of countryside? Were they doomed, like the
wilderness itself, before the march of man?

It wasn't long before she began to see them.

A harsh croak pierced the air as a great raven landed
nearby. Dana knew immediately it was no ordinary bird,
for it was the size of a big dog and had silver-white eyes
that flashed like lightning. As soon as it landed, it began
to transform. The blue-black feathers melded together
to form a capacious cloak from which limbs emerged. A
layer of dark skin slid over its face as the beak withdrew to
become a sharp nose. Glossy dreadlocks fell down its back.
The raven had changed into a tall and beautiful woman,
both striking and terrifying. Her fierce black eyes, rimmed
with gold, lingered on Dana for one nerve-wracking second and then dismissed her. As the raven-queen strode
away, Dana breathed a sigh of relief.

But now she jumped with fright when a mountain
hare exploded from a patch of heather. She was less surprised when this one turned into a wrinkled old woman,
for Dana knew the superstition that hares were witches.
Again, the creature simply went about her business. As
the Lady had said, the denizens of Faerie assumed Dana

was blind, and she was glad they showed no interest in her. Yet here was the catch to the Lady's gift. Did Dana really want to see what was all around her?

Moving to a lower slope to avoid the biting winds, she came to a stream that ran down a dark crag. At first she thought the waters ran red because of iron in the soil. Then she heard the singing. The voice was mournful and high-pitched, a keening wail. Craning her neck, Dana spied the female figure kneeling on the ledge above. Long straggly hair hid most of her face; her hands were wrinkled and blood-stained. Beside her lay a pile of soiled linen. As she washed the garments in the stream, the waters ran red.

Shuddering uncontrollably, Dana had no choice but to forge the stream. Her running shoes turned pink as she splashed through the shallows. Her stomach heaved. She knew of the *Bean Nighe*, the Washerwoman who scrubbed the shrouds of the murdered. The *Bean Sidhe* was her sister, the green-haired ghost who howled at night outside the homes of those who were about to die.

As Dana fled, almost tumbling down the hillside, the dread voice followed after her.

> *Darest thou go, O child,*
> *Into the night,*
> *Where death awaits,*
> *Lurking in the shadows?*

Dana's fear was spiraling. Dusk had begun to settle over the mountains with a steely light. The thought of being out alone in the dark with such creatures was horrifying. She hurried down on a sheep's track, through a patch of prickly gorse. Was that something behind her? She stopped to look back. There was nothing to be seen. A wild animal, perhaps? A badger or fox? She continued downward, telling herself to stay calm. But a little voice in her head screamed that something was following her. There it was again! Clacking noises, like stones banged together. Suddenly the bushes on either side of her bristled. She glimpsed shapes like giant insects scuttling underneath. Terror gorged in her throat. There was a pack of them!

Dana screamed and ran.

As soon as she did, they charged.

In a headlong scramble, she plunged down the slope, heedless of briars and stinging nettles. Her hands were scratched and bleeding. Wild with fear, she panted like a hunted animal. What were they? Why were they chasing her? Something caught up to her and ran alongside. Small and dark, it had coppery eyes that glinted wickedly. With a shriek, she sprang ahead. Her legs were longer. But could she outrun them? Her heart was pounding in her chest, her breathing shallow. She felt a stitch coming on.

A stone struck the back of her head. She let out a cry. A shower of pebbles fell around her. A few landed ahead.

Broken pieces of flint! Axe-heads, like the ones in the museum. *Fairy arrows*, the old people called them. *Elf-shots*. She tried to dodge the missiles, swerving this way and that. It wasn't easy, running downhill. The ground was uneven. The gorse clawed at her legs and arms. She clutched her side where the stitch cut like a knife.

It was the net that finally brought her down. First came its shadow like wings overhead. Then a blow as the heavy web landed. She pitched forward into a tangle of rope, limbs, and bushes, dragging some of her assailants with her. The air rang with cries and shouts on every side.

Snared like a fly in a spider's web, Dana kicked out wildly. Through the coarse mesh she could just make out squat, mud-colored creatures. They appeared to be half her height, with webbed fingers that were cold and clammy. Despite her disadvantage, she was putting up a good fight, determined to get back on her feet. Wherever her kicks landed, the others would yell and curse, but they clung tenaciously. More and more arrived, leaping on top of her as if to squash her. Soon she was lost in a scrum of small bodies, overwhelmed by the smell of damp soil and grass.

"I give up!" she screamed, terrified that they meant to smother her.

The minute she stopped fighting, they all jumped off, howling with triumph. In a matter of minutes they trussed her up inside the net and hoisted her onto their shoulders.

Then they set off, back up the mountainside.

Stunned and in shock, Dana kept still. None of them had said a word to her, but they chattered away to each other in a mix of Irish and English. Their voices were deep and murky. Most of the time they were calling out warnings and directions.

"Puddle here!" someone shouted from the right.

Dana was immediately jerked to the left.

"Briars!" called one in the front.

They swerved so suddenly, her stomach lurched.

"Nettle patch! *Suas! Suas!*" came too late as the dreaded leaves stung her, fast and furiously like a swarm of angry bees.

"Ow!" she yelled. "Be careful!"

They ignored her.

Dana fought to keep her wits about her. She needed to know what they were and why they had abducted her. From time to time she attempted some resistance, but their grip was too firm. She could hardly move a muscle. In the end, she decided to conserve her strength and wait for the right moment to make her escape. Judging by the heaves and puffs, they were beginning to flag. Eventually they would have to put her down and rest.

At one point, a cuckoo's call echoed from low ground. They all came to an abrupt halt. She could sense them holding their breath as they listened. Now the cuckoo cried again. They let out a cheer.

"'Twas on the right!"

"Good luck for a year and a day!"

Crowing with delight, they continued their trek.

Where were they going? As evening set in, the mountains darkened like giant shadows. The air grew chill. Despite the jiggling and jangling and her unknown fate, Dana was beginning to grow bored. Her fear had subsided. For all that the creatures had attacked and kidnapped her, she didn't get a sense of evil or malice. Though she had bruised most of them when she first fought them off, not one had pinched or poked her. And there was something pleasant about their scent, like freshly mown grass on a summer's evening.

Having long lost track of time and direction, she was almost asleep when they reached new terrain. The feet of her captors squelched in soft ground. There was no more gorse, only tussocks of damp grass. Dana noticed something else. They all seemed to have gained a second wind, jogging along at a livelier pace. They were also talking and laughing more freely now. She suspected they had reached home ground.

"Isn't we the clever boggles? Our first human child stoled in ages!"

"And a girl! A girl!"

Squeals of delight.

"Asha, they don't leaves their childer out and about anymore."

" 'Tis true! No prams outside the house or under the tree."

"No babbies on a blanket in the grass."

"No wains wandrin' to school through the fields on their ownio."

"They guards them better nowadays."

"Feeds them better too!" a little voice piped up. "She be's heavy! Five stone at least."

"Aye, she be's a ton weight," another agreed breathlessly. "The three-year-olds be best. She be's nine or ten."

Though she had intended to keep quiet in the hopes of overhearing something useful, this was too much for Dana.

"I'm twelve!" she said indignantly.

Gasps erupted, followed by a stony silence. It was obvious they were shocked.

"How's it she hears us, lads?" someone ventured at last.

"I knew she seen us! Not just the elf-stones!"

"Some of thems could in the olden days."

"She gots the right spirit. Out in the hills on her sweeney. Runnin' away from home, I bets."

"Well, she be's far away from home now. We'll gets great sport out of her."

They danced about, jigging her up and down.

"Ye means we're not going to eat her?"

This last remark provoked a little cry from Dana that

led to such a fit of giggles, she suspected (and hoped) they were only teasing her. Still, she decided it was time to fight again. With a great roar, she exploded, twisting and turning with ferocious energy.

Caught off guard, they dropped her.

Dana immediately rolled away, tearing at the net like a cat in a bag. In a matter of minutes she was free and on her feet, fists up in the air.

Her kidnappers didn't move.

Boggles, they had called themselves, and to the bog they belonged. No taller than her waist, all were of a muddy brown color, with long scrawny necks and round heads and plump tummies. Their large webbed feet were flat as plates. Some were dour-looking while others were ugly in a comical way. A few glittered with scales of bronze. Their most attractive feature were the coppery eyes, shining like new pennies.

The boggles returned Dana's scrutiny with smug delight, nodding to each other and grinning and whispering. They were obviously sizing her up, pleased with their booty, their stolen prize. With a sinking feeling, Dana saw that they were not in the slightest bit worried that she was free. When she looked around her, she knew why.

They were standing on a vast bog that spread out on all sides as far as the eye could see; a drear place with no sign of a tree or road or anything else. The ground was soft peat, sodden and mossy. The sky seemed immense, dusted with stars like splintered glass. In the distance rose the dim outline of the Wicklow Mountains. She let out a low moan. She was miles off course. In an empty wasteland. No wonder the boggles looked so complacent.

There was no hope of escape. There was nowhere she could run to.

Nineteen

One of the boggles stepped forward. At three feet in height he was the tallest among them and evidently the leader. He was also the only one who appeared to have some kind of hair: a bog asphodel that sprouted from the top of his head.

He bowed to Dana.

"We welcomes the human child to the Boglands. Can we helps make your stay happy?"

"*Leave me alone!*" she screamed, shifting her feet in a threatening manner.

Though they all jumped back, they didn't look alarmed. Some of them snickered. They grinned at each other and shrugged. *Well if that's the way she wants it.* Drifting away in twos and threes, they skimmed over the wet ground on their flat webbed feet, like skaters on a pond.

The moment Dana realized they were deserting her, she panicked. She had no idea where she was. The night was growing darker. She didn't want to be left alone.

"Wait!" she called. "Wait a minute!"

As she hurried to catch up with them, they ran away from her, scattering like sheep on the road.

"Come back!" she shouted, chasing after them. "I won't fight! I promise!"

She had almost reached one of them and was about to grab him, when he darted away in a last-minute sprint. They were all quick and skittish, squealing like piglets if she got too near. One or two stopped to stick out their tongues and thumb their noses. Others cut capers, twirling around like whirligig beetles in a bog puddle.

For a moment Dana thought she was back at home with her gang of boys. Did they really think they were better than her?

"Oh yeah?" she yelled at them. "I'll get you! You'll see!"

Picking out the smallest in the bunch, she tore after him.

"Run, Bird, run!" the others screeched.

But he hadn't a hope. Dana soon caught up with him.

"You're IT!" she roared in triumph as she grabbed him.

Whooping with laughter, Bird broke away and sped after the next target.

The chase was on. A wild game of tag on the windy bog. Leaping over hummocks of deergrass and heather. Jumping across hollows steeped in brown water. Splashing through pools choked with sphagnum moss. The soft ground or *bogach* that gave the land its name squelched underfoot and splattered them with muck.

Laughing hysterically, shrieking with the rest, Dana was utterly caught up in the fun. How wonderful it was to run and play! Not to have worries and responsibilities. Just to be a kid again. It was as if she were playing outside on her street. Sometimes as she ran among them, she didn't see the boggles. They were Liam and Conor and Eoin.

She stopped to catch her breath, resting her hands on her knees. In that moment she looked around her, dazed.

"What's going on?" she said, bewildered. "Where am I?"

"You're home!" came a chorus of cries.

"Don't be silly!" she argued, though her thoughts were slow and muddied. "I don't . . . live . . . here!"

Several boggles came to tug at her arms.

"You does!" they cried together. "You does live here!"

Dana frowned. That didn't sound right. And something niggled at the back of her mind. Something important that she couldn't recall. Wasn't it dangerous to play outside in the dark? Shouldn't she tell Gabe?

"Gets back in the game!" one of them shouted.

"The fun! The game!" the others urged.

They were all clamoring around her now and she couldn't think straight with the noise.

"Oh yeah. The game," she said at last. It seemed such a relief to say it. "What are we playin'?"

"Leap frog!" someone announced, and they all cheered wildly.

Dana's long legs made her the quickest and the best. She flew over the small huddled bodies lined higgledy-piggledy over the ground. Her running shoes were soaked, her clothes dripping with mud, but she didn't care. When the boggles declared her the winner, she punched the air with glee.

"They forgets real fast," one remarked to another.

Dana overheard and felt a twinge of foreboding. In the back of her mind, she knew something was wrong. *So what.* If she was in trouble, she would face the music later. Right now, she wanted to play.

One of the boggles scrambled onto a bank of cut turf.

"I's the King of the Castle!" he proclaimed.

Dana jumped up beside him and knocked him down.

"And I's the Dirty Rascal!"

The games continued till Dana looked pale and haunted. Her lips were blue, her teeth chattered, and she was starving, yet she didn't think to change into dry clothes or to eat any of her food. Her knapsack hung forgotten on her back, as drenched and bedraggled as the rest of her.

The moon had risen to etch the streaks of clouds with light. The landscape shone eerily. The air swarmed with midges and the iridescent flies named after dragons and damsels. The fragrant scent of bog myrtle wafted on an evening breeze. With the moonrise came a change in the boggles. Where their eyes glinted a coppery sheen by day, they now glowed like gold coins.

At last they called a halt for supper. A great bonfire was made with logs of bog oak, and everyone sat on stones around it. Dana's clothes were caked and filthy, her hair plastered to her head. Oblivious, she joined the debates about who won which game and what could fairly be called a draw or an "undecided." Sometimes she got the boggles' names wrong, as she found it difficult to distinguish one from another. Each time she apologized, they waved away her regrets.

"You's all looks alike to us," Piper, the leader, told her. " 'Cept when you's got color. We likes the brown ones best."

Along with Piper and his bog asphodel, Bird was easy to recognize, as he was the smallest and had a beak for a nose. But she would never be able to tell the difference between Butterhill and Silverhill, who were twin brothers, or Snow and Twig, who were not related but looked identical. Then there was Underhill, who was no relation to the two other "hills" but was a cousin of Goodfellow, Lightbow, and Gem. Some had identifying markers. Green did indeed wear a vest of woven grass, while Stone had a little chain of pebbles around his neck.

When the fire was deemed hot enough, a big cauldron was placed at its heart. Ingredients for a stew were tossed in willy-nilly, whetting Dana's appetite with mouthwatering smells. She peered at the flora of the bog bubbling away: dark-purple liverworts as fat as worms, green and black bog moss, leathery bogbean with fleshy stems and hairy flowers, bottle sedge and pondweed with flat red leaves. She wondered a moment if it was safe to eat, but decided she didn't care. This was no time to be fussy. She was ravenous.

While the bog bouillabaisse brewed, Dana shared out her chocolates. Since no one told them not to, they ate dessert first.

At last the stew was dished out into wooden bowls. It was truly scrumptious. Though Dana felt as if she were eating the bog itself, the chief taste was "brown." She was reminded of all the brown things she liked to eat, both sweet and savory: almond croissants, the crusty top of a freshly-baked bread, buttered toast, and peanut butter cookies; but also golden-brown fries, grilled mushrooms, HP Sauce, and the crisp skins of potatoes baked in the oven. They offered her grimy water to drink, but she declined. When she passed around the bottle of cola, they admired its color but spat it out.

"You probably don't like chemicals," was her comment.

"*You does?*"

"Yeah. Tastes great."

They huddled around the fire, leaning against each other like a bunch of homeless kids with dirty faces. Dana was reminded of Peter Pan's Lost Boys. Did that make her

Wendy? Now that things had quieted down, she began to think.

"Right, lads," she announced. "There's something we've got to—"

Before she could finish, the boggles were on their feet.

"Time to dance!" they cried.

Skin drums and panpipes suddenly appeared. Up rose the wildest music imaginable, drumming and thrumming, trilling and thrilling. A contagious cadence that called to the blood.

Despite her protests, Dana was pulled into a ring and urged to hop and skip. The *Celebrate the Kidnapped Child Dance* entailed spinning her around again and again till she was hopelessly dizzy. She laughed so hard her stomach hurt.

For *The Dance of Lights* each had to pick a star and, while keeping an eye on it, twirl and whirl like a top. When the music halted, all came to a stop. Except the earth and sky, which kept on turning, leaving everyone to stagger around, whooping, till they all fell down.

Crack the Whip had them holding hands in a long line and careering recklessly over the bog in sharp zigs and zags that left those at the end clinging on for dear life. This was the dance—which Dana knew as a game—that brought them to the crossroads.

She hadn't noticed that they were racing along a road that bordered the bog like a river. It was the signpost that brought her up with a jolt. Having forgotten human things, she was so shocked to see it that she let go of the whip and went flying into a ditch.

Clambering out again, she ran back to the sign.

It pointed in four directions: Dublin to the north, Glendalough to the south, Blessington to the west, Bray to the east. Now she knew where she was. In the Sally Gap. Backtracked for miles! Completely the wrong way! Dismay and despair flooded through her. Her memory returned and, with it, everything she had forgotten as she played: her mission, her missing mother, and her poor abandoned father.

A familiar sound in the distance caught her attention as yellow headlights beamed over the landscape.

The boggles had also spotted the car. With whoops and war cries, the whip cracked back to descend on Dana.

"No, wait!" she pleaded, as little hands clutched hers. "Stop! *Please!*"

Too late, she was part of the line once more as it scurried away, back into the bog.

The Triumph Herald stopped at the crossroads. Gabriel got out and looked around.

"There's nothing here," Aradhana called gently from the car.

"I'm sure I saw something," he muttered.

He stared into the distance. His eyes were bloodshot, his face ravaged. Was he chasing shadows? But what else could he do? Rescue teams were searching the mountains and the police helicopter was out. Yet still no word of her. He was sick with guilt; sicker with worry. She had obviously run away to protest against the move to Canada. What if something terrible happened to her?

He wouldn't, couldn't rest until he found her.

But where could she be?

Twenty

It was well past midnight. The bog lay still under the black dome of the sky and the cold eye of the moon. The silhouette of the mountains shadowed the horizon. Despite the hour, everything seemed strangely bright, tinted with moonlight. Dana lounged with the boggles around the campfire, watching the stars fall. Whenever one dropped from the heavens, they let out an *ohhhh* or an *ahhhh* as if they were watching fireworks. Then they would shout: "*What is the stars? What is the stars?*"

Though she joined in with enthusiasm, Dana was also thinking hard. In the lull between games, she had figured it out. By some kind of bog magic, she forgot who she was whenever they played. Only when she took a rest did she return to herself. She wasn't worried. The boggles didn't strike her as harmful or malign. But they were sly and mischievous, and she would have to outwit them.

Bird climbed into her lap and offered her a stalk of bog cotton. The tuft of white hair at its tip fluttered like a miniature flag.

"Say 'for a year and a day I promise to stay,'" he begged her.

She smiled down at the big eyes like molten gold, then met the eager looks of the others around her. They were such funny little things. She really liked them. And there was a sad touch of loneliness in how much they needed her. Lost boys, for sure, homeless and motherless and longing for attention.

The boggles held their breath as she twirled the stalk between her fingers. At last she spoke in a solemn tone:

> For a year and a day,
> I promise to stay.

They were about to cheer, when she added quickly:

> —No way!

> But I promise the night,
> Without a fight,
> If you set me free tomorrow,
> Without tears or sorrow.

> Though we say good-bye,
> Our love won't die.

It was such a friendly rebuff, they couldn't take offense. Some even applauded. But looks were passed between the older ones and Dana knew they were about to call another game. She would lose any ground she had gained.

"I know what to play!" she said suddenly. "I bet you don't know this one. It's for clever people."

"We's clever!" they cried.

She hid her grin. She knew they couldn't resist a challenge.

"All the kids on my street play it. It's called 'Moonpenny.'"

The name caught their fancy; again, as she had known it would.

"We wants to play!" a few of the boggles shouted. "What's the rules?"

Dana paused. She could see that many were still frowning. She needed to hook them all.

"That's the game," she said. "I tell you things that are moonpennies and things that aren't, and you have to guess the rules yourself."

"*Ohhh,*" they breathed, eyes wide.

More were curious now, but several had begun to mutter suspiciously. She needed to keep up the momentum, to ensnare them all. It was her turn to make magic, to weave a spell with words.

"Boggle is a moonpenny!" she proclaimed. "Dana isn't!"

That did it.

Every one of them was caught. Their little brows furrowed as they pondered what she had said.

"Does we get more samples?" Piper demanded.

"Of course," she said smoothly. "And you can ask me if this or that is a moonpenny."

There was an explosion of chatter.

"Is the moon a moonpenny?"

"Yes."

Shrieks of delight. It was Bird who got that one.

"Is the sky?"

"No."

A groan of disappointment.

"Is the bog a moonpenny?"

"No."

More groans.

"But the grass is and so is a bluebottle and so is a moon-penny," she announced.

"A moonpenny is a moonpenny?"

They were scrunching up their faces and closing their eyes and rubbing their foreheads and pursing their lips. The strain of their concentration was almost painful to behold. At the same time, Dana had to fight to keep from laughing. For no matter how many things they named, get-ting this wrong and that right, they could not discern the pattern. They could not guess the key. Some were nearly in tears: that a game should exist that a boggle couldn't best!

It was only when they had reached the peak of their frustration and demanded to be told the solution that she dropped her little bombshell (also a moonpenny).

"I'm not telling unless . . ." Dana stopped for a moment to heighten the suspense, ". . . you agree to let me go. Like I said, I'll stay tonight and leave in the morning."

The boggles were beyond arguing or negotiating or even complaining. In a feverish pitch to learn the secret of the game, they agreed in an instant.

Dana laughed victoriously and made her announcement.

"A moonpenny is anything with a *double letter* in it!"

There were howls and screeches and tears and laughter, but they all agreed that she had got them well and good, even as Moonpenny took a hallowed place in the canon of boggle games.

"You goes tomorrow," Piper agreed. The bog asphodel on his head bobbed with his nod of authority.

The matter settled, they showed her where she would sleep that night. All of them had burrows throughout the bog. Called a *pollach*, each bog-hole was a snug little space deep underground with a bend in the tunnel to keep out the rain. Lined with fresh rushes and tufts of white bog cotton, they reminded Dana of her hamsters' nests.

Back at the campfire, the boggles relaxed now that they no longer had to distract Dana with games. Instead, they told her stories of their mischief and mayhem: how they knocked down stone walls to annoy the farmers, stole clothes off washing lines, overturned dustbins and potted plants on the windowsills. Their favorite prank, they confessed, was blowing wind down the chimney till a cloud of soot shrouded the house.

"The housewifes does wail like the Banshee!" they cried gleefully.

Dana laughed at their antics and told some of her own: how she and her gang would ring their neighbors' doorbells, then run and hide behind a hedge, snickering as the hapless victim looked up and down the street. In the evenings, when the yellow lights shone through the lace curtains and people sat in front of their television sets, she and her boys would throw stones at the windows to watch everyone inside jump with fright. But she had to admit, the boggles were far bolder than she.

"I never heard of boggles before," she said, "only the bogeyman."

They all shrieked at once.

"Husha! Don't names him! He scares us too!"

"Black sheep of the family! Black Bart the Bogeyman!"

They began to count on fingers and toes the many members of the Clan Bobodha to which they belonged: boggles, of course, bogles, boggarts, bogeys, bloodybones, brownies, bugbears, hobgoblins, boggy-boes, dobbies, hobthrusts, hobby-lanthorns, tantarrabobs, hodge-podgers, bolls, bomen, brags, flay-boggarts, pegpowlers, pucks, madcaps, buggaboes, clabbernappers, gnomes, thrummy caps, and spriggans.

"Don't forgets the kobolds," Green piped up, "our German kin."

"So many!" Dana said, amazed. "And nobody ever sees them!"

"We stays in the mountains and the far-off places."

"Bets you sees the leprechauns," Underhill said. "They's distant relations thirteen times removed. Lots of them lives in the towns. They passes for humans."

"No, I never—" Dana began, then she stopped. She suddenly remembered all the times she *had* seen them, those little old men sitting on the bus or standing at the street corner. The one who offered her a seat in the coffee shop. The other one who gave her a book in the library— about fairies! Of course! All those little old men with knobbly noses and hairy ears and twinkling eyes. Each time she had seen them, she had thought to herself, *he looks like a leprechaun.*

They had reached that time of the night when secrets were shared and friendship was forever. Dana finally asked the question that was plaguing her.

"Aren't there any girl boggles?"

Their reaction was as quick and blunt as a blow. Bird scampered out of her lap. Everyone recoiled. Many looked away. Some began to fidget, while others busied them-selves tending the fire. They appeared not only silent and evasive, but also deeply sad.

"We don'ts talk about them," Piper said at last. He

stared dismally into the flames. "Our Ivy and Sally, our Flower and Pepper."

"Our Megs and Mags and Pegs and Pogs."

"Our Dew and Dally and Sue and Tally."

"We misses our girls!"

"Off they went and it had to be."

"All alone are we!"

Their big golden eyes went dim and watery. They started to sniff. Great drops of tears rolled down their cheeks and off their noses, splashing into the fire with a hiss.

"I'm sorry!" Dana exclaimed. "I shouldn't've asked! I'm a big Nosy Parker! I didn't mean to upset you!"

The boggles were weeping and howling now. Dana felt like a babysitter who had lost control of her charges, all wailing for their mother.

"They'll come back one day," she said desperately.

"Not if the light don'ts," sobbed little Bird.

As soon as the words were uttered, the others snapped out of their woe. Those nearest to Bird clapped their hands over his mouth.

"Hush! *Dún do bhéal!*"

"Say nothin' and keep repeatin' it!"

"Whispers fly on the wind!"

"It be's bad if he hears!"

Dana was alert to the new change of mood. The air was fraught with tension.

"Who might hear? Why is it bad? Do you have an enemy?"

She was already wondering if their enemy was the same as hers.

They shook their heads furiously. No one would answer. They made zipper motions over their mouths to each other, shutting tight as clams.

Dana tried to think of a way to reach them. Something echoed at the back of her mind. Bird had mentioned "the light." Was it the same light as the one in her message? *Where is the light to bridge the darkness.* Could it have anything to do with her mission?

"Do you know Lugh of the Mountain?" she asked them.

"Lugh of the Wood?" they cried together.

She could see she had made matters worse. They all froze in their places and gaped at her.

Piper stood up stiffly.

"Why does you ask?"

His voice was so taut it almost squeaked. Dana's unease was increasing. Their mood had shifted again. They regarded her with a suspicion that bordered on hostility.

"I have a message for him," she confessed reluctantly. "From the High King of—"

Before she could finish they erupted into wails, this time of terror.

"She be's with the Court!"

"The Gentry sent her!"

"After we kepts them away!"

"The tricksters! To send a human child!"

"How coulds we know?"

Their dread was terrible to behold. Bold children caught out and deathly afraid of punishment.

"What cans we do?"

"An fathach mór 'na lui faoi shuan."

"Yes, he sleeps! But for how long?"

"If she finds him, she wakes him!"

"All the storms! All the rain!"

"Our *pollachs* drownded!"

"There be's floods!"

"There be's a bog-burst!"

They worked themselves into a frenzy, then reached a crescendo and collapsed into silence.

Now another change came over the boggles, the worst one of all. They no longer looked cute, not even Bird. Their eyes narrowed to slits: a cold alien gaze. They bared their teeth, fanged and white in the moonlight. They seemed suddenly like some carnivorous creature of the bog, feral and dangerous.

Dana sensed their ill will and grew afraid.

"We must keeps her away from him!"

"We must hides her!"

She didn't stop to plead or argue. Everything had

changed, changed utterly. She knew immediately that they were her enemy.

She jumped up and ran.

And they ran after her.

She was more of a match for them this time. Thanks to their games, Dana knew the bog and was able to traverse it. She headed for the road. The gray line of tarmac shone dimly in the distance. Slowly winding toward her, the yellow lights of a car blinked like a cat. Who was out in the mountains at this hour? She didn't care. They were her only hope. She waved her arms and shouted, but they were too far away. She needed to hide till the car got closer.

The boggles were hollering behind her and gaining fast. Her mind raced in circles. *Where could she hide?* All around her lay open ground lit up by the moon. She remembered the ditch that bordered the road, the one she had fallen into. A glance at the sky. The night wind was rushing a few clouds across it. In a minute they would cover the moon, granting sweet darkness. But not for long. A quick plan took shape in her mind. Terror gave her an edge. And had some bog magic seeped into her bones? She was still a fair distance ahead of the boggles. Hunching down as she ran, she began to zigzag, hoping to distract their eyes from the road. She herself kept watch on the moon.

Yes!

As the clouds suddenly plunged the land into shadow, Dana leaped sideways into the ditch.

And landed with a thump.

The hard fall knocked the wind right out of her. But the moment she recovered, she scurried madly along the trench till she reached the crossroads. She was crawling on her hands and knees through cold slimy water, but she didn't care. The trick had worked. When the moon came out again, howls of dismay rang over the bog.

She was nowhere to be seen.

Dana heard the boggles splitting up, running here and there. And she also heard the engine of the car as it approached the crossroads. Huddled in a ball, she wouldn't jump up until it was almost on top of her.

Then a gasp sounded above her. Looking up, she saw Bird's face peering down at her. His mouth was open, but not a word was uttered.

"Please," she whispered to him. "Don't. I'm your friend."

His features showed the enormity of his struggle.

"*Please*," she pleaded.

Then out came the shout, hitch-pitched and tortured, but loud nonetheless.

"*She be's here!*"

Dana was barely out of the ditch before the net caught her. She screamed as loud as she could, but the car was still too far away. In a matter of minutes, she was bound and helpless.

By the time the car arrived at the crossroads, she had been dragged out of sight.

"Let me go!" she begged the boggles. "You promised, remember? When I gave you the answer to Moonpenny? Don't be cheaters! I won my freedom! Don't be bad sports! I won't tell on you. I promise. I wouldn't hurt any of you!"

Her pleas fell on deaf ears. They hauled her to an abandoned part of the bog where the turf beds had been overworked and people dumped their garbage. The ground was littered with old refrigerators, torn mattresses, and heaps of plastic bags bursting with disposable diapers and rotten food. The stench was foul.

Freed from the net, but held down by many hands, Dana watched as the boggles rolled away a stone from the front of an old *pollach*. The hole looked dark and dank. When they crowded around her, eyes hard as metal, she knew what they meant to do.

Under the cold and impassive face of the moon, Dana fought her last battle with the boggles. Silently, doggedly, she struggled tooth and nail against them. While there was breath in her body she would not go into that hole. She was as fierce as a wild thing caught in a trap.

And just as powerless.

Slowly and inexorably they pushed her toward the *pollach*. Slowly and inexorably it opened wide to swallow her.

"No! Don't! Please don't!"

She kept on screaming as they crammed her inside.

"We has no choice!" Green muttered through clenched teeth.

"We hast to do it!" Silverhill agreed.

Their words echoed with shame and regret. Little Bird was sobbing as if his heart might break. But no one was about to take her side.

Piper's voice rang out in final judgment.

"We hast to keep you away from Lugh. Let sleeping kings lie! No one must wakes him!"

And they rolled the stone back into place.

Trapped in the dark, Dana didn't see them slink away into the shadows, unable to meet each other's eyes. But she sensed immediately that they were gone. The pall of silence and emptiness was unmistakable.

She stopped screaming. There was no point.

In that forsaken place, in the black of night, she was alone.

Twenty-one

The Mountain King wed his Sky Bride in the autumn, on the Feast of Samhain, when the New Year began for the Sídhe-Folk and all those who followed the Celtic calendar. The fallen leaves of the forest made a red and gold carpet for the nuptial procession, as it wound through the hills. The King's subjects cheered and sang, waving boughs clustered with bright berries.

He wore the colors of his kingdom: a dark-green tunic, a purple mantle pinned with a white brooch, bronze sandals on his feet, and a chaplet of oak leaves upon his head. She was dressed in a gown of lucent blue with silver scintillas sewn into the soft folds. Taming her fiery hair was the winged crown he had gifted her.

He brought her to his palace on the grassy summit of Lugnaquillia. Fashioned of crystal, it turned throughout the day to face the sun, like a gigantic flower. When the first light of morning struck the glassy casements, they would coruscate with rainbow colors. If the sky was cloudy, the walls gleamed a milky blue, opaque as a robin's egg. In the westering sun of *evening, beneath crimson skies, the towers blazed like burning jewels. Then would come the fall of night, and the cooling of the castle to black obsidian spangled with starlight.*

"Is this my home?" she murmured as he led her across the threshold.

"Forever and a day," was his reply.

And the celebrations began.

There was music and dancing and feasts galore. Banquets were served on cloths of pure linen and lustrous salvers, offering all the dainties of the kingdom: candied quince and apples, mint curds and berry pies, wild fruit jellies, honeyed syrups tincted with cinnamon, sweet nutcakes and seedcakes, huge vats of chamomile wine and fraughan beer.

Following that marriage, in the sacred rite of hierogamos, all things that were bright grew brighter still. It was a time of splendor and delight, a Golden Age, and every creature, great and small, sang with joy: the hawk that swooped like a falling stone, the fish that leaped in shining flashes, the barking otter, the spear-beaked birds.

Never had two lived so well together. Forever young, forever beautiful, they danced on the summer lawns of Lugnaquillia. They rode the cold currents of the winter winds. They swam in the seas by their lands on the Murrough. And any who chanced to overhear their laughter would feel their hearts lift.

He would hold her close and touch her as he would a precious harp, singing to her sweet ballads of love.

Were every brown leaf in the wood turned to gold,
Were the gray stone of the peaks, the purest silver,
I would give it all away,
For you, *a stór*,
I would give it all away,
For you, my treasure.

One evening they lay together in the warm grasses to watch the stars fall.

"*Tell me of your Home,*" *he said to her.*

Her laughter was light, yet a veil dimmed her eyes.

"*Do not seek to know too much about me. You are of the earth and I, the sky, and we have met in your realm, not mine. Accept what is and do not delve. For I have forgotten much, and perhaps that is best for our happiness together.*"

Did he suffer a moment of disquiet, just then? Did he feel the darkness of the shadow cast by events to come? Did he sense the approach of the stranger and the pain that lay in wait for him?

Twenty-two

D ana huddled in shock. The hole was pitch dark and stank of moldy earth. Buried alive! She struggled to keep control, not to let the fear win. There was barely room to move around. Her body ached from the fight. When the tears started to roll down her cheeks, she couldn't stop them. Then she did what most children do when they find themselves in an unbearable situation. She fell asleep.

Turning over, she realized she was at home in Wolfe Tone Square. The yellow duvet felt soft and warm. The light in the hall shone into her bedroom.

Gabe offered her a cup of warm milk. It tasted of honey with a sprinkle of nutmeg.

"You were riding the night mare again," he told her gently. "I'll stay with you."

He sat in the chair beside her bed and smiled at her reassuringly.

It was just a bad dream!

Happy and relieved, she finished her milk and went back to sleep while her father watched over her.

When Dana woke to the reality of the cold dank hole, it

was all the worse. She let out a cry as the darkness engulfed her once more. Scrunching into a ball, she held on to herself tightly. Every part of her hurt, and the uneven ground jabbed into her. The taste of clay was in her mouth. A foul-smelling mud coated her clothes, skin, and hair. After the sweet dream of home, it was too much to take. She started to howl like a baby.

Without knowing it, like all the times she had cried in bed at night, Dana called for the mother who never came. Her sobs were deep and painful. Her store of tears ran deep. How long she wept, she didn't know, but it seemed forever.

Then she stopped crying.

And lay perfectly still.

I've got to do something. I've got to get out of here.

Moving slowly in the cramped space, she began to push against the stone that blocked the *pollach*. It wouldn't budge. Bracing her back against the wall behind her, she used her feet. Not even an inch. If only she had something to use as a lever! Her eyes were growing accustomed to the dark. She began to notice the spaces around the stone that let in air and faint traces of light. Was dawn arriving? She had no idea of time. Her throat was parched with thirst and she was hungry. The boggles had taken her knapsack. She had nothing to eat or drink. Would they come back to feed her or had they left her there to die? She wasn't going to wait around to find out. She would dig herself free. Clear away the soil around the stone and widen the entrance.

Dana groped around for pieces of flint or stone. Nothing. She would have to use her hands. The clay was caked and gluey. She could remove only bits at a time. Her nails scraped against the stone. Though it seemed hopeless, she kept at it. If she persevered, she was bound to see some progress.

She had been digging for some time when she heard a noise behind her. Twisting around, she held her breath to listen. There it was again! A tapping sound, as if someone or something was on the other side of the hole. How could that be? Wasn't there only boggy earth beyond? Pressing her ear against the wall, she was surprised to hear faint strains of music. The boggles? Unlikely. Though they slept underground, they lived and played in the open.

A vein of gold suddenly ran through the clay. There *was* something on the other side! As light and music poured into her prison, Dana peered through the crack to have a look.

She was gazing into a miniature hall! White tapers flickered in chandeliers. Crystal pillars rose to a high gilded ceiling. Galleries were garlanded with green leaves and bright flowers. Tapestries adorned the walls. Across the marbled floor, dancers twirled in jewels and finery.

How Dana yearned to be there instead of the dark hole!

The glittering company seemed unaware of the breach in their world and the one who was watching them. Then a young man, dressed like a page in hose and doublet, hurried toward her. With furtive glances over his shoulder, he produced a jeweled cup from under his short cape. Nodding curtly, he shoved it through the crack.

Startled, Dana looked down at the tiny hand gripping a tiny goblet. A whiff of cinnamon filled the *pollach*, cheering her instantly. But the moment she took the cup between her thumb and forefinger, it turned into a hollow acorn with a drop of dew.

The young man gestured to her to join him in the hall.

"How can I?" she whispered. "I'm way too big. I won't fit."

He pointed to the acorn.

Dana hesitated for the merest second. A fleeting thought of Alice passed through her mind. *Drink me.* Yet no matter what the consequences might be, her situation could hardly get worse.

She put her tongue to the acorn.

A tiny taste of honey.

The results were instant. She shrank like a balloon releasing its air and, before she knew it, she had fallen through the crack to land at the page's feet.

He helped her up.

"*Fáilte romhat!*" he said. "Speak to no one but she who comes for you!"

Then he sped away before she could thank him.

Disoriented, Dana looked behind her, half expecting

to see a rend in the air and the dark *pollach* beyond. There was no sign of either. She was gazing through a diamond-paned window over a courtyard. In the distance shone a beautiful country of fair hills and sunshine.

A burst of laughter brought her back to the hall. The revelers were stepping around each other in figures of eight. It was some kind of nature dance. All the dancers held objects in their hands—leaves, ivy, tufts of fleece, twigs—which they wove together as they moved. Something was slowly taking shape in their midst. A finely-wrought cradle? Or was it a little boat?

Dana backed against the wall, half hiding behind a golden curtain. Whatever magic had brought her there had failed to clean her up. In that splendid setting, her soiled clothes and her scrapes and scratches looked even worse.

One of the dancers broke away and came toward her. Despite the mask of peacock feathers, Dana recognized her immediately. The Lady! Her sky-blue gown flounced around her, and a silver mantle fell to her feet. Pearls braided her long fair hair.

"Come!"

Grasping Dana's hand, she hurried her past the dancing crowd, out of the hall, and down a glass staircase.

"I have remembered my name!" she said with great excitement, before Dana could speak. "It is *Honor*. No one addresses me that way, which is why I keep forgetting it. And my husband calls me 'beloved' or '*a stór*.'"

"*Husband?*" Dana was surprised. The Lady looked too young to be married. And yet she did seem different this time. Happier and more confident. "I thought you said you couldn't come here?"

"It was no lie. I have broken the rules!"

Dana heard the mischief and delight in the older girl's voice. So the old stories were true. Fairies *did* love being bold!

"For your sake, my human self defies the law! Except for my page, who gave you the drink, the others do not even know where we are."

"What?" said Dana, astounded.

They had almost reached the end of the long flight of stairs.

"'Tis easy enough for a fairy." Honor smiled blithely. "We can roll up a world like a map and pop it inside another dimension. It's pure magic. Or pure science. Whatever you want to call it. I've brought the whole Court—lock, stock, and barrel! And I have given them a task to distract them. They are weaving a robin's nest for one whose mate was killed by a cat."

Now great oaken doors opened before them, ushering them out into the courtyard. Dana gaped. The castle was a fairy tale classic, with elegant spires, ornate balconies, and brightly colored banners waving in the breeze. The walls were made of glittering stone. The turreted roof was thatched with white feathers. When a sudden gust of wind carried the plumes away like a swirl of snow, the roof re-thatched itself in an instant. At the center of the courtyard stood a marble fountain. Around it grew nine slender trees. As their branches dropped hazelnuts into the waters, five silver salmon rose to consume them.

Dana was dazzled. She couldn't think or speak. Everything shone with mystery and meaning, like an important dream.

When Honor led her to the fountain, Dana drew back at the sight of her own reflection. She looked so dirty and disheveled. The Lady signed to her to take a drink, but Dana wouldn't. She didn't want to pollute the glorious waters. The older girl smiled and, scooping a handful, brought the water to Dana's lips. Never was there a more refreshing drink! She could feel it tingling through every part of her. Then, with a gasp, she saw that she was perfectly clean. Not a spot of mud. Even her cuts and bruises were gone!

"It is the Well of Living Waters," Honor said gently. "Now, let us away. I have remembered something I need to tell you."

"I've something to tell you, too!" Dana said suddenly. "The boggles—"

But Honor wasn't listening. Clasping Dana's hand once more, she hurried her to the bronze gates that led outside the castle.

"I came not only to free you," she explained, "but also to warn you. There are things I keep forgetting in my confusion of self. I promised you your heart's desire, but know this: King Lugh is the one who will grant you your boon, and you must ask it of him on the feast-day of *Lá Lughnasa.*"

"August day," Dana said, quickly translating the Irish. "You mean August first?"

"Yes! 'Lammas' some call it. You must reach Lugnaquillia by then. That is when you may request your wish."

"The day after tomorrow!" Dana was dismayed, yet she knew that time was the least of her worries. "Things are even worse!" she told Honor. "The king is fast asleep. And the boggles have something to do with it. I think they're the ones who've been keeping everyone out. They don't want him to wake up."

The Lady stopped so abruptly that the mask slipped from her face. Her pretty features reflected her bewilderment.

"How can this be? Why would they do such a thing? They are harmless creatures. Oh, I know they kidnapped you, but they were just being naughty. They get carried away with their games sometimes. They would never have hurt you."

Dana was hardly convinced and was about to argue the point when they passed through the gates. The words died on her lips as a beautiful scene unfolded before her.

Twenty-three

It was Ireland and yet not Ireland; the fair country she had seen from the castle window. Hills and woods, lakes and rivers, all seemed to shine with intensity, as if the world were newly born. Multicolored birds flitted through the air like butterflies. Warm winds wafted the sweet scent of apple blossoms. Melodious music resounded from every quarter.

"Is this Faerie?" Dana asked breathlessly.

"Yes," the Lady answered, "and no. You do not go to Faerie, you become a part of it. And in a heartbeat you may live thus for a year and a day . . . or for a thousand years. This," and she waved a graceful arm, "is *Magh Abhlach*. The Plain of the Apple Trees. It is an aspect of the Summer Land that is favored by the Gentry of the High King's Court. I moved *everything* to allay their suspicion."

Dana was awed by what Honor had done, but she was worried too. There were often fairy helpers in the tales Gabe told her. Though many had powers just like the Lady, they usually paid a price for aiding humans.

"Will you get into trouble?" Dana asked anxiously. "Might they turn you into a frog or something?"

"I don't believe so," came the reply, followed by a peal of laughter. "Though that would be funny."

Dana didn't think it would be funny at all. It was unsettling the way Honor could be serious one minute and flighty the next. And she had yet to respond to Dana's bad news.

"You've got to tell the High King about the boggles," Dana insisted. "And about Lugh being asleep."

The older girl's mood changed again. She was suddenly grave.

"The High King is away. On a mission of his own, tracking a demon. Otherwise I could never have fooled the Court. But even were he here, I would prefer not to ask for his help. This matter he has entrusted to me and it is something I need to do. To prove myself. Do you understand?"

Dana didn't really, but she nodded all the same. The Lady was almost pleading. Given that Honor had literally moved heaven and earth to help her, Dana was prepared to give her what support she needed.

Honor continued earnestly. "I will discover what is happening in the Mountain Kingdom, I promise you. I am already resolved to help you as best I can. I've broken the rules once, I'll do it again. Desperate times call for desperate measures."

"Thanks," said Dana quietly, and she meant it.

She trusted the young woman and was beginning to consider her a friend.

"Don't thank *me*," Honor cried. "It's the least I can do! I am ashamed that They . . . that we . . . have not done more to aid thee. While I don't regret being with them, there are things about the fairies I find difficult to countenance."

Not for the first time, Dana was struck by the strangeness of the other's position: half in, half out, half this, half that. Sometimes the older girl seemed so human, and other times, pure fairy. Even the way she spoke was betwixt and between, a jumble of courtly and modern speech. Dana's curiosity peaked.

"Did they steal you? When you were little?"

The Lady sighed. "It's a long story, the length of a book. Perhaps one day I shall tell it to you, but there is no time now."

She took Dana's hand, and they were suddenly running as fast as the wind.

The landscape hurtled past them, like scenery outside the window of a speeding train.

Then just as quickly they came to a halt, making Dana's stomach lurch.

They were on a green common that hosted a country fair. A great wooden Ferris wheel twirled above the crowd, twined with holly and ivy. The noisy throng milled over the grass, dressed in bright costumes and rainbow-colored

cloaks. Many looked human; young men and women
with their arms around each other, old warriors with
mantles and their swords sheathed, mothers with babies
tucked into fringed shawls. But there were also giants and
dwarves and other strange creatures. Voluminous tents
shone white in the sunlight, fluttering with silken flags.
Inside, entertainments took place. A horned man swallowed swords of fire. A bearded lady lifted weights. Dana
lingered at one pavilion where a shadow play depicted the
story of Beauty and the Beast. She was surprised to see
that the Beauty was a fairy princess while the Beast was
human. As well as the tents, there were booths displaying
every kind of ware and craft: bolts of rich fabrics, heaps
of precious stones, porcelain china, musical instruments,
and mechanical toys. Mouthwatering smells issued from
the food stalls where sweetmeats sizzled in great pans and
pyramids of pastries balanced precariously.

Honor handed Dana a velvet purse bulging with
coins.

"You need provisions for your journey. And buy yourself new clothes. A cloak to keep you warm in the mountains. You must haggle or they will cheat you, especially
the cluricauns. They're the ones with the red noses."

"*Haggle?*"

Dana pulled a face. She hated shopping at the best
of times; the thought of arguing over the price was a
nightmare.

"You can do it," the Lady assured her in a big-sisterly tone. "Now I must return to the Court to ensure they are still occupied. I'll return as soon as I can. Shop till you drop!"

Despite her initial reluctance, Dana was soon wandering happily from booth to booth. It was nothing like a supermarket or shopping mall. She had never seen so many fascinating things. At one stall, a golden-haired seamstress offered to embroider a triskele on the leg of her jeans. Dana couldn't resist. She did say no, however, to the blue-faced imps who wanted to paint her elbows and knees. But could she make use of a bracelet that turned her purple? Or a ball that bounced as high as the clouds? At the sweet stall, she was mesmerized by the array of candied lollipops, liquorice, toffee sticks, and old-fashioned fruit ices. She bought a stick of fresh strawberries to dip into the fountain of molten chocolate. And after that, she got a cinnamon bun and a cup of hot cider. There was a moment before she put the little cake into her mouth when someone passed behind her and muttered quick words.

"*Má itheann tú ná má ólann tú aon ghreim istigh anseo, ní bhfaighidh tú amach as go bráth arís!*"

Dana spun around, but whoever it was had disappeared into the crowd. She felt uneasy. Why the warning against eating and drinking? She had already done it more than once on the quest. And Honor hadn't spoken of it.

With a fatalistic shrug, Dana polished off the food. *In for a penny, in for a pound.* Then she got down to business.

"Out dancin' under the moon with boggles, I see!" snorted the leprechaun manning the cobblers' booth. "And bejaney mack, would ye look at the state o' dem. Like somethin' that died and was buried."

She had brought him her running shoes, waterlogged and clotted with mud.

The fat little shoemaker was dressed all in green. He had an apple-shaped face with red hair and beard. The pockets of his leather apron were filled with nails of every size and description. Bunches of them also protruded from the corners of his mouth, like a pincushion. As he scraped, sewed, and buffed her shoes, he continually complained that she had ruined them beyond hope. But when he was finished, they looked brand-new.

Chastened, Dana handed him a gold coin and told him to keep the change. As he bit into it, the leprechaun's face lit up. He looked not only mollified but hugely pleased. Just before he returned the shoes, he drove a tiny silver nail into the heel of each.

"That'll give ye a bit of *umph*," he said, winking. "But steer clear o' dem bogs!"

Next, Dana outfitted herself in new clothes suitable for traveling outdoors. Keeping in mind the chill of the mountain peaks, she chose green trousers of strong cotton, a white cambric shirt, and a yellow knitted vest.

Her finest purchase was the long flowing cloak of golden-brown wool with a capacious hood. Finally, she bought a leather satchel to replace her lost knapsack, then stocked it with apples and oranges, curranty bread, chunks of cheese, fairy buns with icing, and a bottle of ginger beer.

It was time to find Honor. Dana wandered through the crowds, looking for the older girl. Had she disguised herself again? She might be hard to detect, seeing as she tended to change not only her appearance but her personality as well! At last Dana spotted her sitting alone on a rock beyond the fair green. But something was wrong. Honor's head was buried in her hands, and her shoulders shook as she wept.

Dana hurried toward her, growing more alarmed as she got nearer. Honor was dressed in human clothes, but the faded jeans and T-shirt were soaking wet. Her hair was drenched, too, and plastered to her head. Her skin was deathly pale with a bluish tinge. Strands of seaweed clung to her arms and legs.

Dana reached out to touch her. The girl felt icy cold.

"What happened! What's wrong?"

"I . . . I remembered . . . shopping with my sister . . . before . . . I died."

A shudder ran through Dana.

"What do you mean? You're scaring me!"

Her words had an instant effect on Honor. She jumped to her feet, and in a transformation so swift it was almost imperceptible, she was the Lady once more. A golden tint flushed her features, and she wore jewels and finery.

"There you are!" she said to Dana, beaming a smile. "I *love* the cloak! Did you enjoy the fair?"

"But . . . you . . ." For a moment Dana considered letting the incident pass, but then decided she couldn't. There were too many mysteries. "You said something about your sister?"

"I did?"

Honor's smile faded. She looked shaken.

"Is she a fairy too?" Dana persisted.

"No. She lives in your world." There was a sad echo in her voice, then she quickly apologized. "I don't mean to be like this. I'm being pushed and pulled betwixt and between. And it's my own fault, really. I yearn for my old life sometimes, the way there are those in your world who long for Faerie." She shook her head ruefully. "It's not good to pine for one place when you belong to another. It can cause soul sickness, even unto death." Now Honor drew herself up. "I do not wish to speak of this further." She brightened visibly, and her smile was warm. "Show me what you have bought!"

Dana frowned. It was as if a door had closed. She felt uneasy, sensing something tragic on the other side. But it was Honor's business, not hers, and she had no right to pry. Shrugging off her disquiet, Dana gave back the purse, which was almost empty, and produced her purchases.

The older girl approved of everything, but was shocked by the prices.

"You were robbed!" she cried. "The bold things! And will these supplies last the trip? There are miles to go yet."

"They should be enough," Dana said. "I ate as well." She hesitated, remembering the warning at the booth. "But is it okay for me to eat fairy food? All the stories say you shouldn't, and that if you do, you can never go home again."

Honor laughed as she linked Dana's arm.

"Oh, you need not worry about that, my dear. You are already ours."

Dana felt a chill run up her back. What did she mean? The words were ominous, yet Honor spoke them so lightly, as if they meant nothing. Was Dana wrong to trust her? The Lady was so changeable. Could she be wicked as well as good? Dana knew she ought to demand an explanation, but she kept silent. Was that fairy magic too? Or was it simply that she didn't want to loose her wish?

The merry sounds of the fair faded behind them, as they strolled away from the green and down a winding road. There on the path before them rose a giant archway made of two great standing stones with a capstone over-head. Dana knew what it was. There were dolmens and cromlechs all over Ireland. It was generally believed that they were portals to the other world.

But now a gloom was settling over Dana. She had enjoyed the fair and Honor's company. The prospect of returning to the mountains to wander alone was not a happy one.

The Lady regarded her pensively. There was pity in her eyes.

"You do not have to do this," she said suddenly. "If you want to go home, just say the word and I will send you back."

Honor sounded defiant, trembling with emotion. Dana wondered if she was thinking of her own situation. The offer itself was tempting. The quest had turned out to be much harder and more terrifying than she could have imagined. And what about Murta and the red thing on the cliff? She had said nothing about them, fearing that the mission might be canceled. And on top of everything, Dana was worried about Gabe and missing him badly.

But she wouldn't go back. Not until she found her mother. And for all that the quest was scary, it was also the greatest adventure anyone could have! After enduring so much, she felt stronger and more confident than she had ever been. Only now did she truly believe that her dream was possible and that she might succeed.

"Thanks, but no thanks," she said finally. "I want my wish."

Honor looked thoughtful. "The longing for home is

the hero's greatest obstacle. It can keep us from the true path we must take."

It was time for Dana to go.

The older girl started to fuss as usual, tightening Dana's cloak and pulling up her hood.

"Will the doorway bring me to Lugnaquillia?" Dana asked.

"Alas, no," was the answer. "There are some rules that cannot be subverted. This is your journey, not mine. Though I may assist you, I cannot bring you to your goal. Listen carefully, dear heart. When you pass through the dolmen, call on the gods of your people. Ask for guidance and aid. This is the right of every traveler."

There was one last sisterly hug, then Dana broke away.

Stepping into the shadow of the dolmen, she found herself standing at a fork in the road. Two paths confronted her. The one on the right led straight into her bedroom in Wolfe Tone Square. There stood her wooden wardrobe with the cracked mirror, the scuffed walls covered with posters of the Irish World Cup team, the chest of drawers with her jeans and T-shirts, and the high bed in the corner built by Gabe. He was sitting on it, on the yellow duvet, holding her pillow and weeping out loud.

"*Da!*" she called, without thinking.

He looked up, startled, but couldn't see her.

The path on the left led into the mountains. It was nighttime and she could feel the icy breath of the wind on her face.

Some part of Dana turned to go into the warm light, to lie on the duvet, to hug her poor dad . . . But she was already taking the harder path, the road less traveled, shivering as she stepped into the cold and the dark.

Twenty-four

As Dana passed through the arch of the dolmen, she did as the Lady told her. She called out with all her heart and soul for help on her journey. When she reached the other side, she found herself returned to her own height and back in the Wicklow Mountains.

It was almost dawn. The first rays of sunrise were seeping into the sky. She stood on a grassy slope overlooking a narrow glen, quilted with woods and farmland. A river wound across the valley floor. She knew where she was: on the western side of Brown Mountain, above the Glenmacnass Waterfall. Friends of Gabriel's owned a nearby farm. Their sheep, daubed with red paint, grazed the lower pastures. Though it was very early in the morning, she worried that she might be seen. She needed to reach the trees on the other side of the river.

Dana was making her way down the hillside when something caught her eye in the distance. There again she could see the sleeping giant in the mountains. Now that she knew for certain he was King Lugh, she studied him more carefully. Why did the boggles want to keep him asleep? Was he a cruel tyrant? They had talked of floods and drowning. Was that how he punished them? And did she really want to meet someone like that? She was trying to discern his character from the outline of his features when a jolt ran through her. His head had begun to turn toward her, as if to face the rising sun. And his eyes were open! Was he waking up? She caught her breath. Was it her imagination? The pain in those eyes looked like madness. But the impression was too brief, for the eyes closed again and he slept once more.

Haunted by what she had seen, Dana made her way off Brown Mountain and across the road. Thoughts circled in her mind. Was the King dangerous? Would she have to wake him to give him the message? How could she do that? And what would happen if she did? She shook her head, mystified. These were things she knew nothing about. But didn't the Lady promise to investigate the matter?

When Dana came to the river above the waterfall, she forged it by jumping across the stones. Expecting to get wet, she was surprised to reach the other side dry as a bone. Pleased with her progress, she plunged into the woods.

It was an old spinney, mostly oak in full leaf. A pale-green lichen furred bole and branch. The undergrowth was matted with fiddlehead fern. As the sun rose beyond the treetops, a mellow light fell through the leaves. It was a perfect place for breakfast. Sitting down on a mossy stump, Dana took out an apple and some bread and cheese. Munching happily, she looked around her.

They were everywhere. Trails of color with wings and tresses flitted over wildflowers. A man in a black cloak rode past on a dark mare. From his saddlebag he tossed glittering dust into the air. Wherever the dust landed, mushrooms sprang up: elf-caps, yellow fairy clubs, plump boletus, powdery puffballs, and the red-and-white parasols of amanita muscaria.

The more she saw, the more Dana understood how thin was the veil between the two worlds, and how closely nature was entwined with the supernatural. She found herself wondering, if the countryside disappeared would Faerie die too? Honor's words in the Glen of the Downs came back to haunt her. *The destruction of the forest is the beginning of the end of our world.* Then she remembered something Big Bob once said to a panel of politicians and businessmen who argued in the name of economic progress. *For what shall it profit a man if he shall gain the whole world and lose his own soul?* Was Faerie the soul of Ireland?

Dana was more eager than ever to resume her mission. In her heart she acknowledged that it involved much more than the gaining of a wish. Along with her dream of finding her mother, she now wanted to succeed for the Lady's sake and for the good of Faerie and her own world as well.

Come hell or high water, the King of Wicklow would get his message.

Her route was straightforward. She had traced it on the map. She would continue through the woods and over the peak of Brockagh, through Glendalough and on to Lugduff, then across Glenmalure on the last lap heading westward to Lugnaquillia. Could she do it in two days? She would have to push herself to the limit.

Her meal finished, Dana set off through the forest. After a while she noticed that the leaves on the trees were hissing like green tongues. Listening closely, she began to understand what they were saying.

> *Elm do grieve,*
> *Oak do hate,*
> *Willow do walk,*
> *If you travel late.*

She shivered. It was an ominous whisper, cold and unfriendly. Looking over her shoulder, she saw a tree move. A slender willow. Its roots seemed to wade through the earth as if it were water.

> *Willow do walk,*
> *If you travel late.*

"It's not late!" she called out nervously.

The willow promptly planted itself down, but something about its offended air made Dana wonder if it weren't trying to warn her.

Moments later, she knew it was.

Oak do hate.

She was hemmed in by oak trees on every side. Then she saw they weren't trees at all, but arboreal giants. They had leafy clusters for hair and twisted knots for eyes. Their skin was ridged and knobbled like bark. Each carried a huge club that he swung in the air as he tramped toward her.

Oakmen do hate.

Their malevolence was palpable. They hated humans. Humans killed trees. An image flashed through Dana's mind. The tree trunks at the Glen of the Downs splattered with the white crosses that tagged them for felling; that marked them for execution.

An eye for an eye. A tooth for a tooth.

She tried to protest that she was young and powerless and had done her best, but they weren't interested. Or perhaps they couldn't hear her. They had begun to roar. Or was it a war song? Great hawing sounds that grew in volume.

She had to get away. Spying a weak spot in their

advance, she ran wildly toward it and ducked under their arms. A loose branch whacked her ears. She let out a yell. But she managed to avoid the club that came swinging at her. To her amazement, she discovered she could move with lightning speed. The silver nails in her shoes! The gift of the leprechaun! Without them she would have been crushed, as the blows rained down like missiles. The ground shuddered with the thuds. But no matter how fast she was and how deftly she evaded them, the Oakmen kept forming new circles around her. And each circle was closer and tighter.

They were too near. Dana knew it. One of them was sure to hit her. She needed to get out of that murderous ring. In a last hopeless dash, expecting to be struck at any moment, she charged forward with a screech and attempted a jump.

She made it!

With a flying leap!

Legs pedaling the air as if she were on a bicycle, she cleared the Oakmen.

And even as they missed their target, they crashed into each other, many of them toppling like timber.

Dana sped away through the forest, dodging and darting around the trees. Some seemed to block her path. Others thwacked her with their branches. But the forest was thinning out ahead of her. Would the Oakmen pursue her into the open?

But now as she neared what she thought was safety, Dana choked with new terror. There before her, barring her way, stood a new foe, fierce and ravenous, with fangs bared in a snarl.

A huge gray wolf.

The great shaggy beast seemed as tall as she. Its eyes glared like yellow agate. Rising on its haunches, it leaped toward her.

There was no time to think. No time to run. No time even to cry out. Yet the moment itself slowed down and stretched into infinity. The gray streak of animal drew an arc in the air. The yellow eyes narrowed like two golden scimitars. The red jaw gaped.

A strange calm came over Dana, somehow inspired by the wolf itself. The splendor of that vault! The wild freedom! The beauty of the beast! Despite the threat of her own extinction, some part of her thrilled. A thought crossed her mind, perhaps her last: if she must die, let such a noble creature be the cause.

She didn't die.

The wolf continued to soar through the air, right over Dana's head.

And landed in front of the Oakmen.

Stunned, Dana turned to see the giants strike out at the beast. But they were too slow. Their blows pounded the ground. The wolf bit and clawed. The Oakmen roared.

Dana knew she should run while both her enemies

were busy, yet she hesitated. Though she suspected the wolf was just guarding its dinner, she couldn't be sure. Was it possible that it was trying to save her? She knew a little about wolves from a television program. They rarely attacked humans. And she was vaguely aware of something else, some bond with the animal that she couldn't explain. To run away seemed cowardly. Looking around for a weapon, she found a hefty rock and heaved it at the Oakman nearest to the wolf.

Good shot! It landed with a *whump*. The giant howled with fury and lurched toward her. The wolf cut off his charge. Dana continued to hurl rocks, but it was soon obvious that the wolf didn't need her help. Snapping and snarling, dashing around at great speed, it appeared to grow in size the more it fought. As it mangled and tore, gnawed and clawed, it drove the giants back. Other than forming defensive circles, the Oakmen had no tactics to fend off their foe. In the end, they thundered away, dragging their clubs behind them.

The wolf stood alone, jaws open, tongue lolling, great fangs dripping. Now it turned its yellow gaze to Dana.

Rooted to the spot, Dana could only stare back.

Twenty-five

T he wolf was still panting from its exertions and kept its jaws open. Paralyzed with fear, Dana stared into the dark-red maw. Her legs felt so weak, she thought they might buckle. In the bizarre way that shock affects the mind, she found herself remembering a time when she was six years old. A mad dog had wandered into her street, foaming at the mouth. When it went straight for her, one of her many canine friends broke its charge. The speed and ferocity of the fight had been horrific. The tearing and mauling. The snarling and biting.

Her father had come running from the house to snatch her up.

"It's killing Prince!" she screamed, as the dreadful sounds continued behind her. "Do something, Da! Save him!"

She had struggled wildly to get out of Gabe's arms, to go back and help, but he had bundled her into the house and slammed the door. Outside, a siren wailed as a police car sped into the square. Too late, Prince lay dead on the ground. But not before he had torn out the other dog's throat.

Now Dana's hand went to her own throat. The memory of the blood and the awful sounds told her what to expect. It would hurt. A lot.

She was wrong.

"Prince died to save you," came a female voice, deep and husky. "A noble deed. Praise his name."

The wolf was speaking to her! Of all the strange things that had happened, this was surely the strangest.

"H-h-how do you know . . . ?"

"I was there." The wolf moved closer. "Do you not know yet?"

Child and beast gazed at each other.

What a beautiful face, Dana thought. The sleek snout was that of a thoroughbred. The eyes were pure gold, and the ears, elegant. Despite her fear, Dana didn't back away.

Again came the voice, as rich as wild honey.

"Do you not know who I am?"

Dana felt a thrill at the core of her being, but her mouth was dry. She couldn't speak.

The wolf's eyes shone with a warm yellow light.

"In the tongue of your ancestors, what is my name?"

After a moment's confusion, Dana realized what she meant.

"You are the *faol.*"

The wolf butted her gently.

"Think, little cub. Why does the feeling of kinship conquer your fear?"

Dana caught her breath. A surge of joy rushed through her as she realized the truth.

"I am a *Faolán*. I belong to you!"

The wolf growled her approval.

"And I to you. For I am the totem of your tribe. The guardian of your clan."

Dana understood. Didn't her father often speak proudly of his roots? He had told her how, in the mists of time, the earliest peoples of Ireland were named for the animals from whom they believed they were descended. The oldest families still had those names, anglicized now as the Irish language declined. Whelans. Whalens. Phelans. Phalens. All were *Faoláns*: of the Clan of the Wolf.

"If you were fully grown," the wolf continued, "I would savage your limbs and tear your throat. I would dismember you and then restore you. In doing this, I would take from you what makes you weak, what holds you back. You would be a daughter of the wolf. But since you are a cub, hard lessons are not called for."

Dana straightened her back. She had cried out to the gods of her people, and the guardian of her clan had come to guide her. It was an honor beyond reckoning. She stared at the wide jaw and the sharp canine teeth. *Oh, Grandmother, what big teeth you have.* But she didn't feel like Little Red Riding Hood. Nor did she want a forester to save her. Instead, she would have fought the forester to defend the wolf. Dana thought about her mission. How hard it was proving. All the setbacks. All the things she had done wrong. She made up her mind.

"I want to be a daughter of the wolf," she said. "It's not fair to count age. Go ahead. Tear me apart. Make me strong."

Bracing herself, she closed her eyes and clenched her fists.

The wolf's laugh began as a bark and ended on a howl. Dana opened her eyes, surprised. The beast loomed over her, massive in bulk. The great head hovered near. The fangs came so close it seemed she might grant Dana's request. The gamey breath was hot.

But she didn't bite.

Instead, she licked Dana's face.

When she spoke again, her voice was gentle.

"Adults must be torn apart because life defeats them. They lose hope, they grow weak. They squander their inheritance. Children need not be torn, for they hold to their birthright. Their hearts are as wild as the hearts of birds. They have the courage of the wolf."

Dana knew her words were true. Gabriel was wounded and weakened by the loss of his wife. He had given up hope, stopped searching for her. Dana was stronger. That was why she had taken up the mission. She had to do what her father had failed to do.

Once again the wolf breathed on Dana, a wild steamy breath.

"Time grows short. We must go west, young cub."

Then she raced away, calling out behind her.

"Follow the greenway! Run wild, run free!"

For a moment, Dana hesitated. Would the nails in her shoes allow her to keep up? In her heart she knew they wouldn't. Speed was not the question. It was a matter of being. When she ran with the deer, she had become one of them. Was she or wasn't she a daughter of the wolf?

Her guardian had already disappeared through the trees. If Dana didn't move fast, she would be left behind. She felt the cry of the wild inside her. It rose like a pressure against her ribs, propelling her forward. Before she knew it, she was running as if she had four legs. A lupine force had invaded her limbs, powering every sinew and muscle. It wasn't long before she caught up with the wolf.

They sped together through the forest—a blur of leafy green—and headed upward for the ridge of Brockagh.

To run with the deer was a gentle union with nature, harmony and light, sweet grass and sunshine. *Blessed are the meek.* To run with the wolf was to run in the shadows, merging with the dark pulse of life, the instinct for survival. A fierceness that was proud and lonely, a tearing, a howling, a hunger and thirst. *Blessed are they who hunger and thirst.* A strength that would die fighting, kicking, screaming, that wouldn't stop till the last breath had been wrung from its body.

The will to take one's place in the world: to say *I am here*. To say *I am*.

They ran into the west. The terrain was chiefly blanket bog, damp mountain grasslands of sedge and heather. Over Brockagh's windy summit they flew and along the peaty ridge that headed north for Tonelagee. They were already in sight of Lough Nahanagan, glistening in the midday sun. Traveling downward through swaths of purple heather, they crossed the Wicklow Gap and arrived at the lake. Cradled in its corrie below Turlough Hill, the lough was shadowed overhead by the reservoir that sat like a lid on top of the hill.

"We will rest here a while," the wolf declared.

Dana stood on the stony shore, hot and sweaty. They had come many miles in a few short hours. The wolf was already in the water, leaping like a dolphin. With a quick look around to make sure no one was there, Dana stripped off her clothes and plunged in. The lake was icy cold. She shrieked with the shock. Turning to swim on her back, she felt something moving beneath her. Before she could react, the wolf had tossed her into the air! Shrieking again, she landed with a great splash.

They played for ages, wrestling and diving and darting around each other. Dana laughed like a child without a care in the world.

She was deep underwater when the memory came. *The two of them in a lake similar to this one. Mother and baby with*

their arms around each other. White bathing suits like water lil-
ies, immersed in the green sunlit element. Her mother's skin was
soft. Strands of her red-gold hair flowed all around them.
Now they rose up in a shower of spray, both of them laughing
and squealing. On the shore, a younger Gabe with thick dark
hair called out to them to have their picnic. The perfection
of the moment: a pearl found by chance inside an oyster.
Her first full memory of her mother! The joy and the pain
was overwhelming.

Dana surfaced from the water to put her arms around
the wolf. Burying her face in the soft fur, she hid her tears.

They decided to have lunch on the lakeshore.

"What meat have you?" asked the she-wolf eagerly, as
Dana dug into her satchel.

"None. I'm a vegetarian."

Dana spread out the curranty bread, cheese, iced buns,
and fruit.

"A *herbivore*? But you have the canines of a flesh-eater,
as I do!"

Dana mumbled through a mouthful of bread.

"I won't eat anything that had a face."

The wolf shook her head, mystified. After chomping
on an apple and nosing under the stones for insects, she
loped away up the nearby slope.

Dana had finished eating and packed up her satchel,
when she heard the cry. She raced up the hillside toward
the sound.

There stood the wolf over the remains of a wild rabbit. Blood smeared her snout and the heather around her. She was chewing raw meat.

"The poor little thing!" Dana cried, thinking of her own beloved pet. "How could you? I thought you were good, not evil!"

Finishing her meal, the wolf licked her chops. Then she trained her golden gaze on Dana.

"I do not hunt on a full stomach, as your kind do. And I honor the creature who dies that I may live. In turn, my death will give life one day. It is the Great Round." She growled low in her throat. "Climb on my back, little cub. I will show you evil so that you may know the difference."

Though she was still upset, Dana did as she was told. It was like riding a pony who ran like a racehorse. She held on tightly as the landscape sped past. They traveled north, leaving the mountains behind as they moved into the lowlands around Blessington Lake. Dana cringed at the sight of tilled fields and farmhouses, meadows with cattle, and pine plantations. She was afraid they might be sighted; but they passed no one, and she wondered if the wolf had arranged that somehow. At one point she was shocked to spot her own face staring back from a poster on a telephone pole.

HAVE YOU SEEN HER? MISSING CHILD. REWARD.

She hunched down on the wolf's back as if to hide.

They came to a forest protected by a wire fence and

a gate with a sign: WILDLIFE SANCTUARY. With one great leap the wolf cleared the gate and landed on the other side. Dana slid off her back.

They crept through the trees, the wolf leading the way.

Dana heard the loud laughter before she saw them, and immediately hunkered in the undergrowth. Crawling forward, she came to a clearing.

There were three men sitting on fallen logs, drinking beer. Empty cans were strewn around them, as well as cigarette butts and plastic cartons of leftover food. It wasn't at the men that Dana stared in horror, but the cages stacked around them. All were crammed with terrified animals—rabbits, hares, squirrels, even cats. One cage held a fox that stared bleakly through the bars. Each animal was wounded in some way, its fur streaked with blood. Some were half dead, kicking feebly. Others lay still and would never move again.

"Will they take them if they're dead?" one of the men said, kicking at the fox's cage.

Beyond hope, the small creature didn't react.

"Doesn't matter either way," said another. "No questions asked. They're skinned at the factory . . . kids' toys and accessories."

As Dana gazed, sickened, at the cages, the wolf rested a paw on her shoulder. Images streamed through her mind, things she had seen on the television and in Gabe's animal rights magazines: trucks jammed with cattle, sheep, and horses crossing Europe without food or water; battery hens crammed into boxes, laying eggs until they died without ever having seen grass or sky; scenes of the daily torture in the laboratories of scientists and pharmaceutical, pet food, and cosmetics companies. Her stomach churned. So many animals, countless numbers, strapped into machines with their innards exposed, trembling in the snarl of electrodes or suffering the agony of toxic testing. As well as the cruelty, it was the powerlessness that struck her. They could not fight for their lives, as was their right.

"Where there is no respect for life," the wolf said quietly, "*there* you will find evil."

Dana couldn't bear it any longer. The poachers were gathering up their snares to set them again. Enraged beyond thinking, she burst out of the trees.

"Can't you *see*? What's right in front of you? Can't you see how much they suffer?"

The three men jumped to their feet, dropping their equipment. They looked beyond her, for an adult, perhaps the game warden.

Then one peered drunkenly at her.

"It's the missing kid from Bray!"

Greed replaced the fear on their faces.

"There's a reward for her!"

Dana was suddenly aware of how big they were and how many, but she had no intentions of abandoning the animals. As long as the silver nails kept her moving, she would open as many cages as possible before they caught her.

The men stepped menacingly toward her. She was about to dash out of their way, when she saw the terror in their eyes.

Behind her, the wolf growled.

As the poachers ran screaming into the woods, Dana hurried to release the animals. The fox was gone in a flash of red. Many of the others scratched and clawed her in their panic to escape, but she didn't care. She only wished she had gotten there sooner. But even those who were badly wounded and missing a limb managed to drag themselves away.

As the last disappeared into the underbrush, Dana picked up a rock to smash the traps and cages.

"We must go!" the wolf urged her. "The hunters will return with weapons."

"We've got to get rid of these!" Dana cried fiercely, breaking up a snare.

The wolf was right. Somewhere nearby, car doors slammed. Soon the first poacher came crashing through the trees with a rifle in his hand.

Dana scrambled onto the wolf's back. A shot rang out. She screamed. In a gray streak of motion, the wolf raced away.

Twenty-six

There was blood on the wolf's flank.

"You're hurt!" Dana cried.

She kept insisting they stop, but the guardian wouldn't halt until all sounds of pursuit had died out and the Wild-life Sanctuary was far behind.

Dana slid off the wolf's back.

"We've got to get help!" She looked around wildly. They were back in the mountains. Out in the middle of nowhere. Not a house or telephone box in sight. She was wracked with worry and guilt. "It's all my fault. If I'd—"

"Peace. It is only a scratch," the wolf said mildly. "His drunkenness threw off his aim." She licked at her wound. "You were right to act as you did. It is when good people do nothing that evil thrives."

Dana was comforted. The graze looked clean and was no longer bleeding.

They were about to set off again when the wolf suddenly pricked up her ears. She sniffed the air, nose quivering. A low growl murmured in her throat.

"What is it?" Dana said, instantly alert and on guard.

She could see nothing around them but rolling hills and bog.

"I do not know," came the answer, low and pensive. "But I can name its nature. It seems our lesson on evil has not yet ended. Follow me."

Once again Dana ran with the wolf, though she was mystified by her guardian's words. She was also surprised that they were traveling southeast, instead of southwest where Lugnaquillia lay. The mystery deepened when they drew up on a height above the Wicklow Gap, overlooking the road. In the distance a jeep approached. Dana's stomach lurched. Was it the poachers? But how did they get there so fast? And why would the guardian want to meet them? The wolf's hackles had risen and she was growling again.

Dana panicked. They were visible on the hillside. And in rifle range.

"We've got to hide!"

There was no cover on the grassy slope. The roadside ditch was their only hope. Dana raced down the hill with the wolf behind her. They had just tumbled into the wet hollow when the vehicle stopped nearby.

Dana's heart pounded as she heard a car door open and the tread of boots on gravel. Whoever it was seemed to be moving slowly. Was he looking around? Had he seen them on the hill? Afraid to raise her head, hunkering as low as she could, she imagined the man with his gun. What if he found them? She wouldn't let him kill the guardian. The wolf's lips had curled back in a silent snarl, but her breathing was steady. She wasn't afraid. As the warm lupine body pressed against her, Dana's courage rose.

A man's voice rang out, talking loudly on a cell phone. Dana's heart jumped.

Murta! Again?

He was giving directions to his location.

"Yeah, well, plans change," he said curtly. "This is where I am. Step on it."

He lit up a cigarette, and flung the burning match into the ditch. It landed near Dana, hissing as the damp ground extinguished it. After a while, a cigarette butt followed. Then more matches and more butts. It seemed forever before the second car arrived, bringing another man. Dana was now determined to find out what was going on. Why was Murta wandering in the mountains? And what did her guardian want her to know?

The two men stood near their cars, speaking in low tones. Dana needed to get closer to hear what they were saying. Before the wolf could stop her, she had crawled along the ditch and beside the vehicles.

The men were arguing.

"I don't care what it takes!" said the new arrival. He was a Dubliner, with the kind of educated accent Dana considered posh. "Call a meeting, throw a party, whatever. Just create a diversion and get them out of the way!"

"You're not listening!" Murta said angrily. "They aren't complete idiots. They won't leave the site!"

"Look, time's running out on the European grant. The date is set. August first. It's up to you to get them out of the damn trees. Can you do it or do we need to find someone else?"

Murta spat on the ground.

"It's *my* job. What time are you moving the equipment?"

"Sunset. A bit of darkness always helps. We won't be working long. With the first line cut, we'll have won the battle. It'll knock the fight out of them." The stranger let out a short laugh. "You can't put a tree back up when it's down."

Murta laughed too, but it sounded more like a cough.

There was a rustle of paper.

"I work for the company, not you," Murta said coldly.

"Consider it a bonus. There's a lot of brown envelopes flying around. Might as well grab your share."

The two were parting when the Dublin man made a startled noise.

"What are you doing with a gun? Are you planning to murder someone?"

Murta coughed up another laugh. "I like to hunt. Gets the blood pumping."

The other man snorted in agreement. "I love the thrill of the kill myself, but I prefer to do it in court."

When the cars drove off, Dana waited for a while

before climbing out of the ditch. She and the wolf stood alone on the road.

"I've got to get back! I've got to warn Big Bob and the others!"

To her surprise, the wolf disagreed.

"We cannot turn back."

"You don't understand!" Dana said urgently. "If I don't go back, we'll lose the woods! We'll lose the battle!"

The wolf's tone was grave.

"If you do go back, we may lose the war."

Dana looked at her, stunned.

"What do you mean?!"

The wolf didn't answer right away. She stood silent and brooding. A growl rumbled deep in her chest.

"Evil I sensed and evil it is," she said at last. "Both the human and the thing that feeds on him. I can protect you from the first, but the second . . ."

The guardian sounded troubled and uncertain; she who had seemed so invincible till now. Dana felt the ground shift beneath her feet. She suddenly remembered the time when she was little and she found her father collapsed on the floor, sobbing violently, a photo of his wife crumpled in his hands. Now, as then, she felt overwhelmed and terrified.

"Courage, dear heart," the wolf said quietly. "Whatever comes, we shall face it together."

They resumed their journey, heading westward once

more. Though they kept a steady pace, they no longer ran like the wind. Dana noticed that her guardian seemed strangely weighed down, as if by some invisible burden. She wanted to ask what was wrong, but was too afraid. She was already sick with worry. Murta's betrayal of the eco-warriors plagued her thoughts. Would he succeed in tricking them? There was also the question of what he was doing in the mountains. Who or what was he hunting? A shudder ran through her, and she drew closer to the wolf.

By the time they came in sight of Camaderry's peak, evening had caught up with them. Dusk brought a haze of gray light. Stars pinned the wisps of cloud. The broad ridge they traversed wound for miles, overlooking the deep valley and the lakes of Glendalough.

As the wolf led them south along the top of the esker, Dana surveyed the landscape with growing unease. She had expected to cross over to Lugduff and continue west to Lugnaquillia.

"Where are we going?" she asked, after a while.

The answer surprised her.

"To the heart of the Vale of the Two Lakes."

"Glendalough? We can't go there! It's always packed. We'll be seen!"

Her guardian's voice was firm.

"Glendalough is the destination of all *peregrinni* who quest in these mountains. That is what you are, little wolf—a wanderer, a pilgrim, one who seeks. In the Vale of the Two Lakes you will find food and rest, and the guidance you need for the next step of your journey."

Dana's alarm was peaking. As well as her fear of being recognized, there was something else about Glendalough that niggled at the back of her mind.

"But why—?"

Before Dana could say more, the wolf loped ahead. Nose to the ground, she sniffed her way onto a track that snaked down the steep slope. Then she let out a bark. Dana hurried to catch up. There, hidden halfway down the mountainside, was the entrance to a cave. The wolf crawled in first and Dana followed.

It was snug and dry and sheltered from the wind. Moonlight seeped through the opening. Dried bracken and tufts of fleece littered the ground, perhaps left by a previous occupant, a fox or a hare. Dana swept the debris into a pile in one corner and placed her cloak over it. After a short supper of bread and fruit, she and the wolf settled down together for an early night's sleep.

But Dana couldn't sleep. She was restless and unhappy. Something didn't add up.

"Why do I need help in Glendalough," she said suddenly, "when I've got you?"

She heard the deep sigh in the darkness, felt the warm wolfish breath on her face.

"I will not hide the truth from you. It is a wrong your

kind do to their children. This evil that has come to the mountains . . . I must do what I can to protect you from it."

Dana's heart clenched. She sat up.

"What do you mean? What'll you have to do?"

The wolf sighed again. She, too, got up and nudged Dana to the mouth of the cave. On the ledge outside, they sat together under the lambent eye of the moon.

The wolf's raspy tongue licked Dana's forehead.

"Let us sing together, little cub. Let us sing of wonder and catastrophe. Of life and death."

Raising her head, she started to howl.

It was a primal cry, wild and intoxicating. A rich unending bay that echoed over the mountains and resounded through the glen. Dana was electrified. It was if lightning shot through her veins. The song of her tribe. The cry of her ancestors. She threw back her head and howled too, her throat wide open as the sound poured out like blood. They howled for ages, singing to the night. They sang of hope and courage; of fate and longing; of the joy and horror of life lived in the valley of the shadow of death. When they were finished, a deep peace settled over them.

Back in the cave, Dana felt drained and exhausted, but she still fought off sleep. Her time with the guardian seemed suddenly precious. She leaned against the warm furry back.

"Do you have cubs?"

"I did. Long ago. Proud sons and daughters who roamed these hills. The forests were our haven; but when the great woods were cleared, our days were numbered, as were the days of the Gaelic order. For the trees hid both wolf and rebel.

"Even as your people were laid low, Dana, so too were mine. Humans have always seen us as evil. Your folk tales make us so. Yet we do not prey on men and we rarely fight, even amongst ourselves. We live in clans and we care for our young. Our food is deer, birds, fish, insects, and berries. But we also take the occasional sheep or cow, and that makes us your foe.

"Government acts were passed to oversee the slaughter. Bounties were set. All over the country, we were killed with spears, guns, traps, snares. The last Irish wolf died at Wolf Hill in the North in the late 1700s. The land is bereft of my kind. We are no more of Ireland."

"Except you," Dana murmured. "You're still here."

Her eyes were already shut. The wolf's voice had lulled her beyond all resistance. And even as she drifted into the depths of sleep, the thought sank with her: the one that had nagged at the back of her mind.

The last wolf in Wicklow was killed at Glendalough.

TWENTY-SEVEN

Dana woke at dawn to a sense of dread. She didn't feel like eating, and only nibbled on an apple at the wolf's insistence. Her guardian was also in a somber mood, and the day itself was oppressive; heavy and muggy, with a hazy sun rising over the mountains. Even the birds, so plentiful in the glen, sang in muted tones.

As the two headed down the hillside, Dana argued once more against going to Glendalough. She pointed out that she was bound to be recognized, while the wolf herself would draw too much attention. When her guardian didn't respond but continued downward, Dana finally gave up. As it was, she had to concentrate on her footing. The rough track they followed belonged to the feral goats who lived in the glen, and it zigzagged precariously around rock and briar.

Reaching the bottom, they set off on the trail called the Miner's Road.

Dana started again. "Why can't we go straight to Lugnaquillia?"

"I am your guardian, little wolf. I do what I must to protect you."

"I don't understand! Why won't you explain?"

Though the path they walked was commonly used by hikers and visitors to Glendalough, it was too early in the morning to meet anyone. The narrow waters of the Glenealo River flowed beside them, meandering over moss-covered stones.

"You called on me to guide and help you. Trust me."

Dana fell silent as they reached the ruins of the old mining village. The skeletons of the stone houses stood gray and empty. The stream that used to wash the ore cut right through the village. The site had been abandoned for over a century, but the toxic lead still leached into the marshes and lakes beyond. The ruins were overshadowed on both sides by jagged cliffs of scree. The steep slopes of frost-shattered granite seemed to bear down menacingly, devoid of any life or greenery. Dana felt as if she were passing through the Paths of the Dead.

The wolf walked slowly beside her, as if fatigued. The great head hung low to the ground, and the golden eyes were sorrowful. From time to time she let out a deep sigh.

Dana rested her hand on the furred neck and kept it there.

Once they had left the village behind, the wolf picked up her pace. As they approached the Upper Lake the landscape changed. Tall Scots pine bristled on the hillsides; the wide blue lake reflected the sky. Here the valley was rich and green and loud with life. Red squirrels scampered on the spiny branches of the fir trees. Ravens and peregrine circled the cliffs. The air rang with the trills of songbirds from the oakwoods ahead. To the right, overlooking the lake, hung the craggy forehead of the height called the Spink.

Now Dana grew aware of another change, though it was nothing she could see or touch. Everything was suddenly fresh and vibrant, as if a window had been opened in a stuffy room. A still quiet voice whispered in her mind, telling her a story.

The old road she walked had been trod for centuries. Countless pilgrims, refugees, exiles, and outlaws had all passed this way; for every road and path that wove through the mountains converged here, at *Gleann Dá Loch*, the holy Vale of the Two Lakes.

> *Monastic City of the western world*
> *Is Glendalough of the Assemblies.*

A fabled hermit founded the site in the sixth century A.D. *Caoimhín* was his name—Kevin—meaning "fair-begotten" or "beautiful born." The son of a princely line, it was said that he had come over the mountains in the company of an angel. Fleeing the world of men, he chose to live in that green and hidden valley. His bed was a cave on the dark side of the lake where no sun shone for six months of the year. His food was wild berries, herbs, and nuts from the forest. Regardless of the weather, he prayed outdoors, with tiny birds perched on his head and shoulders.

Word of his hermitage spread throughout the country and on into Europe. People came from far and wide to pray with him. First a small community took shape around him, and eventually a monastery rose on the site. By the tenth century, long after its founder had left the world, Glendalough was known throughout Christendom.

As Dana continued toward the Lower Lake, she saw that she and the wolf were no longer alone. Columns of people trod the road alongside them. Overlapping in time and space, they seemed unaware of each other: Gaelic chieftains wrapped in broad woolen cloaks; medieval ladies with rosaries dangling from their waists; barefooted peasants with hungry faces; Victorian matrons in feathered hats; men in the dark suits of the 1950s; modern tourists with their cameras and guidebooks. Many were on foot, some rode on horseback, and still others came in vehicles, from horse-drawn carriages to modern cars and buses. Layers of pilgrims through layers of time.

When Dana stumbled on a stone, layers of hands reached out to steady her.

Slowly she walked beside the wolf, but the feeling of dread had left her. The hope that inspired all pilgrims surged in her veins. Whether young or old, rich or poor, in couples or families or walking alone, traveling on foot or in stylish carriages, even those who had fallen by the wayside, all of these people shared the same destination: the same destiny. The Feast was laid out and all were welcome at the table.

Thus Dana arrived, with her companion guide and the spirits of fellow seekers, at Glendalough of the two lakes and seven churches.

The monastic site stood at the heart of the valley, just beyond the two lakes. Again, Dana gazed through the strata of time. She could see the earliest huts of Kevin's disciples amid the stone cells and round tower of later construction. Overwhelming these were the contours of the medieval monastery—cathedral, scriptorium, workshops, bakery, monks' quarters, and visitors' dormitories. The present-day silhouette dominated the others with its Visitors' Center, hotel, and souvenir shops catering to the tourists who roamed the ruins.

The multifarious images threw Dana into confusion. She didn't want to enter modern Glendalough, as there was too great a chance she might be seen; but nor did she want to step into the past, for she sensed the wolf's doom waited there.

The wolf spoke softly.

"Stand beside the earliest crossroads and ask of the old paths, where is the way to good?"

"I'm afraid." Dana's voice trembled. "Not for me, but for you."

"Be of good courage, *a fhaol bhig*. Whether great or small, each of us has a part to play. Let me do what is right."

Dana threw her arms around the wolf's neck.

"No! You can't! Please don't! If I'd known you'd be in danger, I'd never've asked for your help!"

The wild breath of the wolf warmed her face. The rough tongue rasped her forehead. But though Dana clung to the wolf with all her might, the guardian was stronger. She broke from Dana's embrace.

"I will not tell you to turn away. Be ready to face all that comes to you in life—whether good or ill. Who's afraid of death? Not I!"

The wolf threw back her head to howl; one long last howl to echo over hill and glen.

As if in response came the winding horn of the tantivy: the cry of the hunt at full gallop.

And after the horn came the clamor of the wolfhounds, baying for blood.

At first Dana wasn't sure what she was seeing. Murta's jeep was suddenly driving furiously toward them, bumping over the rough trail. At the wheel, his face glared red with rage. Then Dana's sight wavered. Now she saw the horsemen with fitted jackets and tall black boots, swords at their waists and firearms in their hands. Running alongside them were shabbier men, carrying boar spears and pikes. Was that Murta in the lead, whipping his steed into a frenzy? Back in his jeep, he drew it up with a jolt. Clambering out, he gripped his rifle in both hands. Red bloodshot eyes settled on Dana.

What was going on?

Now Murta raised the gun to his shoulder, and Dana knew in that moment that he meant to kill her.

"Run for your life!" the wolf barked at Dana. "Up the hill! Into the trees! *Run!*"

Mind reeling, heart pounding, Dana scrabbled up the ridge into the shelter of the woods. The silver nails in her shoes gave her speed and agility. She didn't turn or look back until she heard the shot. Something was wrong. The sound came from a different direction! Surprised, she stopped. That was when she realized the wolf wasn't with her. Overwhelmed with fear, she hurried back. From the cover of the trees, she could see the road. Utterly disoriented, she spied a figure who looked exactly like her, racing toward the monastery.

And standing on the road below was Murta. Reloading his gun.

Dana's sight blurred again. Now she saw it was the wolf who ran, with hounds and horsemen close behind.

It was a noble and splendid run. A silver-gray flash against the dark greenery. Legs high to paw the air. Eyes glowing gold. A cry for freedom. A cry for the wild. The last run of the last wolf of Wicklow.

"No," Dana whispered, not wanting to believe what she saw.

The hounds raced ahead to drive the wolf back. Back toward the lead hunter.

Murta shouldered his rifle.

"*NO!*" Dana cried.

The shot rang through the mountains. The wolf somersaulted in the air.

Then fell to the ground, dead.

And Dana, who was a daughter of the wolf, let out a death-cry as she too fell to the earth.

Twenty-eight

Dana lay on the ground, convulsed with weeping. She didn't think about Murta or whether he might be near. She was beyond caring. It was a while before she noticed the change. She was shivering uncontrollably, at first with shock but then also with the cold. Something soft and wet drifted around her. *Snow!* In the middle of summer? She sat up, dazed. The valley was bathed in an icy-blue light. The oak trees stood bare, their branches forked like antlers. The mountainsides were cloaked with snow. The faint tracery of small animals, hares and birds, inscribed the ground. A winter's sun shone palely.

She jumped to her feet and ran out of the wood. There was no sign of the hunters, nor of Murta and his jeep. The road itself was gone, and so too the monastic site and all its layers. The deep vale was still and lonely. Sheets of ice rimed the lakes. A raven cawed overhead. The only evidence of life was a camp fire on the shore of the Upper Lake, near a little stone house shaped like a beehive.

Dana let out a cry. The wolf's body had vanished too.

Frenzied with grief, not knowing what she did, she ran to the spot where her guardian had died.

Mama. Mama.

She fell to the ground once more.

"Where have you gone?" she wept. "Where are you?"

The gentle touch of a hand on her shoulder brought Dana back. A quiet voice spoke.

> *Hear my cry, O God,*
> *Listen to my prayer:*
> *From the ends of the earth,*
> *I cry unto thee.*

> *When my heart is faint,*
> *Lead me to the rock,*
> *That is higher than I,*
> *For you are my refuge.*

She looked up. He was a young man, barely out of his teens, dressed in deerskin vest and leggings, with his arms and feet bare. The dark curly hair fell in tangles to his shoulders. His skin was brown from sun and wind. But though he looked a little wild, he wasn't frightening. A light shone in the gray eyes that regarded her kindly, and his features were serene. She knew who he was—the saint of Glendalough.

Kevin spoke to her in Irish.

"A dheirfiúr bhig," he said softly. "My little sister. What has broken your heart?"

"Brother," she said, dissolving into fresh tears. "I have lost my . . ." the word that best described the wolf came easily in her mother tongue, ". . . *anamchara.* I have lost my soul friend."

Kevin helped her to her feet, but she was weak and shaky. The days of wandering in the mountains had taken their toll; the twists and turns of her strange adventures, the fitful meals, the sleeping rough. And now the devastating loss of her dearest companion. She was ill and in anguish.

He led her into the beehive cell that was sparsely furnished but clean and dry. It was for guests, he explained. He himself lived in a cave overlooking the lake.

Dana lay down on the sweet-smelling rushes, and a woolen blanket was placed over her. Kevin brought her a bowl of soup with a chunk of wheaten bread. She couldn't speak but she sipped on the hot broth. He tended her quietly, the way Gabriel did when she got sick. Dana burst into tears again. She wanted her dad. She wanted to go home.

"Sleep, child, it will ease your pain," he promised her. "I shall go and pray for you."

When Dana fell asleep, she fell into a nightmare.

She was running with the wolf again. Hunters and poachers pursued them with guns. A shot rang out. The bullet pierced her flesh. She cried out in agony.

Now the young saint entered her dream. He stood on the shore, where the lake water lapped against the stones. His arms were open.

Come, sister wolf, I grant you sanctuary.

Dana and the wolf leaped into his embrace. He held them both as they lay dying.

Tá tú ag imeacht ar shlí na fírinne.
You are going on the way of truth.

When Dana woke, her face was wet with tears, but she felt rested and stronger. Had she slept for days? Leaving the little house, she stepped into the brightness of a sunny morning. The snow on the mountains dazzled her. She shielded her eyes with her hands. And that was when she saw him. Kevin stood waist-deep in the icy lake. Arms outstretched, eyes closed, he turned his face to the sun as he prayed out loud.

Fada an lá go sámh,
Fada an oíche gan ghruaim,
An ghealach, an ghrian, an ghaoth,
Moladh duit, a Dhia.

Long is the day with peace,
Long is the night without gloom,
Thou art the moon, the sun, the wind,
I praise you, my God.

As he spoke, ripples broke the calm surface of the water. To Dana's horror, a monster rose up from the depths, green and scaly, with a reptilian body and a horse-shaped head. Coiling and curling, it twisted around the saint till they were face-to-face.

Dana was about to scream, then stopped.

Kevin had opened his eyes and was smiling at the beast. A beatific smile. He leaned toward the serpent and rested his brow against its forehead: a gesture as light and affectionate as a kiss. The two remained that way for an eternal heartbeat, like a zoomorphic design in an ancient manuscript. Then the monster slid back under the water.

Catching sight of Dana, Kevin waded out of the lake. Though his lips were blue with the cold and his teeth chattered, he made no effort to dry himself.

Dana was still amazed.

"The old stories say you fought the *péist* and banished it to the Upper Lake. But you are friends!"

He laughed, the carefree laugh of a young man.

"The truth is twisted in many a tale. I carried the creature upon my back from the Lower to the Upper Lake, not to vanquish him but to keep him out of harm's way. They would have hunted him down and killed him."

The saint gazed over the water.

"He is something old, very old, but he is not the enemy. We are the ones who make him evil."

When Dana looked confused, the saint explained:

"Each of us has a 'monster' inside. If we do not find it in ourselves and make peace with it, we cast it out into the world and make war with it there. *Blessed are the peacemakers*, for everything monstrous is, at heart, something that needs to be loved."

They were walking around the lower shore of the Upper Lake. The wooded cliffs towered over them on every side, quilled with the wintry silhouettes of birch and oak. Against the white of the snow, great holly trees painted splashes of green and red. Across the lake, a deer stopped on the high ridge to regard them. A rust-colored fox darted out of view.

"You will face your monster soon, little sister," Kevin said quietly. "No one can save you from this. None of us may be kept from the truth; it is an appointment we meet either in life or at death."

Dana shuddered as some dark thing heaved in the depths of her mind before returning to its slumber. Yet the monster within was not the only one she feared.

"But something evil *is* chasing me," she told him. "I don't even know if it's human or fairy. What can I do?"

Kevin stopped a moment and closed his eyes. His lips moved wordlessly in prayer. Then he opened his eyes again.

"When you make peace with your own monster, you diminish evil's power—over yourself and in the world."

"What?"

Dana's tone made it clear that she was hardly reassured.

Kevin sighed. "In time you will understand my words, but know this: the evil you speak of is not new to the world. It has been here before, sowing darkness to aid some greater design. You will play your part against it, but you are safe for now. Your enemy believes it has killed you, since the wolf died in your place."

Dana let out a cry of guilt and grief.

He laid his hand on her shoulder.

"You must accept her gift. Her sacrifice. Her love for you."

She nodded, even as the tears fell.

He didn't try to stop her from crying, but kept his arm around her shoulders as they walked together.

They came to the Poulanass Waterfall which tumbled down the ridge of Derrybawn. Kevin dipped his hand into the waters to wipe her tear-stained face. His care and concern steadied her.

"Don't you get lonely?" she asked him. "Here all by yourself?"

He looked a little abashed.

"I will confess to you. This is no hardship for me. I am not very good amongst my own kind. I fled the monastery where I was made a monk. It is easier to live with the birds and animals. Humanity is too loud and fractious for me."

"Birds fight too," she pointed out, "and loudly!"

Kevin laughed in agreement, yet it seemed that the birds around him didn't fight. Several different kinds were perched on his shoulders, chirping away happily. Mimicking their calls, he spoke to them and stroked their heads. Dana was suddenly reminded of the eco-warriors in the Glen of the Downs, all the young bearded men who were so passionate and idealistic.

"Thanks for being here," she said, and gave him a hug. He blushed.

It was time for them to part.

"Climb this hill and go through the forest beyond," he directed her. "Travel northwest over the peak of Lugduff. There is another valley you must cross, the Glenmalure, but by then you will be in sight of Lugnaquillia. You must reach it today, little sister, for it is *Lá Lughnasa*."

Dana was halfway up the ridge when she turned to wave a last farewell.

Below stood Kevin, his arms outstretched like a human cross. In each hand a blackbird was making her nest. At his feet curled a badger and her cubs. Dana's heart swelled. First the guardian of the Faolan clan and then the saint of Wicklow County; the gods of her father's people had answered her cry. Once again she acknowledged that there was more to her quest than simply carrying a message and gaining a wish.

Was she ready to face what it was leading her to?

Twenty-nine

Dana was nearing the top of the ridge when she found herself back in her own time. The forest around her was less wild and overgrown. She was standing on wooden steps that bordered the waterfall. Around her were crowds of people. Like returning swallows, the summer visitors had flocked to Glendalough. Families and tourists, young and old, foreign and Irish, they strolled through the ruins, around the two lakes, and up past the waterfall. Fifteen hundred years later, people still came to Kevin!

No one had noticed her arrival. Everyone was staring at the sky. Dark clouds roiled menacingly. The air grew chill. Gusts of wind shook the trees. As the first spatters of rain fell, everyone charged for cover, down the steps and toward the Visitors' Center.

Except Dana, who ran into the woods.

The trees creaked around her. Branches thrashed about. The rain poured down in sheets. This was not good, not good at all. Summer storms could be disastrous in the mountains, causing flash floods. She had to reach

Lugnaquillia before the day ended. How could she travel in this weather? Lightning flashed overhead. The first roll of thunder grumbled. At least she knew where she was going. The marked pathways of the Wicklow Way led directly from Derrybawn to the peak of Lugduff. Hood pulled over her face, cloak wrapped tightly, she hurried along the trail.

Barging blindly through the rain, Dana didn't see the small creature scurry in front of her until it was too late. They crashed into each other and fell together onto the muddy ground.

Despite her shock, Dana recognized immediately what had tripped her up. She jumped to her feet and grabbed hold of the boggle. Maintaining a firm grip, she looked quickly around.

"Where are the others? Are they hiding? Leave me alone! All of you!"

"You leaves me alone! Why's you grabbing me?"

The voice was the first clue. Higher and lighter. Then the dress. Though sodden and soiled, it had puffed sleeves and a little petticoat.

"You're a girl!" said Dana, amazed.

"Course I's a girl!" She was obviously offended. "Ivy's my name. Could I be's anything else?"

Of course she couldn't. Though she had the same rounded shape as the boy boggles and the webbed feet, she had curls of green hair like fiddlehead fern. The big eyes that shone gold in the gloom had long lashes like a doll's.

"Let me go," Ivy pleaded. "I must keeps going before the storm be's worse!"

Dana maintained her hold, unsure what to do. The wind raged around them, flaying them with rain. They were both soaked to the skin.

"Why should I? After what the boggles did to me!"

Ivy looked surprised, then concerned.

"Hast the boys been bold? I knew they'd gets up to mischief without us! What hast they done?"

She looked so sincerely distraught that Dana released her. The girl boggle didn't run away, but stood her ground and waited for Dana's answer.

"They kidnapped me and put me in a hole."

Ivy's eyes went huge.

"Oh, what coulds make them be that bad?!"

"I . . . I don't know," said Dana, through chattering teeth. After what had happened the last time, she wasn't about to mention her mission.

Ivy stared at Dana, disbelief and uncertainty rife in her features. The golden eyes glowed with intelligence.

They were both struggling to stay upright in the wind.

"There be's something wrong here," Ivy said finally. "I needs to know what. There be's one in this forest, old and wise. I thinks it best we goes to see her, you and me."

It was Dana's turn to be suspicious; but there was something about the girl boggle she liked. Besides, the storm was growing worse. She wouldn't get very far on her own. She needed help.

"Okay."

The storm was whipping itself into a frenzy. Trees leaned backward under the force of the gale. The rain fell sideways. After slipping and sliding on the wet ground, the two girls clasped hands as they made their way through the woods.

At last Ivy stopped in front of an ancient oak. It appeared to be hollow. Dana thought they were going to climb inside for shelter, but then she saw the door. A canopy of bracket fungus arched overhead, and there was a little brass handle and matching knocker engraved with the words MANNERS MAKETH THE MAN.

Against the howling wind, Ivy clattered on the knocker.

The last thing Dana expected was to know the person who opened the door; yet there stood the little old lady she had met in the restaurant in Bray and again in the mountains when she set off on her quest.

"Mrs. Sootie Woodhouse!" Ivy cried. "We needs your help!"

"Come! Come!" The old woman bustled the girls in out of the rain. "We meet again," was all she said to Dana.

Under the frilly bonnet, her narrow face seemed to have grown more whiskers. Her yellow dress had a full-length skirt and a lacy apron. The black beady eyes twinkled merrily.

They stepped into a hallway that had a wooden coat stand and framed pictures of woodland scenes. Carpeted stairs led downward under the ground. Mrs. Woodhouse lit a candle to show them below.

Though Dana had seen many wonders in her travels, this was the place that delighted her the most. The rooms were small and low-ceilinged. She had to duck her head to keep from hitting the roof. In the living room was a stone fireplace with pink ceramic tiles, and two stuffed chairs with cushions that stood by the hearth. A carved dresser held china dishes and brown crockery. Rugs of multicolored weave covered the earthen floor, while bookshelves and family portraits graced the walls.

"What a dotey house!" said Dana.

Mrs. Woodhouse scooted them into the bedroom to dry themselves off. The four-poster bed was covered with a patchwork quilt and matching canopy. At its foot stood a wicker trunk of fresh linen. A blue porcelain jug and bowl stood on a washstand.

"Wash your hands before lunch, girls!" Mrs. Woodhouse called in to them.

"This be good news," said Ivy.

They were soon dry and ready to eat. A little feast had been laid out on the round table in the living room. There were bowls of chestnut soup with white rolls fresh from the oven, a platter of hard cheeses, fresh dandelion salad with strawberries, and a blackberry syllabub and a crab-apple pie.

Before they could start on the meal, Mrs. Woodhouse bowed her head and spoke quietly.

"We thank the Mystery that makes all things grow and breathes wonder through the world."

"We does," said Ivy.

"Me too," said Dana.

As she helped herself to a bit of everything, in the back of her mind Dana worried about time. She already trusted Mrs. Woodhouse and had decided to confide in Ivy too. She was waiting for the right moment to mention her mission and to ask for their help. Though all was safe and snug in the little underground house, the storm raged above. Could they get her to Lugnaquillia?

Mrs. Woodhouse looked upward.

"His heart breaks yet again," she said sadly. "Will he survive his memories? Will we?"

"Maybe he gots to wake," Ivy said, though she sounded uncertain. "Maybe it be's best for him."

Dana was surprised. She had come to think of Lugh as a tyrant whom the boggles kept asleep in order to

protect themselves. But Ivy and Mrs. Woodhouse
showed no fear, and their voices expressed only warmth
and concern.

"I thought the boggles didn't want him to wake up?"
Dana said. "That's why they imprisoned me!"

She told them what had happened when she was in the
Boglands.

Ivy was very upset. Her cutlery clattered onto her
plate.

"The bad boys! They's not supposed to steal childer
anymore! But they's even badder to put you in the hole.
Stupid boys! They don't knows the story. The King wakes
already. I's on my way to tell them that."

Mrs. Woodhouse stayed calm.

"You bear a message for Lugh of the Mountain, Lugh
of the Wood?"

Dana nodded. "It's from the High King of Faerie to
his Tánaiste. I've got to get it to him by today."

Her words were no sooner uttered than the other two
were galvanized into action. The meal was over. They had
to leave at once.

"But what's going on?" Dana asked, in the rush of coats
and cloaks being donned. "Why was Lugh asleep? And
why's he waking up?"

"It be's a long story," said Ivy.

"We shall tell it as we go," Mrs. Woodhouse promised.
"It will shorten the road." Her nose quivered with zeal as

she fastened the brass buttons on her cape. "We have dallied long enough, girls. The High King's message must be delivered."

"We should link arms together," Dana suggested, "so no one will get lost or blown away by the wind."

Mrs. Woodhouse's laugh was almost a squeak. "By all that shines, we are not going outside, my dear!" She unlocked a round door on the far side of the room. It opened into a passageway. "*Under hill and under mountain.* That's the fairy way. We shall reach Lugnaquillia before twilight, dry as a bone."

Sheltered from the storm, they set off through the tunnel. As they went, Dana was told the tale of the Mountain King and his Sky Bride.

Thirty

Long were the seasons of their love in the green and gold regions of the world. Little did they dream of the blood-dimmed tide of Fate that would loose itself upon them. For who can plumb the river where flows the waters of existence? Who can glimpse the shadow behind the sunshine of the day? All things contain their opposite. Eloquence is born of dumbness, blindness of vision, and darkness may lie hidden inside that which shines. It is said the Singer of Tales and the Lord of Misrule are one and the same.

One day she vanished.
Without sign or word or warning, the Sky Bride vanished!

At first some thought it a game of hide-and-seek, as the Queen was merry and loved to play tricks. But the King knew by the stillness of his heart that she was gone. Stern and silent, he set out to search the heavens for her. Through zaarahs of darkness and deserts of light he journeyed, under the architraves of immense constellations, past rushing planets and the blazing of suns. Across black starry seas and

*eternities of twilight he voyaged into realms still unrevealed
and newly quickening to the Voice that was older than all.
Out beyond height and width and depth, he plunged over
the abyss, into brighter boroughs even more mysterious which
swam in dark oceans like glittering sea serpents swallowing
their own tails.*
    And all the time he called out to her.

Tá an oíche seo dubh is dorcha,
Tá an spéir ag sileadh deor',
Tá néal ar aghaidh na gréine,
Ó d'imigh tú, a stór.

This night is cold and dark now;
The sky is weeping tears;
The sun is eclipsed in shadow,
Since you departed.

He did not find her.

*Each time he returned from his journeying, more wretched
than a starving crow in winter, the nobles of his Court would
plead with him.*
    *"Be at ease, O King. Be at rest. Let her go. She has
returned to the sky from whence she came. She heard the
cries of her sisters on the lunar winds, calling her home to the
Lands of Light. You must let her go."*

Deaf to their entreaties, he would set out again, for bitter were his days without her, and he would not abandon hope.

Love is as strong as death.
Passion as fierce as the grave.
Its flashes are flashes of fire, a raging flame.
Many waters cannot quench it.
Neither can floods drown it.

Then came the day when all could see that he had gone mad with sorrow. He lay down among the mountains, his face to the sky, and raged against the firmament. So great was his anguish that his tears flooded the countryside: rills turned to rivers, rivers were in spate, trees toppled, fields drowned. Day after day and night after night, his grief was a monster that ravaged the land.

The King's people were at a loss, for he was beyond all aid and reason. Wherever they gathered to shelter from the storms, they spoke of his plight and of their dilemma. The mountain bogs were sodden. If the downpours continued, they were likely to explode. A bog-burst could only mean catastrophe: a deluge of mud and liquid peat gushing down like molten lava, swamping everything in its path. They would all perish in the King of the Hill's sorrow.

Something had to be done.

• • •

And as is the way within the worlds, when the powerful bring all to the edge of doom, the small and humble rose to save the day. It was the little boggles who came to the mountain to see what they might do.

It has been told in many a tale that there are three great gifts to fairy songs: some make you laugh, some make you weep, and some bring the sweet comfort of sleep.

And it is known throughout the Realm that the girls of the boggle family possess the third gift. In the olden days, when human babies were stolen by the fairies, it was the girl boggles who sang to them so they wouldn't cry for their mothers.

Now the girls gathered around their fallen king, where he lay weeping below the cairn of Lugnaquillia. They kissed his brow and closed his eyes and hushed and shushed him with a fairy lullaby.

Soon his head nodded upon his great chest. Then, with an exhalation like the breath of the wind, he turned his back to the sky and plunged his face into the earth. Sinking deeply into the warm embrace, the deep womb of sleep, he was freed of all memory, of all grief, of all pain.

Then it was the turn of the boy boggles to work their magic. Their power over stone. They rolled the weight of a mountain onto the King's back, to pin him down that he may not rise up again. And they placed markers all along the Wicklow borders to keep outsiders away who might disturb the sleeping giant. For there was no guarantee that if Lugh woke, they would be able to put him to sleep again.

With these tasks accomplished, the boys returned to the Boglands alone and sorrowful. For it was their duty to keep watch on the borders, even as the girls remained with the King to keep him asleep.

Thus was their family sundered for the good of all.

†HiR†Y-OПE

Mrs. Woodhouse and Ivy took turns telling the tragic tale, for the former knew more of the beginning, and the latter, the end. As the story unfolded, the three made their way through the souterrain under Lugduff. At first it was a long narrow corridor, snug and dry and smelling faintly of small animals; but soon it widened into a breathtaking cavern scooped out of the immense ridge. Dim alcoves and recesses arched on every side; a cathedral of stone with glistening pillars of feldspar and quartz. It would have taken hours to cross, but Dana's companions moved faster than humans and the silver nails in her shoes helped her keep apace.

Even as Dana listened to the fairy tale, she stared around her agog. Strange marvels were to be seen on every side, some of which she could barely comprehend. At one point they passed a dark cave where a single shaft of light fell from miles above. There in the shadows, a lone figure sat cross-legged, head bowed toward the light as if in prayer. Then came a field of white columns that rose to the dome above. Each pillar was topped with a crescent-shaped helmet that opened like a mouth. All issued in unison notes of such beauty that the three travelers walked below in silent awe.

By the time they had reached the far side of the cavern, the story of the Mountain King and the Sky Bride was finished.

"So he never found his queen," Dana said sadly. "What could've happened to her? Does anyone know?"

Ivy piped up. "I heards a demon stoles her."

"I heard this rumor too," Mrs. Woodhouse agreed. "And Lugh fought the demon but was defeated. They say it was this failure that drove him mad. Whatever the truth," and she let out a sigh, "we all know the outcome. His grief nearly destroyed him and us as well."

They entered a tunnel through which a train could fit. It was very dark, with only faint glimmers of light from streaks of mica in the walls. The other two took Dana's hands to guide her. Mrs. Woodhouse explained that the passage ran under Conavalla and on to Table Mountain where the underground artery forked out in all directions. They would journey south from Table to Camenabologue and then onward to Lugnaquillia.

Dana was glad she wasn't alone. From time to time she saw wraithlike creatures slipping through the shadows, blind-eyed and albescent. From Ivy, she understood that these were the denizens of that mazy underworld; and while they didn't stop travelers from

using their highways, they were a reclusive and xeno-
phobic race.

"I don't likes to come here without Mrs. Woodhouse,"
Ivy murmured.

"Me neither," Dana whispered back.

Table Mountain was, indeed, a grand central station
with tunnels branching off into a vast network. The colos-
sal walls swirled like terra-cotta meringue, dwarfing the
three of them. Dana was staring curiously at the fossils
that stippled the rock, when she let out a gasp. In the
shadows towered the gigantic skeleton of an embedded
dinosaur.

"Ah," said Mrs. Woodhouse. "Those were the days of
the great dragons."

"You were there?" Dana asked, amazed.

"Not at'all," came the reply, with a little laugh. "Tales
have come down through the generations."

They took a passageway traveling southward. It was
lined with white gravel where the quartz had crumbled
into cave pearls. They were still deep in the granite spine
of the mountains, far below the surface; but now they
could hear the distant roar of the storm, like rumors of
war. The tunnel felt damp. Water trickled down the walls.
They were nearing Lugnaquillia, the heart of the tempest.

"Why is the king waking up?" Dana asked Ivy. "Did
the girls stop singing?"

"We's still singing," the little boggle answered. "We

don'ts know why he wakes. Could be's a bad dream. He gets them lots. And we hast to sing more and more to puts him deeper in the spell. But it be's harder this time."

"He gets nightmares?" Dana shuddered, remembering her own. She grew pensive. "Could it be something else? *A shadow of the Destroyer has entered the land.* That's part of my message. Maybe he's trying to wake so he can fight it?"

"He was the best of kings before tragedy struck," Mrs. Woodhouse said, nodding. "He cared for his people."

"So we want him awake," Dana concluded. "The Lady who sent me says he'll know what to do."

That was the moment when Ivy let out a cry, as if she had been hit.

"What hast I done? Stupid stupid boggle! He can'ts do anything if he wakes! He be's under stone! Bog magic binds even the King!"

Dana stopped in her tracks. She was trying not to panic, but her mind was reeling. This was disastrous. What use was her message if the King was trapped? She had assumed he would be free once he woke. There wasn't enough time to go all the way back to the Sally Gap to fetch the boys. A good part of the day had already been spent in the caverns. Even with the silver nails, she couldn't possibly reach the Boglands and get back to Lugnaquillia before midnight.

Ivy's golden eyes welled with tears.

"When I mets you I's going to the boys. To makes a

plan! Now I's done it all wrong! I be's a bad leader. All be's lost because of me!"

Her small body shook with sobs. For the first time since Dana had met her, the girl boggle looked lost and helpless. Dana thought of the boy boggles crying for their girls. How much these little people had suffered!

"There, there, sweetling," said Mrs. Woodhouse, patting Ivy on the shoulder.

But Dana saw that the old lady was also upset as her nose twitched anxiously.

"We'll have to split up," Dana decided suddenly. "It's the only thing to do. It's hopeless, but we've got to try anyway."

Mrs. Woodhouse nodded and looked at her proudly. "I had hoped to guide you, my dear, to the end of your quest, but it seems that cannot be. We each have our part to play, whether big or small. Ivy will bring you to the King. No matter what happens, you must give him the message. I will go to the Boglands to collect the boys. If Lugh cannot free himself, they are our only hope."

"The bogs are miles away," Dana said worriedly. "Can you—?"

She was stopped in mid-sentence by the old lady's chuckle. The black beaded eyes gleamed.

"Do you not know yet? After all the good care you gave my kinfolk? Your hamsters. Sure, I can run like the wind!"

As soon as Mrs. Woodhouse darted away, Dana

understood. Bonnet, cape, and skirts were shed like leaves from a tree as the old woman shriveled and shrank. A whip of tail flounced in the air. A squeak of laughter echoed after. Then the gray fairy mouse disappeared down the tunnel.

Dana and Ivy looked at each other. They were like two children suddenly separated from their mother.

"We can do it," Dana assured her companion.

"We be's fine," Ivy agreed.

They hurried down the passageway, glancing behind them.

And, just as they had secretly feared, things soon got worse.

The roof of the tunnel grew steadily lower until Dana had to stoop. Eventually they were pinched into a crawl-way. Scrambling on hands and knees, round twists and turns, they wondered if the burrow would ever widen again.

Then Dana heard a noise behind them. She grabbed Ivy's arm.

"Did you hear that?" she hissed.

They both stayed still, holding their breaths.

"I only hears my heart," Ivy whispered.

Dana knew what she meant. Her own chest pounded. But there was no other sound. They continued on.

When a circle of light appeared ahead of them, they both quickened their pace, delighted.

And when they reached it, they both cried out in dismay.

There was just enough room for the two of them to stare downward over the lip of the tunnel: into a dark sinkhole. Directly opposite, as if just across the road, was a wall of sheer rock.

"A dead end!" said Dana, stunned. "But how—?"

Ivy dropped a stone over the edge.

It was some time before they heard it land. The plop was unmistakable.

Water!

"But Mrs. Woodhouse was bringing us this way," Dana said, baffled.

"And it be's the only road to Lugnaquillia," Ivy pointed out. "There be's no other tunnel from Table to the south." She stopped to think a moment. "Holds my feet, so's I can look."

As the little boggle leaned further and further over the edge, Dana gripped the webbed feet. She had expected them to feel cold or slippery, but they were soft and warm as if covered with down.

"I see's it!" Ivy cried, excited. "It be's there! A shelf! And steps! We's got to jump to it!"

The boggle went first, confident of her agility. She arrived safely, landing like a frog.

For Dana, it was a frightening prospect. The lower ledge wasn't directly under them, but slightly over to the left.

"You cans do it!" Ivy called up to her.

"Sure I can," Dana muttered, dangling her legs over the side.

And down she dropped.

There was a terrifying moment when she felt solid ground under one foot and nothing but air under the other. She teetered over the abyss.

Then Ivy grabbed her.

"Thanks!" Dana choked.

"You be's welcome," said her friend, grinning.

In that short distance, the view had changed completely. Carved into the rock was a great stairway that ran downward for hundreds of steps, arching under the tunnel they had left. Carefully making their way down it, they were ushered from darkness into a dusky glow. At the bottom, they discovered the source of the brightness.

They stood on a shore of sand that glistened with its own light, like stars ground to dust. But it was the river that truly sparkled, as its waters flowed with the same scintillating crystals.

Several wooden skiffs lay upturned on the beach. Dana looked around for their owners, but Ivy was already pushing one into the water. They both clambered aboard. Too small to row, Ivy sat in the stern to give directions while Dana struggled with the oars. As it turned out, her job wasn't difficult, for the current carried them like a leaf; she had only to keep the boat in midstream.

The voyage was thrilling, despite all their worries about the mission and the passage of time. With breathtaking speed, they raced past walls of white granite and quartz that towered on each side. It wasn't long before they reached the river's own destination: a subterranean sea.

The surface lay still and dark like black ice, as the shining crystals sank to the depths below. Overhead, a vast rocky vault disappeared into shadow. The air was dim and heavy. Silence hung like a shroud over all, broken only by the splash of the oars in the water as Dana began to row. She was barely breathing. Ivy's eyes shone gold in the gloom.

They both heard it.

The sound of other oars dipping into the sea.

Peering through the murk, they saw nothing. Was it an echo of their own oars?

Dana stopped rowing. There it was! A dip and a splash! Then silence.

Another boat was following them.

Too terrified to even think of bluffing, Dana began to row frantically. The paddles smacked the water. The other boat increased its speed also. That their pursuer no longer tried to mask the sound was even more ominous. Yet they could see nothing in the deep shadows.

Dana felt the sweat break out on her body. Her hands were raw. The sea felt as if it had turned to mud and she was dragging the oars through it. She kept straining to peer through the dimness, both wanting and dreading to know what was there. Her stomach churned. It was like one of her nightmares; where she couldn't flee fast enough from the thing that chased her.

At last, the pale glimmer of a shore in the distance! Despite her exhaustion, Dana doubled her efforts. Soon they were moving through the shallows and onto the beach.

Now Dana's heart leaped into her mouth. The glowing light of the sand allowed her to see the other boat as it approached. There was no doubt about the figure who rowed furiously toward them.

Murta!

Thirty-two

Two petrified children, the girls held hands as they raced across the sand and into another tunnel. It was dim and narrow but had a high roof overhead. They knew they were nearing Lugnaquillia. Rain streamed down the walls from the storm above. Their feet splashed through puddles and flooded gullies. Fear drove them on. Behind came the sounds of pursuit: a heavy body displacing water.

"Do you . . . know . . . where to go?"

Dana panted as she ran. As always the silver nails gave her speed, but she had a stitch in her side and was gulping air. She felt faint with terror. What would they do if Murta caught up with them? There was only one solution: stay ahead.

Ivy's breathing was also labored.

"*Om . . . phalos,*" she gasped. "The . . . center."

It was only when they arrived at the core of Lugnaquillia that Dana had any understanding of what Ivy meant.

White and gold were the colors of the immense circular chamber. The walls sheered for miles above, pale granite streaked with veins of golden ore. At the heart of the cavern was a great white saucer of burnished stone. Was it some kind of altar? Covering the vast floor was a luminous layer of gold and white sand that swirled in patterns like a giant mandala. The designs were in a state of constant flux: spirals, fractals, and figures of eight forming and re-forming before their eyes. Who changed them? Whose breath blew over them? For a moment Dana stood enthralled; then she heard the footsteps in the tunnel behind her.

"How do we get out of here?" she cried to Ivy.

"The bowl be's the way!"

Still holding Dana's hand, the boggle pulled her into the glittering dust.

There was no time for questions. As they raced across the floor, the shining sands rippled and eddied around them. It was like splashing through the sunlit shallows of the sea.

They had almost reached the bowl when Murta arrived.

A blood-curdling screech erupted behind them.

They didn't turn or slow down.

Dana felt a rock strike the back of her knee. She let out a cry and almost buckled. But she recovered and kept going.

Now Ivy screamed as the next rock hit her and knocked her to the ground. The sands went into a frenzy around her.

Dana tried to pick the boggle up. Ivy was still conscious, but blood trickled from the back of her head. Her eyes widened as she stared past Dana, and when Dana followed her gaze, she too quailed.

Murta looked hideous. His skin was red and blistered, his clothes soiled and torn. He looked as if he had been dragged through the tunnels. Worst of all, a thin red vapor oozed from the corner of his eyes, like blood.

With a terrified whimper, Ivy scurried on her hands and knees to hide in the folds of Dana's cloak.

That made Dana braver. Somewhere in the back of her mind, she heard a wolf howl. Straightening up, she turned to face Murta. She would protect her friend. She would be her guardian.

The shining sands withdrew from Murta as he stepped through them. He himself acted strangely. Walking slowly, as if in a dream, he gazed around the chamber like someone delirious. His face worked with emotion. One was naked greed.

"Look at all this gold! It must be worth a fortune!"

Then he focused on Dana.

"What the hell—? What are you doing here, kid? And how did *I* get here? Did we fall down a hole or something?"

She could hear the fear in his voice, and it only confused her more.

Then his features distorted and something else was

there. Something that wasn't Murta. Wasn't human. It glared at her with such savage hatred that she recoiled. When it spoke, the voice was cold and heavy, like iron; but she heard an echo of doubt.

"I shot you dead, human child. Yet here you are. It seems you are more than you appear to be." Suddenly the eyes flared like jets of fire. Rage and confusion threw him off balance. "*You!* I came to kill the King, but you—"

Before he could say more, a screech broke out behind Dana.

"You can'ts kill our king!"

And Ivy charged.

The fury of her attack caught him off guard. Flying at Murta like a miniature harpy, she aimed a swift kick to his groin. He staggered back with a screech. Leaping on top of him, Ivy punched and scratched. He recovered quickly. Seizing her with both hands, he began to throttle her.

It was all so fast and violent, Dana was slow to react; but the moment she registered Ivy's peril, she moved. Grabbing the two rocks Murta had thrown at them earlier, she jumped toward him with the speed of her silver-nailed shoes.

And smashed the stones against his head.

He toppled to the ground, unconscious.

Coughing and choking, Ivy scrabbled away from him.

"Are you all right?" asked Dana, anxiously checking the little boggle.

Ivy nodded, but she was trembling all over.

"He be's worse than the Bogeyman," she whispered. "Be's he the demon that stoles our Queen?"

"Could be," said Dana, still in shock herself and studying Murta with alarm. "For sure he's the shadow in my message. But he's inside a creepy human. What'll we do with him? He's going to wake up."

Even as she spoke, Murta's limbs began to twitch.

They looked at each other, horrified.

"What about your gift?" Dana said suddenly. "Can you put him to sleep?"

"I can'ts!" Ivy said with dismay. "I needs another to help. There must be's a word-weaver and a tune-maker."

"What about me?" Dana said desperately.

Murta's eyelids were fluttering. She couldn't bear to think of those red eyes looking at her. She gripped the rocks in her hands, prepared to bash him again.

"We's can try," Ivy agreed, biting her lip. "You does the words, 'cause I knows the tune."

"Right, let's do it," said Dana, taking a deep breath.

She had already chosen her song; the lullaby Gabe sang to her when she was little, and still used sometimes if she was sick or had a nightmare.

They both hunkered down near Murta, but not too close. Dana kept the rocks handy, just in case. She was jangling with nerves, but as soon as she heard Ivy's tune, an unexpected peace came over her. The air was somehow familiar. Then she recognized the notes from the field of white pillars back in the first cavern.

Dana opened her mouth and began to sing.

Go to sleep, my baby. Even as she sang the words, she heard her father's voice in her mind, steadying her. Making her feel safe. *Close your pretty eyes.* As her voice echoed through the glittering chamber, she noticed that the sands danced in unison with her. *Angels up above you, peeping at you dearly from the sky.*

Then Murta's eyes began to open. The heavy lids lifted slowly, like a dozing snake's. Hatred burned through the slits. *The same old moon is shining.* His limbs twitched. He flexed his long fingers. Dana felt her throat constrict. *The stars . . .* she faltered over the words. Still crooning, Ivy reached out to take her hand. Nodding, Dana resumed her song . . . *begin to peep.* The demon was now glaring at her, open-eyed. She tried to look away, but found she couldn't. Every part of her trembled with horror. She was singing a lullaby to something that wanted to murder her! *And now it's time for you, pretty baby, to go . . . to . . . sleep.*

And it wasn't working.

Murta's arms and legs moved as he surfaced into consciousness. He tried to sit up.

"You gots to sing more!" Ivy urged her.

Dana was choking with panic. She didn't know any other lullabies. And what was the point in repeating the one that failed? She gripped the stones, ready to use them again. Then her eyes fell on the sands that sparkled around her like sunshine on still water. Was she imagining winged forms inside the motes of light? A little sunburst exploded in her mind, as if in response to their dance.

She sang new words.

Seothó, a thoil, ná goil go fóill,
Seothó, a thoil, ná goil aon deoir,
Seothó, a linbh, a chumainn's a stóir.

Hush, dear heart, no need to cry,
Hush, dear heart, no need for tears,
Hush, my child, my love and treasure.

And this time it worked.

For the most part.

Murta fell back as if pinned to the ground. But though he lay like a corpse, the eyes were alert, glinting with red rage.

"The demon's still awake," said Dana, shuddering.

Ivy had stopped crooning and was studying Murta with a mix of satisfaction and puzzlement.

"The sleep spell does be binding on all mortals and fairies. This demon be's something else. But it can'ts move without the human."

Dana suddenly thought of zombies and wished she hadn't.

"We've got to get out of here," she said to Ivy. "*Now!*"

THIRTY-THREE

"We goes in the bowl!" said Ivy.

Before Dana could ask what she meant, the boggle hurried to the stone saucer a few feet away and, scrambling over the rim, disappeared inside. Then her head popped up.

"Quick! Gets in!"

Despite her bewilderment, Dana ran to join her friend, happy to escape the demon's glare.

The interior of the saucer was deep and wide, with enough room for at least six people. The sides were smooth and polished. Dana slid into the center where Ivy reclined against the curve.

The boggle's eyes were huge with excitement.

"I loves this," she said, shivering with anticipation. "You wills too. It be's great fun!"

"What—?"

The bowl began to rock gently like a cradle. Dana clambered up the side to investigate. The first thing her eyes settled on was Murta's prone body. She shuddered, thankful that he wasn't moving. The glistening sands were still avoiding him. Her mouth dropped when she saw what else they were doing. Like waves to the shore, from all over the vast chamber, they were converging on the saucer. Gathering beneath it. She suddenly realized what was about to happen. With a yelp, she let go of the rim and slid back to her friend.

"Holds on to your hat!" Ivy giggled.

Soon the sands garnered enough force to thrust the bowl upward. Up, up it flew, at ever-increasing speed, hurtling past the walls of glistening rock. The girls screeched with the same joy and terror of children on a carnival ride. It was as if they were shooting through a column of white and gold light. As the ground dropped miles below them, a glimmer appeared overhead, slowly widening like an open mouth. Dana wondered, with a pang of fear, if they would spurt out the top and into the air! But the saucer began to slow as they neared the summit, finally coming to a gentle stop inside a crater.

They had arrived on the peak of Lugnaquillia. Beyond the walls of the crater, the storm raged. Winds tore in howling circles. Rain whipped the air. Lightning crackled, setting the sky ablaze. Thunder roared like the throat of war.

But the weather was the least of their worries.

They had just climbed out of the saucer and turned to watch it drop below when they discovered they had not been the only passengers. Engrossed in the ride and staring upward, they hadn't noticed the hands that gripped the rim behind them.

There stood Murta, eyes leaking red.

Paralyzed with horror, Dana didn't move as he lurched toward her. His feet dragged over the ground. His arms hung limp. The demon was using all its will to propel the sleeping body. And it wouldn't be long before the spell broke.

Dana grabbed hold of Ivy, who was frozen beside her.

"*Run!*" she screamed.

Scrambling up the bank of the crater, they fell out onto the summit of Lugnaquillia.

Where the full brunt of the storm struck them.

It was merciless. Fists of wind hammered them. The rain lashed like cat-o'-nine-tails. The ground underfoot oozed with muck, sucking at their feet. Only Dana's fairy cloak kept them moving. The moment she drew Ivy into the folds, it closed around the two of them like armor.

At least the storm would slow the demon. Or so Dana hoped. A quick glance back at the crater showed no sign of him. Directed by Ivy, she fought her way across the summit toward the southernmost edge.

Lugnaquillia was the highest mountain in the Wicklow chain, towering over the surrounding landscape. Its flanks were carved with three great cirques. Its peak was a lofty plateau as wide as a soccer field.

Ivy peered around her in dismay.

"This be's the dancing lawn . . . where we hast our parties . . . That be's the spot the bonfire's lit on Midsummer
nights . . . We feasts at long tables under the stars . . ."

Dana couldn't imagine such happy scenes. The place
looked like a battlefield.

They reached the edge of the cirque called the South
Prison. Its slopes sheered down into a natural amphithe-
ater. On the ridge to the west, a saddle of blanket bog lay
between Lugnaquillia and the smaller mountain of Slievemaan. Ivy pointed to the bog.

"Do you hears them?"

At first the wails of the wind drowned out all other
sound. Then Dana detected a faint ululation rising
through the maelstrom. High sweet voices, like a choir of
seraphim, sang a lullaby that was also a lament.

> *Tá an croí á réabadh sa ghleann, sa ghleann,*
> *Tá an croí á réabadh i ngleann na ndeor;*
> *Ceo is gaoth sa ghleann, sa ghleann,*
> *Ceo is gaoth i ngleann na ndeor.*

> *The heart is torn in the valley, in the valley,*
> *The heart is torn in the Valley of Tears;*
> *Mist and wind in the valley, in the valley,*
> *Mist and wind in the Valley of Tears.*

"The girl boggles," Dana whispered.

"Can you see's them?"

Dana strained to see through the veils of rain. At first she could just make out the contours of the giant, embedded face down in the earth. But her sight kept wavering. One moment she saw Lugh, arms and legs splayed, a great boulder the size of a hill on his back; the next, she was viewing patterns of eroded turf topped by a cairn. Then she spotted the erratics: rocks dropped at random by glaciers in ages past. They were dispersed amid haggs of rain-sculpted peat. Both the rocks and the haggs encircled the giant. Now the image blurred and Dana saw the girl boggles, the tune-makers and the word-weavers. Crouched in the rain, miserable but steadfast, they guarded their king.

The giant stirred fitfully. His arms and legs thrashed under the stone that pinned him down. Every time he moved, the storm seemed to worsen. Then all of a sudden, in one huge motion, like a whale turning in the sea, he twisted onto his back. He was still bound, but Dana could see that his eyes were open, dark and deranged with grief.

The girl boggles wept out loud, sobbing as they sang.

Dana thought they cried with fear, for they were surely in danger, but then she saw that Ivy was weeping too.

"Our poor dear King. We can no longer saves him."

Dana shook her head. It was all wrong, like children being responsible for their parents' problems.

"He's the King," she said to Ivy. "He's the father. He's supposed to look after *you*."

Ivy didn't reply, but started to shout.

"The boys! Look! Our boys!"

Below them, the boy boggles scampered through the rain, across the bog and toward the King. Dana was stunned by how fast they moved. Their webbed feet skimmed the rain-soaked land as if they were surfing. The silver lining in the storm: it had sped them all the way from the Boglands!

In front of them dashed a streak of gray fur.

"Mrs. Woodhouse!" Dana cheered.

But her cheer turned to a scream as Murta attacked her from behind.

The sleeping spell had worn off. The demon was in full command of the human. Wrenching Dana's hood back, he gripped her throat and started to strangle her.

Ivy leaped out of the cloak and onto Murta's arm. He let out a shriek as her sharp teeth sank in.

The two girls struggled with the demon on the mountaintop, even as the boy boggles rolled away the stone that held Lugh down.

Now the giant rose up with a roar that shook the land. And as he rose up, bellowing his sorrow, shedding earth and peat and mud, he brought the rest of the bog with him in one great eruption.

In slow oneiric motion, Dana saw the bog-burst explode around her. Avalanches of sodden turf surged down the hillsides, swamping all in their path. Like sluice gates opening, they triggered more landslides throughout the mountain chain. Roads and bridges were washed away. Trees toppled. Wild creatures drowned. Even birds were caught as they tried to flee the branch. As the viscous flow raged on, it skinned the topsoil from the land, leaving raw wet wounds. The girl and boy boggles, along with Mrs. Woodhouse, were engulfed in the brown torrent and carried away. There was no time to cry out, no time to mourn. Dana herself, along with Ivy and Murta, was swept from the summit and into the quagmire.

Immersed in a murky dream of the bog, Dana didn't know if she were swimming or drowning, flailing or floating. Layer after layer churned around her in an upheaval of all that had been buried through the ages: primeval forests and ancient fields; the bones of giant elks and aurochs; and torqued human bodies, corded like black bog oak. Celtic gold that was the wealth of nobles and the pelf of thieves swirled around like debris in a sinkhole—jeweled brooches, coiled torcs, gorgets and armbands, bells and miters, shrine boxes encrusted with precious gems. As with the darkest recesses of the mind, the bog was the repository of the land's oldest memories.

Like a fossil petrified in the peat herself, Dana was caught up in the kingdom's apocalypse. When the gigantic hand plunged into the brown haze to seize her, she didn't think to fight it off. Then she found herself held against the stormy sky, far above the chaos.

Acting on instinct, David facing Goliath, she screamed at the King.

"You're killing everything! Stop it! You've got to stop it!"

Now occurred the strangest thing of all in that turbid nightmare. The giant's eyes settled on Dana and in that instant, he grew suddenly calm. Her presence was clearly a shock that jolted him out of his madness.

The wind stood still. The rain ceased. The storm died.

Dana was back on the summit of Lugnaquillia. Before her stood a young man with craggy features and amber-brown skin. He appeared nothing like the giant freed from the stone. His manner was quiet, his look gentle. He seemed no older than someone in his early twenties, but the shadow of grief made him sterner. He wore earthy colors, bronze tunic and trousers, and a flowing mantle as purple as the heather. A gold circlet bound his black hair.

"Who are you?" he asked her. "How came you here?"

He sounded dazed, but not insane or angry.

Dana was trying to stop shaking. She was still in shock, overwhelmed by the scenes of destruction and the death of her friends. Her voice was barely audible as she started to speak, but once she got going it grew louder and stronger.

"H-h-how can you do this?" She waved her arm to include the devastation around them. "How can you make everyone else pay just because *you're* unhappy? The poor little boggles who did so much for you! And Mrs. Woodhouse and all the animals—" She choked back her tears. She had never been so mad or so sad. But she forced herself to stay calm. "I've got a message for you from the High King of Faerie. But I'm not going to give it to you, unless you put everything back where it was. You're the King. You must be able to do it."

She expected him to explode. To rant and rave again. She braced herself for more storms.

The sorrow in Lugh's features deepened. His look was grave.

"Do you really care for my people, O human child? Then prove your love."

His voice was quiet, but as his next words sank in, Dana jerked back as if he had hit her.

"Today is the feast of *Lá Lughnasa*. The day on which I may grant you a boon. I will restore my land and my people . . . if you *wish* it of me."

THIRTY-FOUR

D ana didn't know whether to scream or cry. Every
part of her protested. *No fair! No fair!* After all the
days and nights in the mountains, the trials and suffering,
the fear and loneliness, the terrible loss of her dear guardian . . . to have it taken away: the dream that had carried
her forward! The promised reward! After all those years of
being a motherless child. The piece that was missing from
her heart, her life: no mother to pick her up from school;
no mother who smelled of perfume and who brushed her
hair; no mother who kissed and hugged her goodnight;
who loved her the way mothers love their girls. She would
rather have it late than never at all. She needed a mother
in her teenage years, to help her grow up, to become a
woman.

She was to give up that dream? That hope of happiness? It was like suffering the loss all over again.

She could refuse. She had the best of excuses. The
wish was for her father as well as herself. He had suffered so much from the loss of his wife. Surely the King
would understand, having lost his own? And now Gabe

had also endured the pain of Dana's disappearance. Didn't he deserve his reward? Didn't he deserve some happiness?

She tried not to think of Ivy or Mrs. Woodhouse or the other creatures in the Kingdom. Were they alive or dead? What if she was their only chance for survival? It was too much to ask of her. She was too young to be called on to make such a choice, such a sacrifice.

"I . . . I can't," she mumbled.

The King regarded her silently. There was no judgment in his look, only pity.

A light breeze warmed her face, like gamey breath. Through the King's features, the golden-eyed wolf gazed out at her.

"Stand beside the earliest crossroads and ask of the old paths, where is the way to good?"

Then the wolf's image changed to that of Saint Kevin. His look was kind and gentle.

"When my heart is faint, lead me to the rock that is higher than I."

Dana couldn't escape the truth. There was more at stake than her own needs and desires. Two worlds were involved and so many lives. How could she think only of herself?

"I . . . wish . . ."

Her voice quavered and broke. She swallowed a sob and clenched her fists.

"I wish that you put everyone and everything back where they were before the bog burst."

As soon as she had uttered the words, the King's face brightened like sunshine after a storm. Admiration rang in his voice.

"*A leanbh, a chroí,* you have done what the best of mortals do. You have sacrificed yourself to rescue Fairyland."

King Lugh raised his arms. His cloak billowed in a purple cloud behind him. The gold circlet on his brow flashed like lightning. He was a giant again, proud and powerful. The King of the Mountain. Lugh of the Wood. Now he began to sing in a beautiful language that sounded like music and birdsong and the rush of rivers. He was chanting and enchanting the land.

It was like a film in reverse. Everything that had been swept away flew back to its place: soil, water, mud, river, flora and fauna, boggle and fairy. Every bird was in its tree, every fish in its stream. The Kingdom of Wicklow was restored to its glory.

Lugnaquillia was bathed in the half-light of a soft evening. The air was fresh after the rains. The sweet scent of drying grasses wafted on the breeze. Peeping out from the greensward were mushrooms of every kind: fairy-ring champignons, gray-scaled parasols, and tiny yellow sulphur tufts. On the north-facing crags of the mountain, a flock of ravens settled into their nests while the first bats emerged for their evening feed.

The sun was setting in the Glen of Imaal. A rosy glow bathed the western slopes of Lugnaquillia. A hush settled over the landscape, breathless and silvered with the last tracery of rain. Lugh drew a sweeping arc in the air. In response to his gesture, a great rainbow swept across the sky. He raised an eyebrow at Dana as if to say, *good enough?*

Before she could respond, the girl boggles came running from the bogs of Slievemaan. They fell on Lugh, like apple blossoms from a tree, kissing his hands and hugging his knees.

"We needs not sing no more?"

"You be's all right now?"

Lugh gathered them up like an armful of flowers and planted kisses on each as they squealed and giggled.

"I am no longer your charge, dearest daughters. I am restored to myself. My thanks to you, ever-loyal boggles. You have done more for your king than should have been asked of you."

When he put them down, they clamored to leave.

"We goes back home?"

"Back to the Boglands?"

"We goes home to our boys?"

The boy boggles had almost reached the top of the South Prison when the King shooed the girls toward them. All met on the slope with whoops of joy, hugs and laughter, cartwheels and somersaults. Then they set off together to return to the Boglands.

"Where's Ivy?" Dana asked, her voice trembling. "And Mrs. Woodhouse?"

Lugh was already gazing over the swell of the mountains. "Mrs. Woodhouse has returned to the forest. She will come to you again, if you need her. As for your friend . . ." He lifted his hand in a beckoning motion.

In the distance bobbed a little pink speck. As it drew closer, like thistledown on the wind, Dana saw it was Ivy floating through the air. The boggle landed beside them, bright and cheerful in a rose-petaled dress.

With a quick grin to Dana, Ivy curtseyed in front of Lugh.

"You's well, dear King?"

"I am indeed, sweet one. Be free from all need to care for me. I would have you go home and live in happiness with your kin."

Ivy had clasped Dana's hand and now squeezed it tightly. It was obvious she was torn.

Gently Dana released her hold. She knew what it was like to be homesick. She was feeling that way herself.

"Go on, Ivy. You've been away long enough. I just hope we'll meet up again someday."

"We will," Ivy assured her. Then the boggle leader addressed Lugh sternly. "Be's that right, *Ard Solas?*"

Lugh smiled down at her.

"Bravest of boggles, you will surely meet your friend again. Your king gives his word."

That was all Ivy needed to hear. With a last hug for Dana and another curtsey to Lugh, she raced off to catch up with the last stragglers heading east.

Lugh watched the boggles disappear into the distance, a pained expression on his face. Then he drew himself up and turned to Dana.

"Now for my message," he said quietly. "All kings and princes look to the High King and I am his Tánaiste. What does the *Ard Rí* say to me?"

The evening had grown cooler as the sun set in the west. Like the boggles, Dana yearned to go home. She was weary and dispirited. Though she had accomplished her mission, her dream was shattered. She knew the message was important, but not to her. Great events were afoot in the Realm of Faerie, the concern of kings and queens. She had played her small part. There was nothing left to do but repeat the words and go home empty-handed.

"*A shadow of the Destroyer has entered the land. Where is the light to bridge the darkness?*"

Lugh frowned as he listened.

"Even as I lay dreaming, I sensed the threat. It was this which stirred me, undermining the spell." He gazed into the distance. "It hides away in fear of me now that I have woken to full strength. I must seek it out."

Dana wasn't listening. She was wondering if the King would take her home or if she would have to make her way back through the mountains alone. She wished she had asked Ivy to wait for her. She could have gone with the boggles. The Sally Gap was closer to Bray. Her heart sank at the thought of the long trek home. And what would she say to Gabe when she finally got there? After all the pain they had both gone through, she had nothing to show for it. Then they'd leave for Canada and that would end any chance of ever finding her mother. A lump formed in her throat. She could hardly swallow. Though she was determined not to cry in front of the King, a sniffle escaped.

Lugh snapped out of his thoughts, and was suddenly aware of her.

"What is wrong, child?" he asked kindly.

"It's . . . things didn't . . . I wanted . . ." The tears escaped and she couldn't stop them.

There was a gentle amusement in his eyes, as well as pity.

"All you have lost is a wish, dear heart. That does not mean I cannot give you what you want."

THIRTY-FIVE

The King made a slight gesture with his hand and everything around them changed.

Dana was still on the summit of Lugnaquillia but apparently not in the same time or space. She was surrounded by trim lawns bordered with flowerbeds and dotted with stone fountains and white statuary. Towering over the elegant grounds rose a crystal palace, its turrets and pinnacles ablaze in the sunset. Lugh led her to the golden doors and into a great hall. Overhead arched a roof of translucent amber so thin it created a honeyed light. The shapes of flying birds could be seen beyond it. In the hall were gathered a shining company, the fairy lords and ladies of the Mountain Kingdom.

They regarded their king warily.

"Stay by my side," he murmured to Dana. *"No harm will befall you; but say nothing of the marvels you see about you or you will break the enchantment that holds you here."*

One of the King's men stepped forward. A slender, silver-haired youth wearing a cloak of green leaves, he carried a small golden harp slung over his shoulder.

"Hail, Lugh of the Mountain, Lugh of the Wood. Help-

less and hapless we have waited for thee. Hast thou returned to thy people, O King?"

Lugh smiled upon his harper and his courtiers, all fey and immortal with sad and glad eyes.

"I heard you weeping as I lay in slumber, your hearts broken with mine. Dear companions, I am truly restored."

Cheers resounded throughout the hall, a tumultuous welcome for the return of the King. A banquet table appeared, laden with a fabulous feast.

As the bright assembly took their seats, Lugh offered his arm to Dana.

"But I'm not dressed for—" she began, then stopped.

In the blink of an eye, her muddy clothes were transformed. She wore a gown of blue silk seeded with pearls and an ivory-white mantle over her shoulders. Her dark hair was caught up in a jeweled comb. Diamonds sparkled on her ears and throat. Though she wasn't one for fashion, Dana swished her dress with delight. It was comfortable as well as beautiful, and even had pockets. She accepted the King's arm.

Two ornate chairs stood at each end of the long table. Dana was surprised when Lugh seated her in one, while he took the other. The nobles of the Court looked startled also, and glanced at her curiously; but the mystery of her presence was left unexplained.

Dana regarded the food ravenously. It seemed like ages since she had last eaten, in the forest of Derrybawn with Mrs.

Woodhouse. *Everything looked delicious. There were ter-rines of soup sprinkled with herbs, wheels of smoked cheeses, mushrooms of every description, artichoke soufflé and pars-nip pie, baby potatoes served with chopped mint, and greens drizzled with lemon and butter. She was already eyeing the desserts. Surrounded by adults, she assumed she had to wait till after dinner. Then she noticed that many of the lords and ladies were sampling the sweets first, helping themselves to the silver dishes of sugared violets, the ginger sherbets and apricot mousse, the hills of chocolate creams, and the tiers of a gigantic hazelnut cake. To wash the feast down were glass goblets of elderflower and rose petal wine, as well as bilberry beers and brandies.*

The courtiers chattered among themselves, but Dana ate without speaking. The food was heavenly. Everything melted in her mouth or burst on her tongue. Yet throughout the meal, she was dogged by the oddest impression. Nothing was as it seemed. *She felt acutely aware of the unseen threads that wove this fragile world together.* Fairy glamour. *And she sensed somehow that any misplaced word or thoughtless statement might tear the delicate fabric asunder.*

Despite her care, from time to time it unraveled anyway. She was about to bite into a peach coated with chocolate when she glimpsed the huge wild berry she held in her hand. She blinked. The peach returned. Sometimes the swaths of lace and diamonds that draped the ladies turned to spider webs sprinkled with dew. The greatest confusion had to do

with size. One minute she felt like a giantess dining with
titans in the Hall of the Gods; then, the next, she was sitting
at a table with other tiny creatures, all fitted snugly inside a
rabbit hole!

Dealing with the quirks of fairy reality was only one of
Dana's concerns. The issue of eating their food had re-emerged.
Would she or would she not be trapped there forever? It was
one of the questions she wanted to ask the King, along with
how she could find her mother. The second matter was the
most important, of course. Though Dana had used up her
wish, Lugh had implied he would help her. She was waiting
for the right moment to remind him of that, but the situation
wasn't ideal.

She had seen from the start that all was not well with the
King and his Court. The tension in the hall was unmistakable. It ran like a dark stream under the pleasantries. Furtive glances were being cast at both her and Lugh. The nobles
appeared to be on tenterhooks, holding their breath. What
were they afraid of? What could possibly happen? The King
himself was silent and brooding. He didn't eat, but sat with
his head in his hand, pensive and preoccupied. Occasionally
he would heave a sigh.

Dana was somewhat wary of him herself. The memory of
the raging giant was still fresh in her mind. The devastation
he had inflicted upon the land. The madness in his eyes. She
was both nervous and in awe of him.

When the banquet was over, the King waved his hand

dismissively and the table disappeared. Now Dana found herself enthroned on a dais at the head of the great hall. The chamber was suddenly thronged, not only with the Court but with countless creatures—birds and animals and other folk of the Mountain Kingdom. Surprised that she sat at Lugh's right hand, Dana couldn't meet the countless stares directed at her. What was happening?

A blast of trumpets rang out. The harper stepped to the fore.

"It is the Feastday of Lá Lughnasa. Lugh of the Mountain, Lugh of the Wood, has returned to his people. Let those who will, step forth and request their boon!"

At first they came timidly, one by one, speaking in low voices to make their requests: a bigger sett in the lee of the mountain; a lost gift found; a betrothal blessed. But as Lugh dealt courteously and magnanimously with each, they grew more confident. He was indeed their beloved King! He had returned to them!

A tall lady glided into the hall. She had emerald skin and hair brown as bark. Her dress was of oak leaves; her crown, of red holly. A whisper rippled through the crowd. Muinchillí Glasa. Greensleeves.

"I have come to speak for the Glen of the Downs," she called out. Her voice was as mellifluous as a burbling brook. "Will you stop the humans from killing the trees?"

Dana suddenly remembered that this was the day the felling in the glen was to begin.

"*The storms have delayed the slaughter,*" Greensleeves continued, "*but they will surely strike tomorrow. Will you intervene?*"

The King regarded her sadly.

"*I will aid those of you who must retreat, but I cannot save the trees. For this is a truth you already know, Muinchillí Glasa. Only humanity can fight human evil. It is not our place in the worlds to do so. If their race fails to stand against its own shadow, we of Faerie must withdraw before it.*"

As Lugh spoke he glanced for a moment at Dana. She shifted uncomfortably. Did he mean her? Was there something she should do?

Greensleeves bowed her head to acknowledge his ruling. Her steps were slow and sorrowful as she withdrew, and the crowd murmured their sympathy.

Many more suppliants came and went. The King dealt with each like Solomon on his throne. It was the final petitioner who created the greatest stir, for she was both beautiful and terrifying. With a shiver, Dana remembered her from the mountains: the tall dark woman who was also a giant raven.

She was over seven feet tall, as straight and slender as a spear, with ebony skin and striking features. Dressed all in black, with leather jerkin, tight trousers, and knee-high boots, she wore a feathered cloak that flew behind her like wings. Her manner was proud and aloof.

"*I am Aróc. Captain of the Fir-Fia-Caw.*" Her voice was

harsh and guttural. *"A boon I ask. Awrrkk. Sad our tale in the West. Pain and loss. We seek new life."*

Lugh listened to her solemnly and nodded when she was finished.

"I grant you the crags of Cloghernagh," was his pronouncement. *"Build and nest as you will.* Tá failte roimhe do cine anseo.*"*

Captain Aróc bowed, but before she could turn on her heels and leave, Lugh signed to her to stay.

"I am curious," he said. *"The marker stones around my borders barred all of Faerie until today. Yet I understand you have been here for some time, scouting the terrain?"*

There was a trace of disdain in Aróc's shrug. Her tone was cold.

"No borders . . . awrrkk . . . in the plains of the sky."

"And if there were?" the King persisted. *"Would you respect them?"*

She glared at him. Black were her eyes, glittering like obsidian and rimmed with gold.

"Awrrkk!" she spat out, with the fierce pride of her kind. *"Fir-Fia-Caw go where they will!"*

Like the rest of the Court, Dana held her breath, waiting for the King's anger. Would he rescind the boon?

A sudden warmth lit up Lugh's face. In that moment he shed the burden of rule and laughed like a carefree young man.

"You will be at home in the Mountain Kingdom, O captain,

my captain. For we are a solitary folk who live by our own governance. No one tells the other what he or she may do. For speaking your truth, I further grant you Corrigasleggan. May the Fir-Fia-Caw enjoy sanctuary as long as the hills stand."

A tremor passed through Aróc, the only indication that she had been caught off guard. Reaching behind her cloak, she unsheathed two scimitars in a silvery flash. Then she knelt before the King and laid them at his feet.

"My loyalty unto death, Liege-Lord."

It was because of Aróc's courage and the King's response to it that Dana decided she would speak at last. It was now or never: she would ask for his help to find her mother. Taking a deep breath, she went to stand up.

But before Dana could move, the King struck the arm of his throne with such force that the report rang through the hall like gunshot.

"The truth! That is all we have when the darkness falls. My harper will make music and I will tell it!"

A ripple of unease raced through the assembly. Eyebrows were raised. Anxious looks exchanged.

"What will you tell, my Lord?" his harper called out.

All gasped in horror at the King's reply:

"The tale of my woe."

Thirty-six

It happened in the early summer, when the hawthorn boughs were laden with white blossoms like brides, and the sun had melted the last snows in the lee of the mountains. On that soft bright morning, the fairy Queen of Wicklow went a-maying with her ladies. Eastward they journeyed, into the rising sun, tripping lightly over rust-colored bogs, down into leafy valleys, and up grassy hillsides. The Kingdom was an endless garden: beautiful were its trees and flowers, its lakes and streams, sweet the music of the birds on the branch and those in the clear air.

When they reached the sugared peak of Little Giltspur, in sight of the blue sea, the Queen's ladies chose a sheltered place to hold their picnic. They fashioned a bower with the mayflowers they had gathered as they went. On a cloth of white linen, they laid out seedcakes dripping with honey and crystal glasses of cool elder wine. Then they called to their mistress to join them.

The Queen only laughed and waved them away as she ran down the hillside. For she was chasing two butterflies, a Holly Blue and a Clouded Yellow. Soon she had left her

ladies behind, as southward she flew in pursuit of her quarry.
After a time, she came to an old forest that crested a high
ridge. Below her fell the steep slope of a glen cloaked with
oak and ash. On the valley floor flowed a narrow stream and,
bordering the stream, a stretch of gray road.

The fairy Queen did not see the road where mortals drove
their noisy vehicles. Having no interest in the other world,
she had never paid heed to its denizens; for she lived between
the layers of their days and behind the veil that they seldom
pierced.

She spied the little Blue hiding in a holly tree, and tagged
him fair and square. When he flew off, she began her hunt
for the Yellow. Then she heard the music. It drifted through
the air toward her, high silvery notes, dipping and gliding
like the very butterfly she sought. Head tilted on her shoulder, eyes closed, she listened. The tune was like nothing she
had ever heard before, powerful and beguiling. Following the
sound, she moved lithely through the trees, drawn downhill,
irresistibly closer.

When she came to a clearing halfway down the wooded
slope, the Queen hid behind a bramble bush. Purple berries
draped her ears and throat like jewels. Peering through the
greenery, she gazed at the young man who commanded the
glade.

He was dark-haired, with long curls that framed his lean
features. His eyes were hazel, the color of acorns; his skin, a
golden tan. He bowed his slender body as he strained to make

music, his red lips pressing against the silver flute. Serenading the trees around him, he delved deep into the roots of sound before surging upward into tremulous trills flickering like leaves in the sunlight.

The Queen was enchanted by what she heard and what she saw. The Queen was enchanted by the music and the man.

She began to sing.

At first he couldn't hear her. The sweet notes that issued from her throat like a siren's song were so low that his ear could barely detect them. Yet his soul resonated as if it were being played upon, and he strove to mirror that secret sound in his music. Only after a while did he realize that the inspiration was coming from outside of him and not from within.

He stopped playing.

She continued to sing as he stood entranced, hardly daring to breathe, listening and looking and finally spying where she was.

Behind a leafy bough was a pale and beautiful face with eyes like stars. His heart felt faint. A strange languor crept through his limbs. He felt his blood slow as if he were dying; but if this were death what bliss it was and he welcomed it gladly, surrendering to his doom. She stopped singing when she saw that he had found her. Like a bird startled on the branch, she went to flee.

• • •

He called out to her in a voice filled with longing.

She was doubly caught now.

A faint motion shook the air, like a veil being drawn aside, as she stepped from the shadows and into the sunlight. She wore a gown of pearl-pale silk that swept the ground. White flowers crowned her red-gold hair that shone like fire.

Enthralled by this vision of a glimmering girl, he ignored the trace of fear that tremored in his mind.

They stared long at each other, fairy and mortal. Both did not really know what the other was. Both were caught in the mystery of being.

He struggled to find speech.
"Hi."
She greeted him in her first tongue, the airy language of the sky.
They looked at each other, baffled.
"Did you say hello?" they asked together.
"What?"
"I beg your pardon?"
Frowns of frustration.
"Where are you from?" he tried again. "What language is that?"

With a sudden smile, she reached out to touch his forehead. A gentle caress.

He shivered.

"There," she said, in English. "Is that better?"

"How did you do that?!"

Her dazzling smile again. All thought abandoned him.

"Now that I know what you are," she said, "I may speak with you. Yet this is not the language born of the land, which my people use also. Are you not of Ireland?"

"Taimse a foghlaim gaeilge, *if that's what you mean,"* he said. *"I'm hoping to learn more Irish while I'm here. I'm Canadian. Of Irish descent. I'm over for the year to collect tunes and work with local musicians. I'm a composer."*

"Gabha an cheoil." *She clapped her hands. "Yes, I heard this in your art. You fashion pure sound into music.* Ceol n'éan agus ceol an tsruháin. *The music of the bird and the music of the stream."*

"A smith of music?" He repeated in English the title she had given him. "What a great thing to call me." Her words fascinated him, for they brought the joining of his thoughts with the sympathy of his heart. "And you're so right about what moves me! I practice in the forest to wake the sleeping muse. I never dreamed you would actually show up in person!"

"An leannán sí faoi shuan? *You call me this? The sleeping muse?"*

Charmed, she threw back her head and laughed merrily.

The sound of her laughter shot through him like quicksilver, scalding his soul. He wanted to hear that laugh again, though he knew if he did he would be lost forever.

His fingertips brushed the white blossoms in her hair.

"Isn't it bad luck to pick hawthorn in May?" he said. "I'm told it's the flower of the Faerie Queen and she punishes anyone who touches it."

That laugh again.

They sat down together on a fallen tree trunk. He played her some of his compositions. She sang along with them. He changed his melodies to suit her rhythms so that new tunes were forged, tunes that were both human and fairy. Tunes that were woven with the thread of new love.

> *Phóg mé ar ais is phóg mé arís tú*
> *Gheill mo chroí don leannán síofrúil,*
> *Is thug mé cúl do gach aon dílseacht*
> *Nuair a phóg mé do bhéal.*

> *I kissed and kissed again*
> *Yielded to the fairy spell*
> *Left behind all love till then*
> *When I kissed your mouth.*

He recognized the ineffable truth that rose in his heart.

"Come with me," he said. "Be my love."

She was already losing her way; yet some part of her remembered as she made her last protest.

"The life of your kind is but a fleeting moment, a raft upon the sea that leaves no wake, the journey of a single day through a sleepy country, a mist dispersing, a petal falling . . ."

But her words drifted away as he kissed her mouth. And she yielded to the spell.

She walked out of the Glen of the Downs that day, hand in hand with her mortal lover.

He did not return to his homeland.

She did not return to hers.

†HiR†Y-SEVEП

*A*s the last strain of the harp resounded through the hall,
the King finished with a plaintive coda.

What is love?
It is a test beyond bounds,
A leap over death,
A thing everlasting.
It is drowning without water,
Grief in the hearty,
A blade in the back.
It is the four ends of the earth,
A battle with a specter,
Heroic deeds in defeat.
It is the wooing of an echo,
The wooing of an echo,
Throughout eternity.
Thus is my love and my passion,
My devotion to she who is my life,
My wife.

Dana struggled to return the King's gaze. She had expected a tragic tale about a queen stolen by a demon. Not this. Like an icy wave it had struck her: the realization of who the young musician was. And with great love and great pain, she had listened to the story of her parents' meeting.

And it was with great love and great pain that the Mountain King regarded her now. Great love, because she was the daughter of his beloved Queen and reflected some of her features. Great pain, because it was Dana's birth that sealed the doom of his loss.

"Thus you have heard," he told her, "the tale that will henceforth be known in Faerie as The Wooing of Edane Lasair by Her Mortal Lover."

Dana shivered to hear her mother's name said with such significance and sorrow.

Lugh's eyes darkened. The sorrow echoed in his voice.

"I searched the heavens for my Queen and through the worlds, thinking she may have lost her way. Yet in my heart I knew some terrible thing had happened. The death of winter was in the air. And though I sought her far and wide, she was not to be found. What dark king had taken her? What demon kept her in his lair?

"I did not think to look for her in the mortal realm, as she had shown no interest in humankind. They were too close to matter, too far beyond the lightness of her being. Then one day a yellow butterfly came to me and, even as his brief life faded, told of last seeing my Queen in the Glen of the Downs.

I hastened there to seek some clue of her fate. To my joy and then my anguish, I found her at last; my anguish, because she wore human guise and, forgetting her true nature, had wedded a mortal man.

"Incredulous and wrathful, I confronted them. I would strike down this man, take back my wife. But though I stood before her as her rightful husband, she did not know me. It was then I drew from their minds the tale of their union, and I saw both had fallen under a spell of love. What is more— and this, I knew, was the seal of my doom—they were await- ing a child.

"I cannot describe the ravages of despair, the rages of jealousy, and the utter powerlessness I suffered. That she had gone to another pierced my heart like a sword. My grief and desolation were beyond containment. I was broken."

It was such a sad story that Dana wept with the King whose wife had been stolen by her father. She could see how all parties were innocent and how all had suffered.

At the same time, she couldn't help the glad feelings that mingled with her sorrow. With a thrill beyond measuring she began to comprehend that her mother was a fairy Queen and she a fairy princess! But her first and overriding emotion was one of relief. At last she knew for certain that it wasn't her fault. It wasn't her birth or some flaw of her character or some terrible thing she had done that drove her mother away and broke her father's heart.

"She must've remembered," Dana said softly. "That's why she left. She must've remembered."

As the truth dawned on the fairy Queen's daughter, the question arose.

Where was she?

That night, Dana lay in her bedchamber in the palace on Lugnaquillia. It was a lady's bower draped with fine tapestries of unicorns in gardens and winged horses in the clouds. The high bed was frothed with white lace embroidered with pearls. A fire burned in the grate beneath a marble mantel. Ensconsed in the bed, Dana gazed up at the glass ceiling that looked out on the night. A star fell out of the sky! And then another! She could hardly contain the huge truth that overflowed her being. Her mother came from those stars and so did she! She was half fairy!

She raised her hand, pale in the dimness. Concentrating, she tried to work some magic. A simple thing: a cup of cocoa.

Nothing happened.

"It is buried deep within you," Lugh had told her, "like a hidden treasure. You must seek it out."

They had spoken of many things as they strolled through his gardens at twilight. The flowerbeds glowed in the dusk, emitting a sweet scent. The fountains splashed merrily.

"I assumed you knew what you were," he said, "as you ate our food without qualm. Because of the silver blood in your veins, it holds little power over you."

Dana's grin was sheepish. "I ate 'cause I was hungry.

And it all looked so good. I was always going to worry about it later."

That made him laugh.

The biggest revelation concerned her mission.

"Do you not know yet? The message belongs as much to you as to me, for it asks about your mother."

Where is the light to bridge the darkness?

That was when Dana's heart began to beat so rapidly that she almost fainted. The interconnectedness of things stunned her. That her mission, her message, and her wish to find her mother were all one and the same!

"Do you know where she is?" she whispered.

The King's eyes dimmed.

"I have striven all day to clear the webs from my mind. Too much was shrouded by the spell. There were times when I lay dreaming that I shared my Beloved's torment; yet each effort I made to wake, so that I might help her, only caused the bonds to tighten. From what I recall, I believe she is a prisoner in Dún Scáith, the Fort of the Shades. How this came about I do not know, for it can only have happened when I lay bound in sleep."

"The demon!" Dana said suddenly. "Saint Kevin told me it's been here before. Doing things as part of a bigger plan!"

Lugh's face twisted with anguish. "Her light is a great weapon against the shadow. Yet it must have taken her."

The same pain struck Dana. "We've got to save her!"

Lugh laid a restraining hand on Dana's shoulder.

"I must kill the demon first. That is my duty. He has been found, lurking in human shape at the Glen of the Downs. It was already my intention to go this night to rid the Kingdom of him. Now I do it also for my Queen. Then I shall free her."

"You go for the demon," Dana said fiercely. "I'll go for my mother! Tell me how to find Dún Scáith!"

She could see that Lugh agreed with her, though other emotions warred in his features.

"Perhaps this is right," he said reluctantly. "The mission was always yours." He continued to struggle until he made up his mind. "So be it. But you must not set out until the demon has been vanquished. I would not have you harmed and nor would she, for you are the child of her heart. Rest tonight. I will send you a message when all is well. Tomorrow you will embark on the last stage of your quest."

Dana was prepared to obey him. For now. She had come to like and trust the King, despite the conflict of loyalties and the final twist in the tale. There would be no reunion of her parents, no return to the family of her hopes and dreams. Her mother was not human but a fairy Queen, whose true husband was the King of the Mountain. With the innate sense of justice typical of the young, Dana accepted that it had to be this way, though she couldn't help but be sad for herself and her father.

He regarded her warmly.

"You might have been my child, Dana. I shall always think of you as my stepdaughter in the mortal realm. Will you accept me as your fairy godfather?"

That made her laugh.

Now Dana turned in the bed and closed her eyes. A final thought wound through her mind before she dropped into sleep.

No matter what happens, tomorrow I'm going to find her.

THIRTY-EIGHT

The next morning, Dana didn't stop to eat the breakfast
that appeared in her bedroom. She dressed, grabbed her
cloak, and ran downstairs to the hall. The first thing she
noticed was the pervasive gloom. Some of the ladies were
weeping. No one would meet her eyes.

The harper came forward to give her the bad news.

"The King has fought the demon throughout the night,
yet still the battle rages."

She felt sick, sensing that the harper hadn't told her the
worst.

"Is he all right?" she whispered.

"His wounds are great," came the reluctant reply. "He is
in peril."

Dana bit back a cry. "I've got to find my mother! The
message says she can fight the darkness. I need to go now!"

The harper blenched. It was obvious he was torn.

"The King has commanded we keep you here until he
sends word. We cannot gainsay him."

"I'm not your prisoner!" she argued. "Look, the light is
our only hope. All I need is someone to show me the way to

Dún Scáith. *If you can't or won't, how about finding me someone who will?"*

The harper's face cleared. He bowed to her.

"My lady, you have wisdom beyond your years. This I can do. Return to your own world. I will send you a guide."

As the harper waved his hand, Dana felt the slight push that sent her through the veil.

The palace and gardens were gone. She was back on the broad summit of Lugnaquillia, surrounded by bog and windy mountains.

Moments later, the harper's promise was fulfilled. A little gray mouse came scampering through the grass and up to Dana. Then it changed before her eyes into a little old lady with a whiskery face.

Dana could have hugged Mrs. Woodhouse, but the situation was urgent.

"Can you help me find my mother? I've got to hurry! For her sake and the King's!"

"Yes, my pet," Mrs. Woodhouse assured her. "I am here to show you the way."

She led Dana to the western edge of the South Prison. It overlooked the bog between Lugnaquillia and the lower slopes of Slievemaan. Dana shuddered. This was the place where Lugh had lain buried and where he had risen up in his madness to cause the bog-burst.

"It is the path you must go," the old woman said quietly, "the dark trail of your story which you must follow.

Be of good courage. Do not fear your own ruin, for there is a treasure within you."

"Are you coming with me?" Dana asked, though she already knew the answer.

"This is your quest, *a leanbh*. Your mission. When a girl goes to seek the Great Mother, no one may go with her. It is a sacred journey she undertakes alone."

"Slievemaan," Dana murmured to herself. "*Sliabh na mBan*. The Women's Mountain."

Mrs. Woodhouse handed Dana the leather satchel she had left behind in the palace.

"You will need this."

Assuming it held provisions, Dana slung the satchel over her shoulder. And with her golden-brown cloak wrapped around her, she set off. Though she felt nervous and excited and almost dizzy with fear, one thought overrode all emotion: *I'm going to find my mother.*

She stopped only once to look back at Mrs. Woodhouse.

The old woman's appearance had changed yet again. Half lost in the rising mist, draped in a gray mantle, a gigantic female figure stood against the sky.

Dana continued on her journey, making her way across boggy ground, past craters of black peat exposed by wind and rain. Clouds shrouded the morning sun. A cold mist streamed over the landscape. Soon she could see only a few feet in front of her. Banks of gray haze hemmed her in on all sides. Lone trees stood out like the masts of tall ships emerging from a fog at sea. Her face felt wet, as if with tears.

She was walking in the Wicklow Mountains and yet she wasn't. To bolster her courage, she tried to imagine the wolf padding alongside her; tried to think of Saint Kevin and his quiet strength. But neither image held for long. Nothing could hold firm in this liminal space on the threshold of the unknown. Though her fear was growing, she didn't think of turning back. Half fairy, half mortal, this was her birthright: to walk between the worlds.

It seemed like hours before the sun broke through the clouds to burn away the mist. She found herself walking in a green valley not unlike Glendalough. The sudden beauty of it made her smile.

Then they came.

At first she thought they were rain clouds speeding over the mountainside and into the vale. Then, as they drew nearer, she saw what they were: a swarm of black crows with their eyes sewn shut. As they poured into the glen, they attacked everything around them: ripping out plants and stripping trees, tearing apart animals, devouring birds and insects. The silence of the slaughter made it seem more terrible. A fog of blood obscured the scene.

When the demon birds departed, there was nothing left.

Dana stood on barren ground. Not a single blade of grass in sight. No bird sang. No creature stirred. A chill wind wailed around her. A gray light dimmed all. Was this *Dún Scáith?* The Fort of the Shades? Or was it *Dún Eadóchais?* The Fort of Despair?

She could sense the suffering of the land. With each step she took, it seeped into her body and withered her soul. *Generations have trod, have trod, have trod.* With a new and dawning horror, she realized she was not walking on solid earth, but over a cesspit of noxious substances. Her stomach heaved as the sweet sickly smells rose up.

And even as she recognized the worst of her nightmares, it began to happen.

The noisome mud gurgled like a throat. Now the ground opened up to swallow her. She fell into a stinking pit. Like a wild thing she tried to claw her way back up; but not even the silver nails in her shoes could help her climb the slimy walls.

She screamed for help.

Her screams fell like stones into a bottomless well.

She screamed again.

And again.

A sudden thought struck her. This was not only her nightmare, but her mother's too! The hellish dream of a light being trapped in matter. It could only mean one thing. Her mother was near!

Dana started to shout at the top of her lungs.

"*MAMA! MAMA!*"

A noise sounded at the top of the pit. Dana gulped back her cries as a white face peered over the edge.

It wasn't her mother.

THIRTY-NINE

Honor!

A slender white arm reached down toward Dana. Jumping to catch it, she hung on for dear life. As she scrambled up the wall, she felt as if she were being dragged from the grave.

"Oh, thank you!" she cried as she clambered out of the pit. "I'm so—"

Her words died as she stared at the older girl.

Honor was shivering uncontrollably. Drenched to the skin, she was deathly pale, almost blue. The jeans and T-shirt were those she had worn briefly at the fair, and once again they were wet and strewn with seaweed.

"Do y-y-you . . . know . . . wh-wh-o I am?" she asked Dana.

Her eyes were dark and empty; her voice, lifeless.

"Oh God," Dana whispered.

Worse was to come. Even as Dana watched, a red stain appeared on the girl's T-shirt, as if she were bleeding from the heart.

"You're wounded!"

Honor shrugged indifferently.

"It c-c-comes and g-g-goes."

Dana could bear it no longer. As the waves of horror washed over her, she backed away from her friend.

"*Help me,*" Dana whispered, pulling her fairy cloak around her.

Only then did she remember her satchel, still strapped over her shoulder. Acting on instinct, she opened it. There inside was a little bronze pan, some pieces of kindling, a tinderbox, and a handful of hazelnuts. She looked around her. She was standing on an empty plain that had been blasted by fire. The stubble of vegetation was burned and blackened. The air was ashen.

Honor followed her look and shuddered.

"N-n-nothing l-l-lives here."

Dana could feel the horror trying to reclaim her, but she fought it off. Removing her cloak, she threw it over Honor's shoulders. The other girl stood straighter as the golden-brown folds enveloped her. Now Dana trembled in the bitter cold, but she knew what to do.

There was enough kindling to start a small fire with the tinderbox. Just as she had hoped, the fairy wood burned without being consumed. The two girls hunkered down in front of the flames. Both kept their eyes on the fire, as if to ward off the shadows that hovered beyond. Dana was silently thanking Mrs. Woodhouse as she placed the pan over the fire and roasted a few hazelnuts. The moment she popped one into her mouth, she felt strengthened; but when she offered the pan to Honor, she was met with a blank stare.

Dana took a hazelnut and put it to the girl's lips.

"*Eat*," she commanded.

Honor obeyed. Moments later, a faint flush entered her cheeks.

"More," Honor whispered.

Between them, they finished what was in the pan.

Dana could feel the courage surging through her veins. Her mind grew calm and lucid, ready to deal with the situation. Honor was clearly restored. When the older girl insisted on returning the cloak, Dana saw that the red wound had disappeared and her clothes were dry. Yet it wasn't the blue-eyed Lady who crouched opposite her, but the human girl Honor sometimes became.

"Dana?" she said at last, her voice shaking with emotion.

"Yes, it's me!" Dana almost cried with relief. "What happened? What are you doing here?"

"This is *Dún Scáith*. The Fort of the Shades." Honor glanced at the desolate plain around them. "I came into the Mountain Kingdom, as I said I would, to find out why Lugh was asleep, and maybe discover what the demon was doing here. I wanted to protect you but . . . I . . . fell into darkness."

"Did the demon capture you?" Dana thought of her mother. "Did he bring you here?"

"Yes and no." Honor gave her an odd look. "I'm only beginning to understand the nature of this place. It's not the monster outside that holds us here, but the monster within. Yet, for me, these two are the same. I can't explain it, Dana, but I can show you: the nightmare I was reliving before you called me from the shadows. If you will, take my hand."

Dana hesitated, balking at the prospect of another nightmarish experience. But she needed to know more about *Dún Scáith* if she was going to free her mother. She reached out for Honor.

As soon as they clasped hands, the landscape changed. The sudden shock of color made Dana's head spin. Instead of the dreary gray, there was blue sky, green trees, and sunlit rock. She knew at once where she was. On the hillside of Bray Head, the small mountain by the seashore of the town where she lived.

Honor was beside her; but when she spoke, her voice echoed in Dana's mind.

Because of the spell on the marker stones, I could not stay long in the Kingdom as a fairy. I donned my human guise. But since that part of me is dead . . .

Dana shuddered, remembering Honor as the ghost of a drowned girl. Was that how her friend had died? But what about the wound? The blood? Where did that come from?

They were standing at the edge of a cliff overlooking the Irish Sea. Cold waters crashed on the rocks below.

This is where I died.

Suddenly they were on a narrow shelf just below the cliff edge. Dana let out a cry as the wind whipped around the corner and made her teeter. A hang glider called out a warning from above. Now a whirring sound came behind her. She glanced over her shoulder. At first she wasn't sure what she was looking at. There was a crack in the air itself. Then a fiery arrow shot through it! Beside her, Honor let out a death cry. The arrow had pierced her back and heart. For one awful second, she was impaled against the rock wall.

Then the arrow dissolved.

Honor jerked back in shock and surprise. That was when she lost her balance. Screaming, arms waving, she plummeted into the sea.

Dazed, Dana saw her friend's body strike the water below. Yet she also saw a luminous imprint of Honor tumble through the rend in the air.

It was like trying to view a puzzle that contained two pictures at the same time. There was Honor sinking through the murky sea. But there she was, also, at the bottom of a well of blue light.

And in that blue well, she wasn't dead; but lay fast asleep, like a pale flower, shining and innocent, a newborn soul.

"Oh," said Dana softly.

Let me tell you what you see. While I died in the water,

my soul fell through the crack into an in-between place. There I slept for a year and a day.

Dana was glad that Honor explained what happened next, for the images were so startling and alien.

A great golden eagle dived into the blue well. Like a gull plucking a shell from the sea, it fished Honor out. Yet the eagle's face was human and seemed to mirror Honor's own.

That is my twin sister. She undertook a mission to save me.

The eagle's wings enfolded the sleeping girl like a shawl of golden feathers that were also tongues of flame. The whole scene exploded with fire. Now Honor stepped out of the conflagration, awake and reborn, with gold-tinted skin and hair crowned with flowers. She glided toward the rend in the air that hung over Bray Head like a fiery mouth.

Look closely! Do you see it?

Dana's heart tightened. There was something caught in the crack. Red and segmented, a writhing shape, it burned in the flames. Dana recognized the thing that had pursued her through the mountains. It was dying in the fire.

But now as Honor stepped through the rend, the red shape broke free and dropped behind her. And when Honor disappeared through the crack just before it closed, the demon fell onto the summit of Bray Head.

The images faded. Dana and Honor were back on the

dark plain in front of their campfire. Honor's voice echoed with guilt and horror.

"The Midsummer Fire would have killed the demon except for me. The shadow of the Destroyer used *my* shadow to free itself. It's all my fault. I am the one who brought this doom upon us; the thing that threatens both worlds! This truth I discovered when I came to *Dún Scáith* and I cannot bear it."

She buried her face in her hands and wept.

Dana didn't know what to say; but she was beginning to see how people got trapped in the Fort of the Shades.

"Don't do this!" she said, at last. "You're only one person. How can you blame yourself for something this big? You didn't ask for the demon to come. And anyway, he's been here before. You didn't start this. You're just one small part of it."

As Dana spoke, she hurriedly roasted more hazelnuts and made Honor eat them. Though she wanted to take some herself, she didn't. She needed to ensure there was enough for her mother.

It took a while for Honor to recover. She smiled at Dana with warmth and affection.

"Thanks," she said softly. Her voice sounded abashed. "I came here to help you and instead you've helped me! Let's go find your mother."

Dana shook her head.

"No, you've done enough. You showed me what I need to know. You can't stay here. You've got to go home."

The golden tint seeped through Honor's skin. Her eyes gleamed like blue stars. But even as the Lady reached out for Dana, her touch began to fade.

"Dear one, *a chroí*. Thou art a trueheart and a braveheart. May you fare well on your own journey into the dark."

Dana stood up slowly. She was alone on the burnt plain, surrounded by shadows. Reluctantly, she turned away from the fire. She knew what lay ahead. She understood. It wasn't the demon that imprisoned the Queen in *Dún Scáith*.

Dana hoisted her satchel over her shoulder and drew her cloak around her. Then she set out.

To free her mother from the private hell she had made for herself.

FORTY

Dana trudged over the bleak plain. In the distance rose a jagged range of mountains. The sky was gray; the ground, ashen. Dread seeped into her bones along with the chill. The strength of the fairy food was leaving her, but she wouldn't take more. She needed the hazelnuts for her mother who had been too long in that place. Would they be enough? Could they draw her from the shadows? And what if they didn't?

Dana pushed the dark thoughts away. She knew they were part of *Dún Scáith*. It would try to attack her with doubts and fears.

She had decided to head for the mountains, though they seemed so far away. She couldn't think of anywhere else to go. But with each step she took, she felt more drained and hopeless, more insubstantial. Would she end up like Honor? A lonely ghost, wandering lost? And if she did, who would call her from the shadows?

Stop it.

Sometimes she cried out for her mother.

"EDANE LASAIR! WHERE ARE YOU? CAN YOU HEAR ME?"

Her words never traveled far, but fell around her like stones.

Sometimes she whispered.

"Mum? You there? Mum?"

Yet she did not falter, nor did she turn back. And as she pushed on, drawing nearer to the uplands, she felt herself turning into a thing of steel and stone; a creature that neither weariness nor despair nor endless miles could defeat. And she began to know in her heart that she would prevail.

Yea, though I walk through the valley of the shadow of death.

At last she reached the mountains and the path that led through them. Soon she found herself on a narrow road that wound along the side of a cliff. The bare rock was dark-red, sheering miles above her and plunging miles below. The air had grown dimmer. Was night falling? Could she continue in the dark?

She was just beginning to wonder if she should turn back, when a light bobbed on the trail ahead of her. It appeared to be swaying back and forth. As it approached her, she saw the hooded figure carrying a lantern, and the donkey behind it, laden with baskets.

By the time the stranger reached her, Dana had given up trying to discern its gender. The features inside the hood kept wavering; one minute, male, the next, female. To further confuse her, the masculine face was sometimes soft and gentle, while the feminine could be cruel and fierce. In the end, Dana accepted that this person was both man and woman, and somehow neither.

"Who are you?" she asked in wonder.

She was glad to hear her own voice. A good solid sound. Not a ghost yet.

"I am the Singer of Tales."

The voice was melodic, yet again lacked the distinction of gender. What followed next had the same bizarre logic of a dream. The Singer pointed to the panniers on either side of the donkey. They were filled with books.

"Choose one."

Dana searched through them tentatively: paper scrolls and Egyptian papyri; tablets of wax and clay; manuscripts of vellum; hand-sewn texts bound in calfskin; even thin sheets of gold with letters worked into the metal. As well as illustrated tomes and glossy paperbacks, there were talking books, computer disks, and videotapes. A metallic box glowed and hummed with laser, electronic, and holographic devices that she guessed were books yet to be invented.

A few volumes she recognized from Gabriel's collection, but most were a mystery to her. *The Book of Time. The Book of Names. The Red Book of Westmarch. The Yellow Book of Leccan. The Book of the Dun Cow. The Book of*

Lindisfarne. The Books of Mica Schist. The Mahabharata. The Mabinogion. The Book of the Dead. The Book of the Living.

She picked one whose title caught her eye. *The Book of Childhood.* The cover showed a wide river flowing through a green countryside. There were hundreds, no thousands, maybe millions of children gathered on the riverbanks. All were drinking the water. Some scooped it up with cracked cups, while others used their bare hands.

Dana was mesmerized by the image.

"What does it mean?" she asked.

"The river is the inexhaustible Source of Life," said the Singer. "The children who drink from cracked cups were loved from birth. Though the cup is flawed, as with all human love, still it is a gift that serves them. The children who drink from their own hands were not given love. They must help themselves to the water of life."

"That's sad," murmured Dana.

"The saddest tale of all," the Singer agreed.

Dana thought of Gabe. Though things hadn't been perfect, she had definitely got a cup.

She noticed a book under the Singer's arm and peered at the title.

The Book of Dreams.

"What about that one?"

"You may not see it. It is a tale to be told in your future."

Dana returned to the baskets, digging further. Here

was the world at her fingertips! Everything she ever wanted to know at a glance. She rummaged through books on dragons, ancient stones, and the creation of the universe. She was about to grab another pile, when she stopped. She could be there forever, lost in thoughts and ideas. Was this the test? A trick or a trap? She tossed the books back.

"You must choose one," the Singer of Tales insisted.

Exasperated, Dana closed her eyes and grabbed the first thing at hand. It was bound in white leather and stamped with gold.

The Book of Obscured Memories.

"How about this one?"

Inside the Singer's cowl, the face changed. Saint Kevin's gray eyes gazed out at her.

" 'Obscured' means secret or hidden away, little sister. Memories may be obscured for good reason. Before you look, take heed and take care. *No one can save you from this. None of us may be kept from the truth; it is an appointment we meet either in life or at death.*"

Dana was suddenly afraid. More afraid than she had been throughout the quest. She wasn't expecting it to come so suddenly and without warning, yet here it was: the challenge of her own dark truth in the Fort of the Shades.

Something stirred inside her, deep in the abyss. Some monstrous memory she had buried long ago. Every part of her screamed. *Put the book down! Leave it shut! Don't look!*

She was shaking so hard, she thought she might faint. Like a small child waking alone in the dead of night, she faced the terror of the unknown. She wanted to hide in the covers. She wanted to call for her dad.

Dana steadied herself. She had no choice. If this was what she had to do to find her mother, then so be it.

She opened the book.

FORŤY-OΠE

The young musician rented a little house near the Glen of the Downs, not far from the place where he had met his glimmering girl. She told him she wanted to live in the woods and close to the mountains, for she abhorred the crowded towns and cities.

On their wedding day, when they went to the Registry Office, she clung to his arm and wouldn't let go. The loud noises of the traffic made her flinch. Her nose wrinkled at the smells in the air.

But when he brought her back to the cottage, she clapped her hands with delight; for it was surrounded by oak trees, and there were wild roses trailing over the doors and windows.

"Is this my home?" she murmured as he carried her over the threshold.

The walls were freshly papered with a pattern of green leaves. The floors had blue tiles and the roof, wooden beams. A fireplace stood in every room. The furnishings were old and old-fashioned.

"Forever and a day," was his reply.

He loved that she was a country girl with simple tastes. Worshipping her, he accepted her quirks without question or complaint. She would not eat salt. Nor could iron enter the house. And there was to be no mention of her family.

One warm summer night, they lay on a blanket outdoors to watch the stars fall over the treetops.

"Tell me something about your childhood," he urged her. "Where did you grow up?"

Her laugh was light, but a veil dimmed her eyes.

"Do not seek to know too much about me, my love. You are from Canada and I am from Ireland. What else do you need to know? Accept what is and be content. I've forgotten a lot about my past and maybe that's best for our happiness together."

Did he suffer a moment of disquiet, then? Did he feel the darkness of the shadow cast by events to come? Did he sense the approach of their parting and the pain that lay in wait for him?

The book contained moving pictures as well as words. Dana drank in every image of her mother, as someone who had hungered and thirsted for such a sight. Edane Lasair made a pretty human, dressed in floppy hats and brightly colored clothes. The fiery hair of her true nature had turned to strawberry blond, tumbling over her shoulders. She often appeared dreamy and distracted, yet her look was gentle and her mouth quick to smile.

Nine months later their daughter was born. She was a sweet-natured baby with her father's dark hair and her mother's eyes that shone like the stars.

Not yet twenty, Gabriel worked hard to support his little family. He coached music students, busked on Dublin's busy streets, and played on the bandshell by the seafront in the summer. They didn't need a lot of money as their rent was small and they lived modestly. Edane made a small garden, growing most of the fruits and vegetables they ate. Flowers brightened every room. Their home was filled with light and music, joy and beauty.

From time to time odd things would happen.

The baby was only six months old when Edane left her on a mat under a tree in the garden. The leaves of the young rowan sheltered the infant while flickering with sunlight to keep her entertained. Back in the kitchen, Edane kept watch on her daughter from the window as she baked a blackberry pie. Turning but a moment to put the tart in the oven, she looked back again to check on her child and let out a scream. The baby was surrounded by wild animals. A fox licked her face. A badger was nudging her out of a damp spot. Birds flitted around her as she tried to catch them.

At the sound of Edane's cry, the animals fled, leaving the infant in tears.

Another time, Edane woke in the night with a mother's instinct and glanced over at the baby's cradle. Light hov-

ered in the air above it. Gurgles of laughter rose up. Hazy with sleep, Edane made a questioning noise. The light disappeared. Silence ensued.

Dana watched her mother's reactions. How she ignored or denied the strange things she saw. How quickly she forgot them. The spell of humanity was woven so thickly around her, it repelled anything that threatened to unravel it.

At three years of age, the child was a stocky little girl with bunches of dark curls and a mischievous temperament. Curious, courageous, she loved to run and she loved to climb trees. No longer a baby, she was growing fast, discovering who and what she might be.

One day when her father was away at work, she escaped from the garden and into the woods. Climbing high into the branches of an oak tree, she found herself unable to get down again. She didn't cry, but waited for her mother to find her. It was Edane who cried and became upset, who called her "a bold girl." The child was put to bed for a nap, kicking and screaming. When her mother went to kiss her, the little girl pushed her angrily away and kept on yelling.

"I hate you!"

Patiently shushing her daughter's shouts, Edane drew the curtains to make the room dim. Then she sang a lullaby.

Seothó, a thoil, ná goil go fóill,
Seothó, a thoil, ná goil aon deoir,
Seothó, a linbh, a chumainn's a stóir.

Hush, dear heart, no need to cry,
Hush, dear heart, no need for tears,
Hush, my child, my love and treasure.

Soothed by the song, the little girl grew quiet. Her eye-lashes fluttered softly; a smile crossed her face.

Edane tiptoed to the door. It was only when she turned for a final look that she saw the glow around her daughter's bed.

Dana was sitting up and gazing at her palms. With a squeal of delight, she cupped her hands and offered them to her mother. They brimmed over with golden light.

Edane's features twisted with anguish as memory slashed like a knife, cutting the spell that bound her. In horror, she backed away from the child who carried her mark, the sign of the Light-Bearer. She backed away from her child as she remembered who she was, her abandoned life, and her beloved, the King, whom she had forsaken. She backed away from her child as her mind and spirit broke.

Then she ran from that place, never to return.

Forty-two

With the force of a blow, Dana remembered that moment. The shock. The agony. The severing of the bond between mother and child. She was a bad girl and she drove her mother away.

Deep inside, the monster rose.

It was something you did. You are the reason your mother left. You are the one who broke your father's heart. It was you who tore your family apart.

Dana dropped the book as if it had burned her. A cry tore from her throat. She ran away from the Singer of Tales, the Lord of Misrule. Away from the truth.

⸻ ☙ ❧ ⸻

Far in the mountains, a child was lost. She stumbled over the bogs, sobbing and weeping. Her feet sank into the soft ground. The winds were cold on her face. She ran without sense or purpose, her heart as wild as the hearts of birds, shattered like an egg that had fallen from the nest. Her cries mingled with the lament of the sheep scattering before her.

Maammaaa.

Maammaaa.

Inside her mind, the serpent coiled, squeezing and strangling.

It was your fault. You are to blame. You are the monster at the heart of your family.

⸺ ⸺

For many long lonely hours, Dana staggered through the wind and rain. Eventually she came out of the mountains and into the foothills in sight of the sea. She passed a derelict cottage with broken windows and an overgrown garden. Now she stood at the edge of a forested ridge overlooking a glen that was severed by a road. Dimly she recognized where she was.

Battered by the storms of the previous day, the tree houses in the Glen of the Downs hung askew like ruined nests. The site was deserted. Led by their betrayer Murta, the eco-warriors were on the farthest side of the vale, digging up an illegal dump. Big Bob patrolled the trees alone, without fear or suspicion. The sun had set. No one worked in the dark.

As twilight descended over the valley, the shadows in the forest deepened.

From where she stood, Dana could see what the eco-warriors couldn't. In the silence of the evening, bulldozers advanced on the glen like a convoy of tanks of an invading army. Behind them came the trucks that bore the chainsaws, the iron machinery of the war on nature.

With her fairy eyes, Dana could also see the lines of refugees leaving the valley. Birds and small animals, the spirits of trees and flowers, all fled the coming destruction of their homes. As Dana witnessed the exodus, images flashed through her mind of similar scenes she had seen on the television: columns of the displaced and expelled, filing down roads or through frozen forests, children and old people and weeping women, all driven before the onslaught of the shadow.

Across the glen, she caught sight of two titanic figures locked in mortal combat on top of the ridge. The King had lost his weapons and grappled bare-handed with a writhing foe. No longer inside Murta, the demon wore its own shape. More chimera than real, it was blood-red and monstrous, with a segmented body and long coiling tail. Every part of it was burned and blistered, yet it raged unabated. Dana's heart quailed. Lugh's limbs looked twisted and broken. He bled from many wounds. Would her godfather die in the struggle?

The first iron blade cut through the bole of a tree. Dana's fairy blood quivered. Sharp teeth sawed through the wood. A slender birch toppled. Sap seeped from the bloodied stump. More trees were set upon. More crashed to the earth. A dimness settled over the woods as life and light were extinguished.

Big Bob came running as soon as he heard the chainsaws. He knew he had been betrayed. Sickened and defeated, he made his last stand by an ancient oak, as the trees fell around him like soldiers on the battlefield.

On the height above, the King had fallen. Shrieking its triumph, the demon lifted him high in the air, ready to hurl him down the ridge. Lugh would die with the trees. His eyes were dark with anguish. He could not save his people. He could not save his Queen.

It was the slaughter of the trees that woke Dana's fairy self. As the silver lightning shot through her veins, she let out a cry of rage for the Mother Earth.

MAMA!

She looked down at her hands. Ever since that fateful day, she had refused to let it happen. She had denied her gift. In that one searing moment, she had learned to hate it, banishing it forever to the dark of her psyche.

Now the monster rose up from the lake of her mind and Dana saw that it was beautiful and shining with light. She smiled with love at the gift of her birthright. She bowed her head to acknowledge its beauty.

By making peace with your own monster you diminish evil's power, over yourself and in the world.

She cupped her hands together. As the golden light welled up in her palms, she raised them to the sky in offering.

Now the light shone out like a beacon to reach the one who was lost in darkness; the one who had heard her cry in the shadowlands; the one whose eyes were beginning to open as she ran toward the light.

A giantess came running out of the west and over the mountains. Her fiery hair streamed behind her like a comet. Her hands gleamed with the brightness she bore.

On the eastern ridge, Dana's palms spilled over to suffuse the sky with a radiant arc. When the giantess stopped on the opposite ridge, her light poured forth to join with Dana's.

Under the glow of the golden bridge, the Glen of the Downs was lit up like day.

Evil works best undercover in darkness, in secret and silence, through furtive action, covert operations and clandestine relations, when no one is certain, where no one can see. Who can fight shadows? What is being fought? But in the glare of the light, the motorists driving through the glen couldn't help but see. The images were too stark to be denied. Ancient trees falling. Chainsaws cutting. Bulldozers ploughing great ruts in the earth. And one man alone, arms around an old oak, face wet with tears.

Everyone knew about the protest. Many did not support it. They wanted the road widened so they could drive faster. They didn't care about trees or nature or the life of the valley.

But there were others who agreed with the tree people, who had made contributions and signed endless petitions. They saw Big Bob standing alone and they knew in their hearts it was time to act. Whether big or small, each had a part to play.

A silver Mercedes screeched to a stop at the side of the road. A middle-aged businessman jumped out. He ran to the nearest tree marked for felling and put his arms round it, placing his body between the bark and the blade.

A secretary on her way home, after working late, pulled up in her little Ford Fiesta. She ignored the mud on her high heels as she picked her tree and ran to protect it.

Now a local builder, out with his children for an evening drive, saw the others guarding their trees. He stopped his van—"FOR OUTDOOR WORK, I'M YOUR MAN"—and he and his three girls tumbled out. Holding the youngest in his arms, he blocked the path of a bulldozer, while the older two stood on either side of him.

As more and more drivers pulled into the shoulder, a human chain of defense quickly formed around the trees.

As below, so above. Even as the light had filled the valley, calling up the resolve of every trueheart and braveheart, so, too, it brought strength to the King high on the ridge. Now the demon screeched and cowered in the brightness. Now Lugh rose up to fight again. Taking hold of the monster, he flung it into the Irish Sea, where it sank beneath the waves and dissolved in the brine.

Following the light that shone over the glen, the eco-warriors came rushing back to camp. In an instant they were shinnying up trunks and swinging on ropes, as cheers and war cries resounded through the valley.

Shortly after came the wail of sirens as police cars converged on the scene. And then the media. All efforts to work halted.

The battle was won.

—∽ ∾—

Dana waited as the shining figure came toward her. Too impossibly young to be a mother, Edane was no longer a giantess but a shy slender woman. She looked at Dana as one who had hungered and thirsted for such a sight.

"Mama?" Dana whispered.

Dana knew her, but didn't know her. She was the mother her child-mind dimly remembered, appearing still to be in her teens. Dana was trembling. She barely heard her mother murmur. *Child of my heart, blood of my blood.*

And though Dana longed to go to her, to be touched and held by her, she was unable to move. She felt cold and stiff.

"Why did you leave me?" The words had been frozen so long inside, they were like jagged icicles as sharp as knives. "Why did you go?"

Pain marred Edane's beautiful features. Tears welled in the blue fairy eyes.

"I was lost, my little one. I fell between the worlds. Between those I loved in one and he whom I loved in the other. I have wandered blind in the dark, unable to find my way out."

"In the dark?" Distrust etched Dana's voice. The old anger flared. The unappeasable rage against a mother who had abandoned her child. "How? You carry your own light!"

Edane held out her hands as if to plead. Gold streamed from her palms.

Without thinking, Dana lifted her hands in response. It was the same movement she had made years ago.

"Don't you see, my daughter?" Edane said softly. "It

has returned to me only this day. I lost the light when I lost you. For I am the Light-Bearer and you are the Light that I bore."

And Dana suddenly understood. Holding back no longer, she ran into her mother's arms.

FORTY-THREE

D ana could have stayed there forever, happy and at peace in her mother's arms. She remembered the softness and the scent of apple blossom. All the things she had ever wanted to tell Edane crowded into her mind and onto her tongue; stories from school, tales of her football gang, the boy she secretly liked but had mentioned to no one, the trophy she had won in the Irish language competition . . .

"Mum," she began.

Edane, a stór! *Edane, my love!*

The King's cries rang out across the glen.

Mother and daughter broke apart. It was an awkward moment. Dana could see that Edane was torn, reluctant to leave her child but yearning, also, to go to her husband. Dana herself felt confused. She cared for Lugh, but didn't want him there. A surge of anger shot through her. She reached out for her mother and held on tightly.

Gently, Edane separated from her daughter.

"I will return to you *soon,*" she said softly.

And like a flame in the wind, she was gone.

Dana watched as the two shining figures met on the ridge opposite her. They stood apart for some time. She wondered if too much had happened between them. If they wouldn't be able to bridge the past. Then they moved toward each other and embraced beneath the stars, and it looked as if they would remain that way forever.

In that moment, Dana felt truly alone.

It was time to go home.

Slowly she made her way down the wooded slope. She would go to the eco-camp and find Big Bob. Get him to ring her dad. As she pushed her way through the bracken and briars, she struggled against the pall of disillusionment. It all seemed such a letdown. She had succeeded in her quest and achieved her dream, yet she didn't feel happy or even glad. Nothing had turned out as she had hoped or dreamed. Though she was overjoyed to have found her mother, she still suffered the same feelings of absence and loss. Edane looked too young to be the mom of a twelve-year-old. And it was already clear that she wouldn't stay with Dana, but would return to live with her husband, the King.

Lost in sad thoughts, Dana didn't see Yallery Brown until she bumped into him.

His brown paper clothes rustled like autumn leaves. His eyes blinked through the straggles of hair.

"Bejapers, there's a face as long as yer arm," he said. "And where on earth do ye think yer off to, missyella?"

"Home," she said, too miserable to elaborate.

"Is yer story finished, then?" He looked surprised.

Dana nodded.

Yallery shook his head, and the long hair danced around him like a bird's nest caught in an eddy of wind.

"What? Did the oul fat lady sing? Are ye tellin' me I missed her?"

Despite herself, Dana started to giggle.

"Asha, it isn't over yet, *a leanbh*," he chided. "Ye look divil a bit like a happy-ever-after."

He was already rummaging in his pockets. Before Dana could say anything, he had taken out a dandelion, and huffed and puffed her away.

When Dana landed on the summit of Lugnaquillia, she found the mountain lit up like a millennium cake. A thousand tall candles and flaming torches illumined the night. The castle itself was ablaze with chandeliers sparkling through the crystal walls. Music wafted out the open casements to be echoed by minstrels wandering in the gardens. Banners and flags fluttered on the parapets. Silken pavilions were pitched on the dim lawns. The air resounded with the revelry of the crowds who danced and sang and played. All creatures great and small, all beings bright and beautiful, had obviously come to celebrate the return of the Queen.

Dana hovered at the edges of the throng. She was hoping to spot Ivy or Honor or anyone else she knew. Still dressed in her traveling clothes, she felt out of place, as if she had stumbled onto some stranger's party. She wished Yallery hadn't sent her there.

Wandering aimlessly, she arrived at the crater that contained the white saucer in which she and Ivy had made their escape from the demon. A shudder ran through her at the thought of Murta. But everything looked different. The hollow was garlanded in sweet-scented roses of white and yellow. There were little ladders and stiles to invite people in. Squeals of terror and delight echoed through the air. Dana climbed up to see.

The crater was packed with odd sods and bods waiting for the saucer, like people lined up for a Disney attraction. With a great whoosh it arrived, carrying a gaggle of screeching boggles. Dana looked among them eagerly, but no sign of Ivy. She spotted Bird at the same moment he saw her. His eyes widened and filled with tears. She could tell he was about to run away.

Before he could bolt, she jumped into the crater and raced to grab him.

"You're it!" she shouted at the top of her lungs. Then she whispered quickly into his ear. "It's okay, Bird. We're friends."

As soon as the others heard her cry, they shrieked with glee. The game was on. Dana smiled as they scattered, but didn't join them. She didn't feel like playing. It was then she admitted to herself that there was only one person she wanted to meet there. And she was suddenly that lonely child again, sitting on the steps, looking up and down the street, waiting and wishing.

She had just decided to leave when a voice chirped at her elbow.

"Here you is! I be's looking for you everywhere!"

Ivy was all dressed up in a skirt of woven bluebells with a necklace and bracelet of lapis lazuli.

Dana was so delighted to see her she picked up the little boggle and swung her around.

"Am I ever glad you're here! I hardly know anyone. I don't suppose . . ." Dana hesitated. She didn't want to spoil the fun, but Ivy was like her best friend. She could be honest with her. "I want to go home. Could you help me get back to Bray?"

Ivy burst out laughing.

"You can'ts go home, silly. This be's your party!"

"What?"

"Don'ts you know? This be's in your honor!"

FORTY-FOUR

F ully restored and resplendent, Lugh of the Mountain,
Lugh of the Wood, stood upon the crest of the ridge. He
saw nothing and no one but the Lady of Light who stepped
toward him, her hair aflame like the sunset.

They did not draw close, but kept the distance of strang-
ers. Each wore a golden mask of pain. Yet they gazed hun-
grily upon each other, desiring to bridge the dark of their
past.

"My Lady, forgive me that I did not come to thy aid when
I heard thee cry out from the shadows."

"You were bound under a spell of stone and earth, a
chroí."

"Still, I should have come to thee."

"My Lord, forgive me that I did break our covenant and
cause thee such torment."

"You fell into a spell of love and forgetting, a stór, and
you suffered for it."

"Still, it grieves me to have afflicted thee so."

As they spoke together, their masks faded away. For love is as strong as death. Passion as fierce as the grave. Its flashes are flashes of fire, a raging flame. Many waters cannot quench it. Neither can floods drown it.

She flew toward him like a bird flying home in the evening. His arms were the branches of a tree on the lee of the mountain.

"My love," they murmured to each other. "My only love."

And lo, the winter is past, the flowers appear on the earth, and the time of the singing of birds is come.

FORTY-FIVE

B efore Dana could say anything more to Ivy, a tantara
of trumpets rang out over the mountain. Now a great
roar rose up from the throng as King Lugh and Queen Edane
arrived. He wore the green and brown of hill and forest, with
a flowing mantle of dark-purple and a chaplet of oak leaves.
She glimmered like the sky in silver-blue and white, her fiery
hair bound with a winged crystal crown. Arm in arm, the
royal couple greeted their subjects with the same love and joy
that was showered upon them.

Dana edged her way to the back of the crowd. Her feelings were jumbled. She could barely comprehend that this
beautiful queen was her mother, and Lugh himself seemed
too majestic and unreachable. Her overriding emotion was
one of dismay. Must it be like this? Would she always be an
outsider?

Silence fell over the huge gathering as the King raised
his hand.

"Pleasant it is, beloved friends, to meet at last on the
summer lawns, after the longest winter the Mountain Kingdom has ever known. This is a time of great jubilation. Let it

be known that there is one amongst us whom we must thank for this wondrous day."

Dana nearly died of embarrassment as all eyes turned in her direction. Both Lugh and Edane were smiling at her with such an intensity of love that she had to look away.

The King lifted his hand to quiet the applause.

"Yet it is not we who shall give her praise and thanks this night, but honored guests who come to our table. Give welcome, my people, to the High King and High Queen of Faerie."

As the horns of Elfland rang out once more, a fatamorgana of sound swelled over the mountain. Bands of multicolored light shot into the air like fireworks, as a mighty stone archway took shape in their midst.

"There'll be talk of UFOs in the Wicklow Hills tomorrow," Dana whispered to Ivy.

"You's for what?" hissed Ivy, but she kept her eyes on the shining portal.

When their High Majesties stepped through the arch, Dana was more than surprised to discover she knew both of them. The High King over all kings was none other than the tall stranger she had met in the glen, the one who had first told her to follow the greenway. Clothed in black like the night, he wore his red-gold hair loose upon his shoulders. On his brow shone the star of sovereignty.

But it was the young woman beside him who surprised Dana the most. No longer caught betwixt and between, no longer uncertain of who she was, Honor stood by her husband with the regal poise of a High Queen. Her silken gown was green and gold, her crown inlaid with precious stones. She addressed the assembly.

"Joyous we are that our Tánaiste, Lugh of the Mountain, Lugh of the Wood, is restored to the Realm. Joyous, too, are we that the Light-Bearer has returned to us. Today a battle was won in the heart of the woods and in the hearts of humanity. Yet more glad tidings we bring to thee."

An expectant hush fell over the crowd. Only Dana was uneasy. She found it hard to catch her breath. Some nameless thing was pressing against her chest, demanding to be recognized. Her heart beat wildly, like the heart of a bird, as the High King spoke.

"Today the mortals saved the woods. As it has always been since time began, it is humanity who must come to the rescue of Fairyland. It is humanity who must fight the shadows of the Enemy. We have many champions in the mortal realm whom we call our dear neighbors. But know this and rejoice, my people. One more powerful than all the rest has entered the two worlds."

The child part of Dana wanted to run. Off down the slope and onto the road and back to Bray. Far, far away from the grand destiny that called to her.

Queen Edane stepped forward with a glad proud look.

"I am the Light-Bearer who bore the Light. Where is the Light to bridge the darkness?"

Dana did not run.

Her mission in the mountains had prepared her for this. Her quest had been her training. Her search was for herself. Deep in her mind, the wolf threw back its head and howled; the monster rose up from the lake to rest its head against her brow.

As the crowds parted before her, cheering and crying out her name, Dana took her place among kings and queens.

Lugh winked at Dana before making the last announcement.

"The formalities are done! Let us play in Dana's name! For what use is life without fun and laughter?"

As the party resumed with even more abandon, Dana turned to her mother; but before they could speak together, Queen Edane was swept away in a wave of well-wishers clamoring to see her.

Dana's heart sank.

"It will not always be like this," a voice said gently beside her. "Your time with your mother will come."

Dana turned to Honor with an air of reproach.

"You're the High Queen of Faerie!"

"Yeah, can you believe it?" Honor burst out laughing.

"Did you know, then? Who my mother was? That I—"

"I did and I didn't," the older girl said quickly. "Honestly, I hardly knew my own name half the time. Midir—the High King, my husband—he knew, of course, he knows everything, well, almost everything, since he's been around

for millennia or more. He says it was better that way, as it let me get around the rules." She shrugged. "Desperate times call for desperate measures."

The High Queen reached for a tray of fairy buns as it flew by them on wings.

"Here, try these. They're fantastic! Those are flakes of real gold. You can eat them."

Dana couldn't resist the cakes or her friend's good humor.

"I did not mean to deceive you," Honor added in a more serious tone. "Know that I, too, was on a mission to find my true self. My husband took a risk bestowing the task upon me, and he did it for my sake as well as yours. Thus you helped me even as I helped you, as is the way in all the worlds."

"I understand," Dana said, nodding. And she did.

With the matter resolved between them, the two were giggling and laughing together when Queen Edane joined them.

"My dear daughter," she murmured, planting a kiss on Dana's head. "I am so proud of you."

Dana's heart swelled, but she was also a little uncomfortable. It would take time to accept that this fairy queen was indeed her mother. Dana had already decided to call her by her first name, the way she did with Gabriel.

"I should go home, Edane. Gabe'll be out of his mind. It's not fair to him."

The Queen slipped her arm around Dana's shoulders.

"*Do not fret, a leanbh. You will return to your father soon. Time is a thing we may order as we will. While you revel here, not one second will pass in the Earthworld. This is your feast, Dana. The reward for all your hard work. Enjoy it!*"

Edane's words melted the last of Dana's reservations, and enjoy herself she did: frolicking with Ivy and the other boggles; dancing with foxes and fairies, tree spirits and giants; singing with the wild birds who nested on the crags; and rolling down the hillsides with parties of pixies.

In between the fun and games, like a silver thread woven through the soft dark night, were all the times her mother sought her out. Together, they would go for a walk along the great cirque beneath the stars. Or meander through the winding paths of the maze illumined by white candles. Or sit together on an ivy-covered swing surrounded by the night perfume of the flowers. And each time they met, stories were told, of the few years they had been together and the many years they had been apart. Sometimes there were tears and sometimes there was sorrow, but love and laughter were always near. Though Dana didn't tell her mother half the things she had intended to say, she knew their true tale was only beginning; and they had all the time in the world to get to know each other.

FORTY-SIX

Starlight shone over the Glen of the Downs as night deepened. The public protest had ended. The day was won. As the national news reported the events, the developers withdrew their equipment and retreated from the site. The surprise attack had failed; a long battle in the courts loomed ahead.

At the central campsite, a small group of eco-warriors approached Big Bob, bringing Murta with them. Two of the young men gripped his arms so that he couldn't escape. He looked as if he had been badly beaten. His body was not only bruised and cut, but burned as well.

"Which of you did this to him?" Big Bob thundered.

The young men were so shocked by the accusation they couldn't speak at first.

"Well, *we* didn't!" Billie spoke up, indignant. "Though we might've wanted to, after we saw him with the others. He showed up like this earlier, when he told us about the dump. You weren't here. He said the private guards had roughed him up when they found him snooping."

"That's why we believed him," one of the others pointed out.

Their leader calmed down and signed to them to let Murta go.

"I trusted you," Big Bob said to him. "You were my right hand. Why did you betray us?"

Murta tried to glare defiantly but couldn't hold the other man's gaze. The past week had been a blur. He assumed he had been infected with some kind of virus, no doubt from living outdoors. He was more than glad that his part in this nightmare was over.

"Just doing my job," he said hoarsely. "I was never one of you. Big companies pay me to infiltrate groups like yours—unions, radicals, troublemakers. It's a living."

"While your soul is dying." Big Bob looked sad. "If you win, you lose, Murta. It's your birthright, too, we're fighting to protect."

Murta spat on the ground. He turned to leave, hunching defensively in case someone tried to stop him. But they all moved away, as if he were leprous.

Big Bob watched him go, then sat down at the fire with a heavy sigh. Billie joined him and two of the men. The other eco-warriors returned to the forest, some to repair their tree houses and others to take up their posts.

Gabriel drove through the Glen of the Downs on his way into the mountains for yet another night's search.

With him was Aradhana, who had stayed by his side since his daughter's disappearance. He slowed the car as he approached the campsite, intending to check in with Big Bob. The eco-warriors had been taking turns to help look for Dana. The people who had joined in the protest had already gone home, pleased with the part they had played that day. A lone police car remained.

As he turned in to the parking lot, Gabriel happened to glance in his rearview mirror. He caught his breath. Halfway up the slope on the other side of the road, a light glinted in the trees. He jumped out of the car to look again. There it was! A silvery glow. His heart pounded. He told himself it was probably a flashlight, one of the tree people patrolling the far ridge. But the coincidence compelled him to investigate. It was precisely the spot he had blocked from his sight for many years now.

"I'll be back in a minute," he said quickly to Aradhana. "Wait for me here."

Aradhana didn't respond, but she followed after him as he raced across the road and into the trees.

It was a steep climb up the slope and the ground was sodden from the storms, but Gabriel knew the way. Knew exactly where he was going. As he neared the clearing, his heart beat so fast his chest ached. He hardly dared to hope.

Please, he prayed.

And then he saw her.

There in the little glade, where the ancient oak withdrew to form a fairy circle, where the bramble curled in berry-laden tangles, there by a fallen tree trunk stood his daughter.

Dana waved shyly.

Still in the shadows, Gabriel stood stunned. There was something wrong. It was weird and disturbing. A strange light shone all around her, making her a ghostly figure. By some trick of perspective, she seemed as tall as the trees. And she wore a golden cloak.

"Can you see her?" Gabriel whispered to Aradhana.

He was beginning to fear he was going mad. Half-crazed with the need to find her, was he hallucinating this vision? He felt seized with a paralysis of mind and body. He was *fairy-struck*.

"I see her," Aradhana said firmly. "Go to your daughter. Bring her home."

It was all the urging he needed. As Gabriel ran toward Dana, the fairy spell broke. She looked solid and of normal size.

As her father came toward her, Dana saw the toll the week's ordeal had taken. His clothes were rumpled, stubble covered his head and chin; his eyes were swollen from lack of sleep and constant weeping. Fear and despair had nearly destroyed him; her dear beloved dad who had raised her on his own and always done his best to make her happy.

She was suddenly a little girl who had endured a great deal.

"*DADDY!*" she cried. "*MY DADDY!*"

And she ran like the wind into his arms.

Gabriel gathered his daughter up, weeping and kissing her and crushing her against him.

"This is the place, isn't it, Dad?" she whispered to him.

He looked around. Everything blurred through his tears, but he knew what she meant. He had known it the minute he saw the light in the trees.

"Yes," he said softly. "This is where I met your mother."

And as he looked toward the spot from where she had stepped thirteen years ago, Edane entered the clearing. She, too, appeared tall and shining at first; but though she diminished to human size as she approached him, she still shone like a star that had fallen to earth. Forever young, forever beautiful, she had not changed one iota since the day he had first set eyes on her.

As he gazed upon his lost wife, Gabriel finally accepted what he had always known but couldn't admit. She did not belong to his world. She was one of the other race who dwelled in Ireland.

The blue fairy eyes regarded him solemnly, as if from a great distance.

"I regret the pain I have caused thee, Gabriel Faolan. It was not my wish and I have suffered also."

Her voice was musical, like his flute. He was already thinking of her as a beautiful tune that belonged to his past.

"I want to thank thee for the great gift of our child," she finished.

"The great gift you gave me also," he said.

And the last strains of their song came to an end.

Still clinging to her father, Dana reached out to clasp her mother. For that one moment, suspended between the two pillars of her creation, Dana's life was a complete circle, as perfect as a pearl. Though they would not live happily ever after together, they would all live happily.

In the shadow of the trees, cloaked in green leaves, a fairy king waited.

"I cannot stay," Edane said, kissing her daughter good-bye. "We shall meet again soon, my dearest one."

Now Aradhana stepped into the clearing. She had stayed where she was as she witnessed the family reunion; but when she saw the shining woman depart, she went to Gabriel and Dana and took their hands.

Together, the three left the woods and made their way to the road.

The last police car was about to leave, when the driver recognized Gabriel and Dana.

"Isn't that the missing kid?" he said to his partner.

They were out of the car in an instant.

"Did the eco-warriors—?" the first officer began.

Gabriel hurried to explain. "It had nothing to do with them. It was . . ." He racked his brain, trying to think of an explanation, then realized the truth was best. "She was with her mother's people."

The policemen exchanged looks. It was often a family matter, these child disappearances.

"Do you want to press charges?"

"No," said Gabriel, with a wry smile. "We'll just have to work out some arrangements between us."

Dana and Gabriel grinned at each other as they walked with Aradhana to the Triumph Herald.

"You okay, kiddo?"

"Couldn't be better, Gabe. You?"

"I'll live."

FORTY-SEVEN

Oh, the thrill of flying! The rush of wind and wings, blue depth of sky, white crest of cloud, and the sun rising! Upward, ever upward, as the world falls away!

It was even more magical than she had imagined.

"Da, this is brilliant!"

Dana pressed her face to the airplane window and gazed down, entranced. Ireland lay below her, like a great green cloth shaken out over the wavering sea. As a deep love for her mother country surged through her veins, she looked upon the land with fairy eyes. There was Saint Kevin by the Glen of the Two Lakes, the boggles chasing sheep through the Sally Gap, King Lugh and Queen Edane in their crystal palace on Lugnaquillia. And there, at the very heart of the tale, enthroned on the royal Hill of Tara were the High King and High Queen of Faerie.

Follow the greenway.

Dana caught her breath. Was that a flash of gray in the trees? Her heart skipped a beat. The pang of hope.

Not all that is gone is gone forever.

She turned to grin at her father. He, too, was brimming over with happiness. Like daybreak after the darkest hour, so many good things had happened since her return. One of the biggest surprises was her wholehearted acceptance of the move to Canada.

"But . . . what about . . . your mother?"

"It's okay. She'll be there too."

He had asked few questions and she had offered fewer details. It wasn't going to be easy, but they had already reached an understanding. He would not interfere with her connection to Faerie and she would not go away without telling him first.

The situation was eased by the presence of a third party.

"Gods, devas, fairies, they are all part of life," was Aradhana's view. "This can be hard for people to accept if they only think in squares and lines."

"Are you calling me a blockhead?" Gabriel had protested, but then was mollified with a kiss.

That Aradhana was an indispensable part of the family was obvious to everyone; but it was Dana who had urged Gabriel to ask the young woman to marry him.

"It's not that I haven't thought about it," he admitted. "I can't stop thinking about it. But all these big changes happening at the same time: you and your mother, Canada, my new job, your new school . . .

could we manage a wife and stepmother on top of all that?"

"Gabe, do you think we could do it without her? Do you *want* to?"

Now Dana leaned across her father to nudge Aradhana, who was reading the airline magazine. Despite the last-minute booking, they had managed to get three seats in a row.

"I promised Suresh I'd take tons of photographs," Dana told her. "He's going to put them on the kitchen bulletin board. Beside the ones of India."

"He's going to miss you," Gabriel said guiltily.

"He will see me at the wedding," Aradhana pointed out. "And he can come and visit whenever he likes. He will have much more money now that he owns the whole restaurant."

Gabriel took his fiancée's hand and pressed it to his lips.

"I hope you won't regret your decision. Your entire life is about to change."

"You swept me off my feet," she replied. "Where I come from, that is what suitors are supposed to do."

Dana went back to her window-gazing. The plane was moving over the Atlantic Ocean. The cold waves rose and fell in slow motion. Life was so strange. Things had not turned out the way she had either hoped or dreamed. A happy ending in real life was very different from a "happily ever after" in a fairy tale. Still, she had to admit she was pleased with how things had turned out.

And, yes, she was happy.

GLOSSARY
Key to Pronunciation and
Meaning of Irish Words

a chroí (aah kree)—dear heart

a dheirfiúr bhig (aah greh-fur vigg)—little sister (vocative)

a fhaol bhig (aah ale vigg)—little wolf (vocative)

a leanbh (aah laano-iv)—term of endearment. Lit. "child"

anamchara (aah-num kara)—soul friend

an cuileann (awn quill-un)—holly

an dair ghaelach (awn dare yaa-luck)—Irish oak

An fathach mór 'na luí faoi shuan. (awn faw-hawk more naah lee fwee hoo-un)—The great giant lies asleep.

an leannán sí faoi shuan (awn laah-nawn shee fwee hoo-un)—the sleeping muse

An Taisce (awn tawsh-kuh)—Lit. "store house
or treasury." Ireland's oldest and most powerful
environmental body. Established in 1948. While it
is very active in planning and development matters,
education, anti-litter programs, protection of heritage
and so on, it does not approve of or participate in more
radical protest activities such as those of eco-warriors.
See www.antaisce.org.

Ard Rí (aar'd ree)—High King

Ard Solas (arr'd suh-luss)—Lit. "The High Light."
Term used when addressing the president of Ireland, as
in "Your Excellency."

a stór (moh store)—Lit. "my treasure." Used also for
"my darling."

Bean Níghe (ban knee)—Washerwoman, i.e., a fairy
washerwoman

Bean Sídhe (ban shee)—Banshee (literally, "Woman of
the Sídhe," i.e., woman of the Faerie Folk)

bobodha (baw-boa)—variant spelling of *badhbh* (bawve),
meaning "bogeyman."

bogach (baw-gawk)—soft ground

Caoimhín (quee-veen)—Kevin

Ceol n'eán agus ceol an tsrutháin (kee-ole nane aw-guss
kee-ple awn s'roo-hoyne)—The music of the birds and
the music of the stream

Conas atá tú, a mháthair? (cuun-uss aah-taw too, aah
waw-hurr?)—How are you, mother? It is an old and
courteous custom to use "mother" or "father" when
addressing the elderly.

Dún do bhéal. (doon duh vale)—Shut your mouth.

Dún Eadóchais (doon ade-oh-case)—Fort of Despair

Dún Scáith (doon scaw)—Fort of the Shades

Éist nóiméad. (aysht no-made)—Listen a minute.

Fada an lá go sámh
Fada an oíche gan ghruaim
An ghealach, an ghrian, an ghaoth
Moladh duit, a Dhia.

(fawdah awn law go sawve
fawdah awn ee-huh gawn 'hroo-um
awn gya-luck, awn gree-un, awn gwee
muhla dit, ah yee-ah)

Long is the day with peace
Long is the night without gloom
Thou art the moon, the sun, the wind
I praise you, my God.

fado (faah-doe)—long ago. Note: *Fado fado* is a
storytelling phrase best translated as "once upon a time."

Fáilte romhat. (fawl-cheh row't)—You are welcome.
As in English used both to welcome someone and as a
response to *go raibh maith agat* (go rev mawh a-gut), i.e.,
"thank you."

faol (fwale)—wolf. Archaic, literary word. In modern
Irish, the more common usage for "wolf" is *mactíre*
(mock teer-uh), literally "son of the land."

Faolán (fwale-on)—a derivative of *faol,* meaning "wolf."
Clan or family name anglicized to Whelan, Whalen,
Phelan, Phalen. Also spelled O'Faoláin.

gabha an cheoil (gou-waah awn kee-ole)—smith of music

girseach (geer-shuck)—girl

Gleann Dá Loch (glenn daw lock)—Vale of Two Lakes

Go raibh míle maith agat. (go rev meela mawh a-gut)—Thanks a million. (Lit. "May you have a thousand thanks.")

Imdha toir torudh abla
Imdha airne cen cesa
Imdha dairbre ardmhesa.[1]

Plentiful in the east the apple fruits,
Plentiful the luxuriant sloes,
Plentiful the noble acorn-bearing oaks.

[1]Note: this is Old Irish, older than Latin is to modern Italian. As the language has changed and developed over thousands of years, no one knows for certain how it was pronounced!

Is breá an tráthnóna é. (iss braw awn traw-no-na ey, as in "hey")—It's a fine evening.

Lá Lughnasa or Lá Lúnasa (law loo-naah-saw)—
August first, Lammas. Named after the Irish god Lugh.

Lasair (lass-eer)—flame, blaze

Lug na Coille (lew nah kwilla)—Lugh of the Wood

Magh Abhlach (maw awv'lock)—Plain of the Apple
Trees (one of the many names for Faerie)

*Má itheann tú ná má ólann tú aon ghreim istigh anseo,
ní bhfaighidh tú amach as go bráth arís!* (maw i-hunn
too naw maw oh-lunn too ane 'hryme ish-tig awn-shaw,
nee why-hih too aah-mawk awss goe braw aah-reesh)—If
you eat or drink anything in this place, you will not get
out of here again!

méaracán gorm (marr-aah-cawn gur-um)—Lit. "blue
thimbles." The same Irish name applies to both harebells
and bluebells, though they are different wildflowers.

méiríní sídhe (mare-eenie shee)—Lit. "fairy fingers,"
i.e., foxglove

mo leanbh (moe laan-uv)—my child

muinchillí glasa (mwinn-killy glaw-saah)—greensleeves

Na Daoine Uaisle Na Gnoic (naah deen-uh oose-leh
naah guh-nick)—The Gentry or Noble Ones of the Hills

ní (knee)—abbreviated form of *iníon* (in-kneen),
meaning "daughter." Hence, Dana ní Edane Lasair is
"Dana, daughter of Edane Lasair."

péist (paysht)—fabulous beast, reptile, snake, worm,
monster

*Phóg mé ar ais is phóg mé arís tú
Gheill mo chroí don leannán síofrúil,
Is thug mé cúl do gach aon dílseacht
Nuair a phóg mé do bhéal.*[2]

(foe'g may air esh iss foe'g may areesh too
yell moe cree dunn laah-nawn shee-frool
iss huug may cool duh gawk ane deel-shawk't
noo-ur aah foe'g may doe vale)

I kissed and kissed again
Yielded to the fairy spell
Left behind all love till then
When I kissed your mouth.

[2] Verse from "An Phóg" ("The Kiss"), Irish and English by Pádraigín Ní Uallacháin, from her CD *Ailleacht* (Beauty), Gael Linn CEFCD 187, used with the kind permission of the singer/songwriter.

pollach (pawl-awk)—hollow place, from *poll* (pawl), meaning "hole"

scéal (sh'kale)—story. Note: *sí scéalta* (shee sh'kale-taah) are fairy tales.

'Sea. (sh'aah)—It is; yes. Abbreviated form of *is ea* (iss ah), meaning "it is."

Seothó, a thoil, ná goil go fóill
Seothó, a thoil, ná goil aon deoir,
Seothó, a linbh, a chumainn's a stóir.[3]

(shaw-hoe aah hoyle nawh goyle goe foyle
shaw-hoe aah hoyle nawh gull ane d'jorr
shaw-hoe aah linn-uv aah huh-munn iss aah storr)

Hush, dear heart, no need to cry,
Hush, dear heart, no need for tears,
Hush, dear child, my love and treasure.

[3]From "Suantraí dá Mhac Tarbhartha," by Eoghan
Rua Ó Suileabháin, c. 1748–1784, *An Leabhair Mór*,
(*The Great Book of Gaelic*) (Canongate Books, 2002).
Translation by O.R. Melling.

Sídhe na Spéire (shee naah spare-uh)—The Fairy Folk of
the Sky

Sídhe Slua na Sliabh (shee sloo-aah naah shleeve)—The
Fairy Host of the Mountain

Siúil liomsa, a chara dhil, suas fá na hardaín,
Ar thuras na háilleacht' is an ghileacht amuigh,
Le go ndeánfaimid bogán de chreagán a' tsléibhe,
Is le páideoga lasfaimid dorchadas oích'.

Ní laoithe an bhróin a cheolfainnse duitse,
Ná ní caoineadh donóige nó doghrainn daoi,
Ach le silleadh a mhillfinnse méala an chumha
Sa phluais sin go maidin ar shliabh na caillí.[4]

(shool lumsa a karra yeel, soo-ass faw naah harrjeen
ayre hoorus naah hoy-lawkt iss awn yiil-awkt am-wee
leh goe nane-fee-midge baw-gawn jeh 'hraa-gawn ahh
    shliv-uh
iss leh poy-juh-gaah lass-fwee-midge dur-kaadass ee-huh.

knee lee-huh awn vrone a 'key-ole-fawn-suh duut-suh,
naw knee cween-aah duh-noy-guh know duh-yriin dee,
awk leh shee-laah aah will-finn-suh male-aah awn c'uh-
    maah
saa fluss shinn goe maw-jinn ayre shleeve naah caah-lee.)

Rise up, my love, and come along with me
On a journey of beauty in nature's sunlight,
To smooth every stone as we walk on the hillside
And with rush candles light up the dark of the night.

No sighing of sorrow I'd ever sing for you
Nor wild lamentation, or sad foolish song;
With a glance I'd disperse the dark clouds of longing
In the cairn on the mountain, from dusk to dawn.

[4] Verses from "Cara Caoin" ("Beloved Friend"), Irish
and English by Pádraigín Ní Uallacháin, from her CD
Ailleacht (*Beauty*), Gael Linn CEFCD 187, used with
the kind permission of the singer/songwriter.

Sliabh na mBan (shleeve naah mawn)—The Women's
Mountain

Slua na h'Aeir (sloo-aah naah h'air)—The Fairy Host of
the Air

Spéirbhean (speer-vaan)—Lit. "Sky-Woman." A type of fairy lady.

Suas (soo-uss)—up

Tá an croí á réabadh sa ghleann, sa ghleann,
Tá an croí á réabadh i ngleann na ndeor;
Ceo is gaoth sa ghleann, sa ghleann,
Ceo is gaoth i ngleann na ndeor.[5]

(taw awn cree aw ray-bah saah g'lann saah g'lann
taw awn cree aw ray-bah iih ing'lann na nore
ky'oe iss gee saah g'lann saah g'lann
ky'oe iss gwee iih ing'lann naah nore)

The heart is torn in the valley, in the valley,
The heart is torn in the Valley of Tears;
Mist and wind in the valley, in the valley,
Mist and wind in the Valley of Tears.

[5] Verse from "Gleann na nDeor," ("Valley of Tears"),
Irish and English by Pádraigín Ní Uallacháin, from her
CD *Ailleacht* (*Beauty*), Gael Linn CEFCD 187, used
with the kind permission of the singer/songwriter.

Tá an oíche seo dubh is dorcha,
Tá an spéir ag sileadh deor',
Tá néal ar aghaidh na gréine,
Ó d'imigh tú, a stór.[6]

(taw awn ee-huh shaw duv iss durra-kah
taw awn spare egg shee-laah jore
taw ny'aal air aye naw grane-ah
Oh jimmy too aah store)

This night is cold and dark now;
The sky is weeping tears;
The sun is eclipsed in shadow,
Since you departed.

[6] Verse from "An Leannán" ("The Beloved"), Irish
and English by Pádraigín Ní Uallacháin, from her CD
Ailleacht (*Beauty*), Gael Linn CEFCD 187, used with
the kind permission of the singer/songwriter.

Tá fáilte roimhe do cine anseo. (taw fawl-chuh riiv doe
kinnah awn-shaw)—Your people are welcome here.

Tá grian gheal an tsamhraidh ag damhsa ar mo theach.
(taw gree-on gyal an sour-oo egg dow-soo air mo hee-
ach)—The summer sun is dancing on the roof of my
house.

Táimse a foghlaim gaeilge. (Taw-iim-shuh aah foe-lumm gwayle-guh)—I am learning Irish.

Tánaiste (tawn-ish-tuh)—Tanist, second-in-command, heir presumptive; in modern Ireland this is the title of the Deputy Prime Minister, second in line to *An Taoiseach* (awn tee-shawk), the Prime Minister.

Tá tú ag imeacht ar shlí na fírinne. (taw too egg im-mawk't air shlee naah fear-nuh)—You are going on the way of truth. This is a literal translation of the phrase Irish-speakers use to refer to the dead. They will say *Tá sí ag imithe ar shlí na fírinne* (taw shee ag immuh-heh air shlee naah fear-nuh)—"She is gone on the way of truth"—to say "She is dead."

Note on the Battle for the Glen of the Downs:
In 1997, the Irish government approved the widening of an existing road that ran through the Glen of the Downs. To allow greater speed for a three-minute journey, it was decided that a four-lane highway would be built through the Nature Reserve, with more than two thousand hardwoods cut. The tree-house protest undertaken by Irish and international eco-warriors covered a three-year period of court battles and campaigns. The incident described in the book—wherein members of the public helped to stop an early cull—did occur. But though

the battle was won, the war itself was lost. In 2000, the protestors were forcibly removed from the site. Thirteen were imprisoned without charge, some for up to two months. The cost of upgrading the small stretch of road was a staggering 85 million euro.[7]

[7]Frank McDonald and James Nix, *Chaos at the Crossroads,* Gandon Press.

Note on the
Irish Language

The historical speech of the Irish people is a Goidelic Celtic language variously called Gaelic, Irish Gaelic (as opposed to Scots Gaelic), and Erse. In Ireland, it is simply called the Irish language or "Irish." For over two thousand years, Irish—Old, Middle, and Modern—was the language of Ireland, until the English conquest enforced its near eradication. Today it is the official first language of Eire, the Irish Republic. Recently it has been awarded official status in the Six Counties of Northern Ireland through the Good Friday Agreement.

As a native language or mother tongue, Irish is found only in a number of small communities called *Gaeltachtaí*, located chiefly on the west coast of Ireland. Sadly, these communities are declining due to economic factors, reduced rural population, social disintegration, intermarriage with non-native speakers, attrition, and the settling of non-native speakers in the areas. Some estimates put the demise of the *Gaeltachtaí* within the next few generations, a loss that would be of incalculable magnitude to Irish culture and society. It must be said, however, that native speakers ignore these rumors of their death with characteristic forbearance.

Meanwhile, the knowledge and use of the Irish language is increasing among the English-speaking population of the island. In the most recent census of 2002 (preliminary results), over a million people in the Republic and 140,000 in Northern Ireland reported having a reasonable proficiency in the language. Census figures for the use of Irish continually increase. Globally, study groups and language classes are popular not only among the Diaspora—those Irish and their descendants who have emigrated throughout the world—but also among non-Irish peoples such as the Japanese, Danish, French, and Germans. In the United States (*Na Stáit Aontaithe*), Irish language classes are available throughout the country, while the Internet lists countless sites that teach and encourage Irish.

Back home in Ireland, the grassroots phenomenon of *Gaelscoileanna*—primary and secondary schools teaching in Irish—is widespread and rapidly growing, despite tacit resistance from successive Irish governments. These schools guarantee new generations of Irish speakers whose second language is fluent Irish. The longstanding Irish-language radio station *Raidió na Gaeltachta* continues to broadcast from the viewpoint of native speakers, while the new television station *Teilifís na Gaeilge* (TG4) caters to both native and second-language speakers. Many institutions both private and public support the language, the most venerable being *Conradh na Gaeilge* (www.cnag.ie).

There are several dialects within the Irish language which express regional differences among the provinces of Munster, Leinster, Connaught, and Ulster. Also extant is Shelta, the secret language of the Irish Travellers (nomadic people who live in caravan trailers) which weaves Romany words with Irish Gaelic.

In whatever form, long may the language survive. *Gaeilge abú!*

About the Author

O.R. Melling was born in Ireland and grew up in Toronto with her seven sisters and two brothers. At eighteen, she hitchhiked across Canada to California, seeking adventure. A year later, she was off to Malaysia and Borneo on a youth exchange program. That set her motto for life, "to travel hopefully." She has a B.A. in Philosophy and Celtic Studies and an M.A. in Medieval Irish History. To date, her books have been translated into Japanese, Chinese, Russian, Czech, and Slovenian. The next book in her *Chronicles of Faerie* series is *The Book of Dreams*. She lives in her hometown of Bray in Ireland with her teenage daughter, Findabhair. Visit her Web site at www. ormelling.com.

This book was designed by Vivian Cheng and Jay Colvin and art directed by Chad W. Beckerman and Becky Terhune. It is set in Horley Old Style MT, a Monotype font designed by the English type designer Robert Norton. The chapter heads are set in Mason, which was created by Jonathan Barnbrook based on ancient Greek and Roman stone carvings.